Enigma Tracer

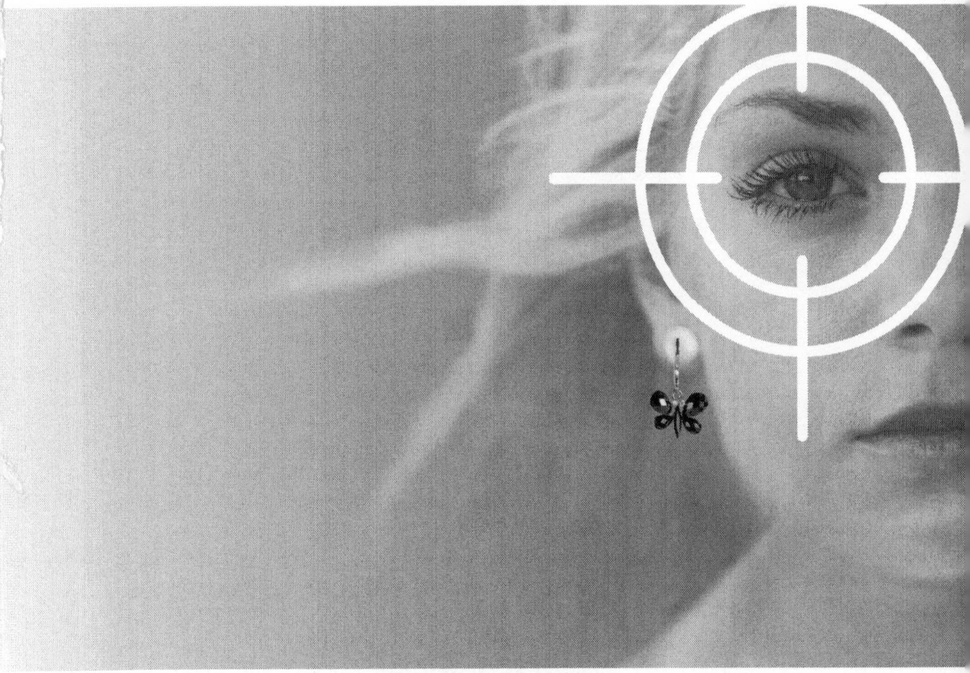

BOOK 1 Enigma Heirs Thriller Series

Enigma Tracer
By Charles Breakfield and Rox Burkey

Published by

ICABOD Press

ISBN: 978-1-946858-65-8 (paperback)
ISBN: 978-1-946858- 64-1 (eBook)
ISBN: 978-1-946858- 66-5 (audiobook)
Library of Congress Control Number: 2022924052

Cover, interior and eBook design:
Rebecca Finkel, F + P Graphic Design, FPGD.com

First Edition
Printed in the United States

TECHNO-THRILLER | SUSPENSE

Novels by Breakfield and Burkey in **The Enigma Series**

Out of Poland (novella)

The Enigma Factor

The Enigma Rising

The Enigma Ignite

The Enigma Wraith

The Enigma Stolen

The Enigma Always

The Enigma Gamers
A CATS Tale

The Enigma Broker

The Enigma Dragon
A CATS Tale

The Enigma Source

The Enigma Beyond

The Enigma Threat

Novels by Breakfield and Burkey in the **Enigma Heirs**

Enigma Tracer

Short Stories

Remember the Future

The Jewel

Love's Enigma

Nowhere But Up

Destiny Dreamer

Riddle Codes

Hot Chocolate

Hidden Target

Caribbean Dream

Fears, Tears, or Cheers

Magnolia Bluff Crime Chronicles

The Flower Enigma (Book 5)

Acknowledgments

We are grateful for the support of our readers. Thank you for providing a review.

PROLOGUE

2½ YEARS AGO

Graduate School

Gracie awoke with a start from the irritating buzzing that grew louder by the second. She rubbed her face to erase the dream that got disturbed and felt the fresh air as she flung off her covers. She heard a familiar yet nearly unintelligible mumbling as if from a cave.

"Gracie, turn off that damn noise," the gravelly voice begged.

The buzz persisted until Gracie's brain recognized the source, so she reached over and pushed the buttons of her phone on the nightstand. Her slender fingers reached the dim bedside lamp switch. She pressed it on and brushed sleep residue from her eyes.

Gracie stretched like a cat, pulled up the covers, and wondered how much time they had to get ready. She pulled her phone, pressed the screen to reveal the time and came to her senses about lounging around. "Oh my gosh," she mumbled as her heart skipped a beat and her nerves ignited like she'd fallen off the edge of a cliff rather than jumped out of bed. "Bailey, get up," she announced. "We've only two hours to get it together and complete set up to face the board to deliver our final. I'll go wash up fast." She gathered a few grooming necessities, for the short trek down the hall.

"I'm so tired," the weary voice replied.

"I know. Me too. We prepped so late, but we'll be fabulous. I'm glad we're on first." Gracie watched the lump of bedlinens move, reminding her of wrestling with her twin brother JJ under the covers when they were kids. "Tell you what, you rest until I finish my shower. Then I'm dumping you on the floor."

The lumpy bed hiding the lithe form seemed to relax, and silence reigned.

Gracie grinned and embraced the smallest increase of light peeking through the wooden blinds she twisted open, proclaiming morning. Hoping the sun would rise early and fog delay until later, she yawned. She caught sight of their matching suits hanging on the closet door frame and pictured them polished and ready for success. They knew one critical element of their final presentation included professional appearance and behavior. She silently gave thanks to her mom, who located the smartly tailored suits, complementary silk blouses, and low-heeled leather pumps. After sixteen grueling months of focused study in the advanced dual degree program at Mary Immaculate College in Ireland, it was thrilling to reach graduation.

Grabbing her towel and toiletries, she dashed out the door. The dorm hallway would remain silent from the rest of the students for at least another hour. That was the reason for the first slot—no contention for the bathroom. Five minutes and the water warmed enough to stop her shivering. She shampooed, rinsed, and stepped out of the white tiled enclosure. Gracie vigorously rubbed her body dry and used the second towel to wrap her light blonde hair. Seeing bright eyes reflected from the slightly steamy mirror, she saluted her image and hurriedly returned to the shared room.

"Bailey," she called. "The water's warm, so get a move on, sister." The lump moved slightly, but Gracie remained unconvinced of the needed follow through. "Ya got till five. One. Two. Three."

The covers flew and landed on the floor as her roommate launched herself to her full height with her thick wavy mane of dark auburn hair framing her oval face. "Okay. I'm awake. Stop counting." She grinned. "Thanks for getting the water warm. I'll be right back."

Gracie's phone rang. "Hi, Mom...Yes, I'm up and showered. Bailey's there now. We're going to be ready and arrive ten minutes early...I know we'll win. We practiced every contingency last night, and Bailey's heart is set on bringing home the trophy...." She drew underwear and stockings from the top drawer of her dresser.

"Our combined marketing and international findings, from the extensive survey we completed, and detailed return-on-investment proof points, will knock their socks off. There are two foreign board members, one from Japan and one from France. Bailey will deliver a portion in Japanese, and I'll do some in French...Yes, ma'am, I know you'll be listening and cheering for us. Thank you for letting me attend this school and find Bailey. She's my best friend, outside of my family....

She chuckled. "Of course we'll take some selfies...

Okay, I gotta get ready. Love you..."

After sliding into her best satin underwear, Gracie checked out her smooth lines in the mirror. Her confidence rose a notch. Then she started on her hair with a brush in one hand and the blow dryer in the other. Drying and styling with practiced moves, she was nearly finished when Bailey returned.

Bailey added her first layer of clothing and stood by Gracie as she finished. "You have great hair, Gracie. I almost wish I was blonde too."

"You're a knock-out with your naturally wavy dark hair and that heart-shaped face. I've watched all these guys check you out from the moment we met. Always you first. Like Sean."

"He's pretty cute and in all our classes. But he's a flirt who ignores no, in any form. Heck, on our coffee date when he expected more, he showed me we had zero future. You said he was self-centered. You were right. My parents taught me to not mistake blarney as sincerity regardless of the spoken and unspoken language. We're the best roomies."

"Yep. He's a piece of work. He and Ian present after us. He won't realize he lost already." She laughed. "Not after our amazing presentation. No way they can win." She passed the handle. "Here's the dryer. I'll do my makeup and then get dressed. I'm so excited."

"I've got butterflies so bad, Gracie. We get breakfast after our preso, right?"

"That's the plan. Besides, I'm too nervous to eat."

Makeup applied, hair fixed in similar styles, and clothes perfect, Bailey and Gracie checked themselves in the mirror. Gracie did a slight turn and peered over her shoulder with a quick smile. "We are professional business women, dressed for the part."

Their images appeared together in the mirror and they grinned. "Seriously professional." Bailey added with a nod. "One blonde, the other brunette."

They hip-bumped and high-fived one another. "Quick, I promised my mom we'd snag selfies."

They each snapped shots of one another.

Gracie scrolled her photos to text to her mom.

"Gracie, how did you get the shot of me?" Bailey asked while she watched over her friend's shoulder. "I looked at the group of pics you're sending your mom."

Gracie shrugged, then chortled. "You sent it to me right after you took it. Boy, you must be nervous. Come on, girlfriend." Gracie hid her guilt with practiced facial control and gently patted Bailey's shoulder. After these many months at school, Gracie hoped her remote snooping of Bailey's phone would not get discovered.

"You're right; I must be. I don't remember." She opened her phone, saw the clock, and found the photo she sent in a text message. Giving her head a quick shake, she grabbed her laptop and nervously laughed. "We're right on time. Let's do this."

Thirty minutes later, Gracie and Bailey strode into the presentation room. They quickly set up the equipment and had time to complete a cursory check before the side door opened. The board of advisors and the visiting business leaders filled the executive-style leather chairs behind the table. Pens and pads for scoring sat on the table beside the folders they positioned for each attendee.

The girls greeted each member by name, and shook hands. Gracie swallowed her nervousness as the first slide of the presentation flashed onto the screen. "The folders can be used to follow along or reviewed later. We've provided the details of the surveys we conducted as back up to our findings." The slides complimented the details of her discussion. At the five-minute mark, Bailey took over.

"We were surprised at the numbers resulting from the investment model. After the third verification, we are confident in our projections of the value-add of our marketing plan."

Gracie glanced at the clock behind the judges and noted the nods of agreement from three of them during the presentation. As Bailey added her piece focused for the Japanese business leader, and the man's features twitched into a brief smile. Bailey passed the final section of their delivery back to Gracie and added a self-assured wink.

Gracie's confidence soared when she delivered the final. "Based on the results, we are ready to publish our findings to the international business journal. We'd like your recommendation."

Applause from the judges echoed in the chamber and embedded the auspicious moment in her memories. The gentleman from France stood as the girls walked the length of the table thanking each judge. "Bailey, Gracie, a thorough presentation. I will review the backup data you provided. If that matches your summary, which I have no doubt it will, then I will sponsor your findings in the publication." Others on the board murmured their agreement with slight grins of approval.

Gracie knew in that moment, their hours of work paid dividends they'd never considered. They gathered their materials used in the presentation and exited holding their heads high. Sean and Ian were in the hallway, getting ready for their time in the spotlight.

Sean smugly commented, "We know you, lassies tried, but now we'll show the board the winning presentation. Let me know when I should set up your remedial training support."

Gracie smiled, restraining Bailey, who turned a bright red as her anger surged. "Sean, no worries. We're happy with what we did, and the grades will tell us in a few days who won. Come on, Bailey. Let's go eat; I'm starved."

Bailey pasted on her false smile. "Yep." She waved. "See ya, boyzzzz." They turned and chuckled as they strutted down the hallway toward the exit.

The girls crowed with excitement the rest of the day. They checked in with their parents and confirmed their arrival for graduation on Saturday.

"Hey, Bailey, what should we do tonight?"

"I know, let's go to the pub for dinner and maybe sing. Tonight's talent night, and you know how I love to flex my voice."

"Sure, we've earned it. I got your back always. Promise." Gracie felt a sense of pride in their friendship and a twinge of regret that they'd soon return to their respective homes.

Changing into fresh jeans and tee shirts, the young women joked as they headed out searching for nourishment. Regardless of the outcome of the presentation, they would receive their dual master's degrees in International Marketing and International Finance made them feel the world was their oyster. Getting the win would be whipped cream on the hot fudge sundae they hoped to add for desert tonight. After months of visiting the local pub, the girls greeted their friend Erin who greeted them with hugs.

"I know you two are going home soon. I'll put you in the corner booth and send over some complimentary wine. I'll miss you both."

"We'll come visit," they replied in unison, crossing their hearts and raising their right hands.

A slight haze of fragrant pipe smoke mixed with the scents of the evening fare greeted Gracie's nostrils as they were seated. She stood a moment inhaling the cedar-scented air and listening to the muted voices enjoying the ambiance and company. The soft, worn leather seats were comfortable and matched the old-fashioned décor. Oil paintings of quaint farmhouses, children at play, and musical gatherings related a sense of the region's history: friendly and welcoming. From here she could see the band stage. It was empty at this time, but the place was otherwise a beehive of activity. The booth was ideally situated, except it was furthest from the privy. She planned to order shepherd's pie and ribs. When she mentioned this to Bailey, her friend agreed with a hearty nod. A few minutes later, the wine arrived. The server had barely finished pouring a glass when she had it in-hand for a toast.

"I love this red wine, Bailey. Make certain I only have two," begged Gracie.

"I'm right with you. It's good but runs to my head."

They tapped to the beat and smiled at everyone who stopped by for a *hey*. Bailey ordered the second round of wine and two glasses of water. "We must drink the water before the next wine, girlfriend."

"That helps?"

"Oh, yeah," Bailey assured. Raising an eyebrow, she softly added, "Incoming from three o'clock."

As the song ended, Sean and Ian swaggered toward their booth.

"Hey, Ian, watch these two cailíní. Folks swear Americans can't hold their liquor," Sean taunted.

Gracie smirked and suggested, "Perhaps, but I'm not American. We Europeans are far more sophisticated than you stogey Irish lads."

"I hope you lads won't feel too bad about taking runner up to a pair of businesswomen like us," Bailey added. "Likely, you'll have to get used to it."

Sean sneered, "Don't you wish, lass. I've not met a lass who claims to be a professional that I can't beat." He laughed uproariously, and Ian joined him as they strolled off.

The girls' drinks arrived, and they downed the waters in short order. Bailey sighed, "Too bad that Sean's so cute on the outside but possesses a devil's heart."

Gracie dismissively flicked her hand "He's just dust in the wind. Please—" she rolled her eyes— "don't give him another thought. You've got a great future ahead of you, my dear friend. When we take the prize over the weekend, we graciously smile. Don't ever let them know what you're thinking."

"I'll be right back." Bailey slid out of the booth. "We need to toast our success when the next glass of wine arrives."

Gracie grinned and nodded in agreement. She wanted the next few days to stretch forever. Once home, she'd need to make a decision on whether she wanted a role in the family business. From her youth she'd trained and learned how to combat the evil forces in the world, but she had the right to choose that more secret existence or plunge into the professional world with humanity. Gracie recognized life would change forever with her choice. She pulled out her phone and texted her brother.

JJ, how did you think the presentation went?

The reply:

I think you nailed it—the guys after you were amateurs by comparison.

Gracie chewed her lip, reflecting on her day.

I love having a brother who looks out for me.

Do you think our folks liked it?

They're proud of you, Sis.

The spotter on Gracie's phone in her hand lit up like a Christmas tree. She inserted her earbud to hear the exchange. It was Bailey, and she sounded scared as she begged, "Stop, Sean. Let me go." Gasping breaths, "Don't drag me outside! Ian, don't let him."

Gracie quickly texted.

Gotta go.

Gracie sprang from her seat. She raced from the table worming around the booths and guests like an obstacle course professional. She hit the toilet hallway and spotted Ian holding the exit door. She wondered, *what in heavens name was going on?* Hearing Bailey's protests, she shoved Ian out of the way. The door swung shut, the image of Sean holding Bailey against the wall by her throat sending her into a rage. Gracie's adrenalin skyrocketed, pushing into her throat as a lump. Suddenly she couldn't breathe. No. She had to help Bailey!

"Sean, I said no," reverberated in her earpiece.

Gracie's training kicked into high gear. No one could hurt her friend and get away with it. Ian reopened the door beside her. She delivered a kick to his stomach, then his head that sent him to the ground in a heap gasping for air.

Sean didn't notice her. Anger distorted his face when he raised his fist to punch Bailey. Gracie rushed over, grabbed his arm and yanked it behind him. The satisfying cracking sound of the dislocated shoulder echoed in the alleyway. She whirled and delivered a perfect kick to his balls. A short scream of agony bounced off the walls, then he passed out.

Bailey slid to the ground hitting her head with a muffled clunk. Gracie dropped to her knees beside Bailey, feeling the sting of the rough concrete on her skin. Bailey was out. She stroked her friend's cheek, willing her to open her eyes, all the while doing a cursory check. She found a bump on the back of her head and a scrape on the forehead.

"Bailey, Bailey, can you hear me?" Her eyes fluttered, yet she did not gain full consciousness. "Gracie," Bailey whispered, "Glad you're here. How'd you find...?"

Gracie teared up. "I'll always know where you are. I sensed you needed extra support, though heaven knows you stand on your own most times."

Bailey opened her eyes and appeared to focus. "My head hurts. Where's Sean?"

"He's in a heap behind me. He won't hurt you now. Ian's out too."

Bailey grabbed onto her friend, trying to pull herself up.

"Let me help you. Do you think you can stand?"

"Yes."

Gracie smiled. "Good." She stood and reached to help Bailey gain footing.

Bailey inhaled and patted her shirt. "I think I'm okay."

"Great, let's get you tidied up before we toast with our wine."

Bailey nodded. Together they made their way into the pub. Bailey cleaned up a bit in the privy while Gracie stood guard.

She opened the door to check Bailey's progress. "Are you alright?"

Bailey finger combed her hair, then fluffed it a bit. Her eyes angrily flashed as she pressed the cold, wet towel to her cheek. "I'll probably find a bruise tomorrow, but otherwise, I'm just mad." Pulling at the rip on her shirt to show the damage, she added, "He wrecked my memento shirt of the Queen. The ass."

Taking off her lightweight hoodie she handed it to Bailey. "Put this on. We'll find another shirt tomorrow. I'm sorry you got hurt." Tears filled her eyes.

"I'm glad you kicked his butt. Ian too. He's jealous of our friendship and I guess still mad that I didn't want to date him." Bailey chuckled. "I'll be fine, but he's gonna remember never to mess with you."

They hugged and laughed. "Not the way we planned to celebrate," Bailey commented.

"We will remember the good parts of the day, over that jerk. Come on." They strolled to their prime spot to toast, eat, and sing with the band.

Reseated, Gracie signaled their pub buddy. "Hey, Erin, a couple of lads were trying to get fresh with Bailey. They're in the back alley and seem *over-served*. Would you be a dear and alert the constable?"

Erin cocked her head until realization dawned. She rushed to make the call.

Bailey said, "Thank you, Gracie. We make a great team."

Gracie fluttered her fingers in between tasting bites of food. She picked up her phone and spent the next few minutes with her fingers flying.

"Message from home?" Bailey asked.

"No. Just making sure things are good for graduation. All good."

"Should I ask for details on how you found me so fast, or is that something I should trust works when I'm with you?"

"Trust me. We all have our family secrets, right? I have some awesome resources. I meant what I said about keeping track of you. You're my friend. Friends stick together."

Gracie saw the color return to Bailey's face.

"Okay, one more sip of wine." Bailey raised her glass. "Cheers, my friend!"

Gracie's phone buzzed for an incoming text.

> Gracie, we'll discuss this later, Mom.
> p.s. Love you.

CHAPTER 1
PRESENT DAY

Changing of the Guard

Finished with the last meeting of the day, Gracie flumped down in her soft office chair and breathed a deep sigh. She took a generous swallow from the cold glass of water, and said to no one in particular, "This two-job thing feels almost like Jekyll and Hyde. Someone should have warned me when I made my life choice."

She'd barely shut her eyes when the phone erupted again. This time she smiled at the incoming caller ID. "Hi JJ, I'm glad you called. It'll do me good to speak with my favorite twin. It's been one of those kinds of days."

She pictured his dark hair and swarthy complexion with the same wiry build as their dad. She favored the fair skin tone, dark blond hair and slender form of their mother. She briefly thought about her daily workouts, whereas children, he bested her half the time. She knew that the next time they saw each other he'd suggest a rematch to see if she kept up her practice.

Sounding dejected, JJ admitted, "Would you be disappointed if I'd called to whine?"

"Only if I get to go first," Gracie chuckled. "I take it you're overwhelmed like me in our new roles."

"I was doing fine in the modest cyber assassin role for the CATS team," JJ confirmed, "And being in charge was a dream come true. That is, until the dream morphed into a nightmare. To be fair, the people I manage are pros. They try to help guide me but my response to most of their questions is a pathetic, *what would you do*? I think they realize I'm a fake."

"Oh, JJ," Gracie sympathized, "I think your role is much tougher than mine. I mean, running the R-Group, the logistics of placing operatives with the right skillset into covert operations and then extracting them in one piece… It must be nerve wracking."

"Hey, wait a minute," protested JJ. "I'm not the one who uses her full-time job at the World Bank as cover for managing R-Group resources poking into stuff around the world. You can't possibly aid all the global customers begging for help with cyber threats from the Darknet. If you think I'm gonna trade jobs for your pressure cooker role, you're several sandwiches short of a full picnic basket. I'm wiser cuz I'm older."

Gracie smirked. "By minutes, JJ. Less than five." She giggled. "Aren't we funny? We've groomed for these roles all our lives. Even though we're complaining, we wouldn't think of shirking our responsibilities. I like that I have someone to talk to, especially since you're so much older and experienced."

She heard JJ's rapid tapping on the keyboard, responding to what she assumed were a few emails, before refocusing on the dialog. "Do you find our cousins helpful with your projects?" he asked.

Gracie looked up into the imaginary window above her head. "Granger and JW are exactly like their fathers. JW's quiet, reflective with old-world manners like Uncle Jacob. When those two join forces on a problem—they take no prisoners. After Granger pulls his head out of the supercomputer he and Uncle Quip rebuilt, he leads with the heart of a smart aleck. I think they'd respond better to your guidance.

"Satya and Auri are delightful pre-teens that respond easily to direction. They display the cutest, inquisitive minds until you realize their computer analytic skills have them operating at a Ph.D. level in advanced mathematics."

JJ chuckled. "I believe that if anyone asked them to map the correlation of peanut butter to jet engines, you'd get that answer in specific, logical detail."

"True that," she agreed. "Next time we meet, I plan to be close when you ask that question. I bet Satya will answer first."

"My money's on Auri by a mile," JJ insisted.

Gracie filed away the bet she'd make for that conversation. She smiled at the picture her mind conjured. "How 'bout your team? I'm pretty sure you inherited a team of alpha personalities. Does anyone seem like a good candidate for a deputy position for your CATS team? Dad supported mom when they assembled the Cyber Assassins Technical Services group. With their experience it would make sense to move one of them into the role to take on some of the management duties. You need to spend time with your lovely bride."

"Some of our operatives returned to their respective governments, like Summit, who went home to India." JJ clucked his tongue in mock annoyance, and protested, "Hey, no fair reading my mind. Yeah, this is what I'm reviewing these days. Mercedes works part-time so she and Jim can take it easy. Our two cyber freebooters, Judith and Xiamara, work on call as contractors. I always have to check to see if they got arrested before sending work their way." JJ cleared his throat and continued, "Brayson shows the best aptitude for becoming my deputy director. He's more like a peer than an employee. I enjoy working with him and his wife, Marian."

Gracie released a breath, annoyed with her frustration. "I'm hearing that we have the best jobs on the planet with some great team members. We need to stop whining."

JJ laughed aloud. “When you put it like that, I know you’re right.”

Almost simultaneously, their cell phones lit up with incoming calls.

Gracie chuckled. “Looks like today’s therapy session is over. Talk later, JJ.”

Gracie chided herself for an unnecessary pity party. “JJ’s dealing, and so can you,” she whispered to her inner self.

CHAPTER 2

How Was Your Day?

Jeff sat on his comfy brown leather couch positioned in front of the windows of his high-rise Manhattan apartment. He'd moved here when he started practicing law. The one bedroom was oversized with a king-size bed decorated in shades of blue covers. The walls adorned with various painted seascapes he purchased while attending college. An adjoining bathroom included a whirlpool tub, ideal for relaxing after a few games of racquetball, which he played now and again. The kitchen was fully outfitted with every necessary gadget to create gourmet meals. Light jazz played in the background.

His emotions felt as tight as harp strings with no song to play. It was like the in-between moments of daytime shifting to evening, and the twinkle of city lights illuminating the view. He reached for his phone and put it down at least five times before he scolded himself. "Jeff, old boy, you got it bad. Wait and let her call you about the speaking engagement in Amsterdam. If you ask, she'll wonder how you found out before her, so wait." His wandering mind postulated, "Of course, that assumes she wants you to go along. With her busy schedule she rarely even stays overnight."

Sounds of the incoming call startled him back to the present. He fumbled to answer. "Hi, Honey, what's up? Did you have a good day?"

"Mr. Wood." He felt like a dog when Gracie complained. "Weren't you going to call me with the good news about the speaking engagement? Did you get busy and forget?"

Staring blankly at the floor, he sat dumbfounded.

"Jeff, honey, are you there? You must be in a bad cell zone. I'll call back later."

He found his voice. "No, wait, I'm here. I was just, uh…how did you know I knew about it? I didn't tell anybody."

Gracie laughed with the sweetness that tickled his heart. "You know I have more than one job. I'm not just some finance quant crunching numbers before approving a loan. My other job is a little more delicate to discuss—information-brokering, in a nutshell. I practice being ahead of the data rather than waiting for it to appear. Jeff, I appreciate you submitting me for consideration to the European committee. A recommendation looks better coming from a third party; it carries more weight."

Jeff moaned, lamenting the lost opportunity of surprise. "I haven't felt this deflated since that time my parents admitted it was them that put the money under my pillow at night, and not the tooth fairy."

"Don't be silly," she pleaded, "I'm delighted you helped me. I know lately we've had limited time together. I'm asking you to attend the conference with me. I miss you. Speaking at this global conference is an important milestone in my career. I want you with me. Afterward, I'd like to introduce you to my family in Switzerland."

Jeff's heart soared as he considered the possibilities of time together. "Really? I'd like that, Gracie. Time with you to lavish affection and meet your family. Count me in."

Gracie chuckled softly. "Perfect. I planned booking one room, and it will include a king-sized bed. What do you think? Am I missing anything?"

"Outstanding. I didn't get labeled as a creeper," Jeff bantered. "But I'm promoted from a keeper to a sleeper?"

Gracie sarcastically groaned, "Did you start celebrating my win without me?"

Unsure if she was teasing, Jeff chuckled. "Admit it, Gracie, I'm cute when you're mad."

The soft answer had the desired effect, and she giggled. It took a minute to catch her breath before she asked, "Where're we going for dinner tonight?"

"I thought I'd cook at my place." Jeff added, "I make a great veal parmesan. I figured I'd add steamed seasonal veggies and rice on the side. Can you supply a nice wine? I'll have the hors d'oeuvres ready to serve at six, if that works with your schedule."

"I can't wait. I'm starved. I can't wait to toast my win for the conference. Thank you."

On her way home to change, Gracie grabbed the perfect wine for dinner. She gathered her coat to head to Jeff's when she received a text from Bailey:

> Gracie. You once told me you had connections that did investigative sleuthing. My team lead, Morgan, needs that expertise. Can I call to discuss?

Gracie studied the text and replied:

> Bailey, please send me the details in email to help me understand. Then we can talk.

Bailey replied:

> Thanks, girl. BTW, congrats on the speaking engagement that just hit the wires. Talk soon.

Gracie pondered the possibilities. It sounded like a new piece of R-Group business. "Should I call Mom and ask about the wisdom of taking a business contract from a friend? I know she'll ask, why be in business if not to help your friends? After all, that was why Grandpa's dad started the business."

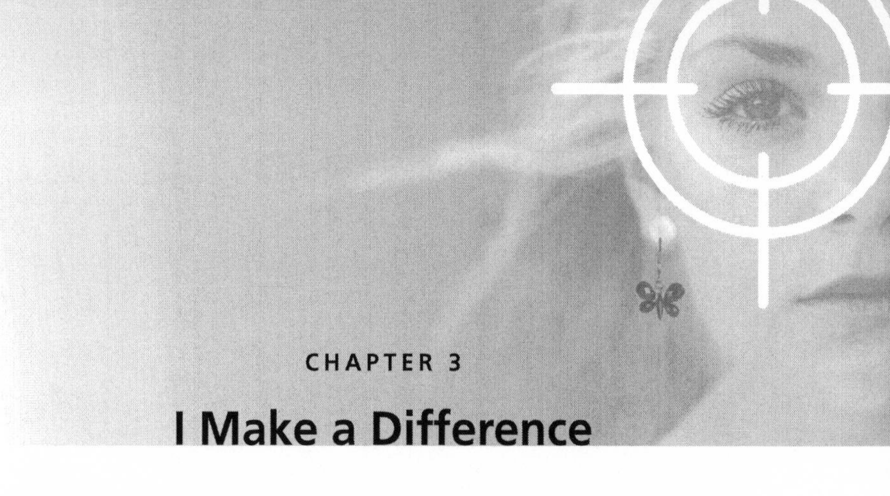

CHAPTER 3

I Make a Difference

Before she knew it, the day arrived to travel to the conference. The direct flight from New York to Amsterdam was textbook smooth with customs a modest formality. Their hotel transport driver had barely raised the name plaque sign when they found him. Jeff assisted with loading the luggage, and they were whisked away to their romantic destination.

Gracie, admiring their surroundings, offered, "Jeff, I love the subtle elegance of the herringbone pattern on this brickwork walkway. It's so even." She performed an exaggerated soft shoe, the toe of her heels marking out The Toren Hotel's stone step entry. She glanced at the façade, then the transfixed Jeff. "The walkway, not my leg."

Jeff smiled and shook his head as if recovering from a sucker punch. "Damn nice legs, though."

Gracie blushed, immediately flashing on the passion potential for their first night in Amsterdam. She stood on tiptoe and kissed his cheek. Finding the suitcase handle, she grabbed it and tucked her other hand into the crook of his elbow. "Let's check-in, drop our bags, and go discover Amsterdam. The Anne Frank house is nearby. I'd love to check it out in the daylight. The skies are clear and the temperature is perfect for walking. Wouldn't you like to stretch your legs after that long flight from New York? Today is our play day."

"Play or walk, tough choice. Gracie, my sweet, this is a side of you I haven't seen before. Are you still a bit buzzed from the champagne on the flight?"

"Maybe," she grinned, "but I'm delighted to be here with you. I'm getting a touch of nerves about the conference tomorrow."

"You're gonna be great. Come on, you, let's get to our room, change, and go sightseeing."

Gracie looked around as if reconnoitering their upcoming walk. "Which way should we go first?"

"We can ask for directions to Anne Frank's, but I vote we start at the bakery next door and snag something sweet and spicey. Doesn't that aroma tempt you?"

Gracie laughed and tugged his arm as she started up the steps. "I can smell the chocolate in the air."

"Your right, honey. But there's something mixed with it, some sort of spice."

She inhaled. "Definitely cinnamon. We'll get the goodies, then walk off the calories."

"Deal."

Jeff joined her, chuckling while they entered the hotel. They approached the check-in desk and handed over their passports to Sophie, according to her nametag. "Good morning and welcome. You're checking in?"

Gracie grinned, observing Sophie's fingers flying across the keyboard.

The clerk slightly frowned. "One moment. I need to verify something." Sophie picked up the phone and quietly spoke into it.

Gracie raised an eyebrow, then shook off her worry and murmured to Jeff. "It'll be fine. We're expected. My admin confirmed when we landed so we're good."

Sophie hung up and smiled. "Someone will be here shortly."

A tall man emerged from behind a door with a serious expression and motioned them to join him at the adjacent window. "Ms. Rodreguiz, Mr. Wood, I'm Daan Jensen, the concierge. We had a booking issue that altered your reservation. Instead of the room you requested here on the ground floor, we've had to move you to the honeymoon suite. It has a wonderful view."

Gracie felt astonished. Jeff looked skeptical.

Daan continued, "There's no additional charge to you for our mistake. We're including the normal perks of the room for the inconvenience."

Gracie glanced at Jeff and grinned. "Daan, this is a stunning windfall. Thank you for finding us a room. We know how crowded you must be with the Global Conference starting tomorrow."

"Yes, madam. We know you're one of the featured speakers."

Gracie delivered a gracious, practiced smile and blinked her eyes. "Thank you, again."

Showing support along with a bit of pride, Jeff grinned and pulled her closer. "Daan, Gracie and I need to drop our luggage and go see your beautiful city after grabbing a bite to eat. Can you provide us directions to a couple of sights we shouldn't miss, especially Anne Frank's?"

"Yes, sir, of course. I'll also call and let Sven know you'll be by after lunch at the bakery He's the best at telling the story and history." Carefully writing down the directions then reviewing them verbally, he handed her the paper.

Gracie secured the directions safely into her purse. "This is great. Thanks, Jeff. Are you ready?"

Jeff accepted the card key from Daan and waggled his eyebrows toward Gracie. "Always for you, my dear."

Grabbing their bags and holding hands, they went to the open elevator. When the door closed, Gracie did a short happy dance and pressed the button for the top floor. "I love how things work out. Isn't it great being us?"

She watched Jeff key the door lock that opened to reveal the suite. The colors and charm were like a movie set. Gracie hugged Jeff with delight and glided into the room, oohing and aahing at the elegant beauty.

"This is a great home away from home for a few days," Jeff commented as he headed toward the bathroom. "You do have a knack for the unimagined, honey."

Gracie laughed. She changed into jeans and walking shoes then expertly unpacked and stowed the contents with the practiced hand of an experienced traveler.

Jeff emerged and rushed to finish the same chore. "Remind me later to draw you a bubble bath."

Gracie sighed, eyeing him from head to toe. "Okay, I'll light the candles while you pour the wine."

"Let's go."

Hand-in-hand, they went to enjoy the recommended lunch venue and go see the historical sites.

Gracie licked her lips as they exited the bakery. "I think the best part was the spice cookie dipped in chocolate."

"I don't know, sweetheart, the sandwich on the flakey roll hit the spot."

She nodded. "It is a tasty place. We may need to stop back again before leaving town." She pulled out the directions. "Let's see what Sven can tell us about Anne Frank." They turned toward their destination as a group of bicyclers steered around them. "Jeff, look at the flowers on some of those bicycles.

"I read that Amsterdam is the bicycle capital of the world. Residents and visitors ride any and all varieties, especially near the canals." Jeff pointed to the array of bike racks lining the waterway. "It seems like a great way to get around."

Gracie tucked her arm in his and turned him right away from the hotel. "Yep. Walking works too. We're headed this way."

Sven greeted them. "Welcome, Daan said you'd be by. I'm delighted to speak to anyone about the brave, inspirational Anne Frank."

"I understand she wrote letters to her friends in her diary," Gracie started. "That confused me when I heard that because I thought she was isolated."

"You're correct. Anne and her family spent the majority of their time in the Secret Annex. There Anne invented a group of friends to discuss the events of her life in her diary. Kitty, Pop, Phien, Conny, Lou, Marjan, Jettje, and Emmy were fictional friends, with Kitty being her favorite, or so she wrote. Anne met Kitty in school while reading the *Joop ter Heul* books, written by Cissy van Marxveldt before going into hiding. She actually finished the series while isolated. She hoped to publish her own stories someday. Thankfully someone helped her achieve that goal."

Sven took them to the area to see the original documents. They marveled at the volume of written work from the young girl.

"How long did Anne stay hidden here?" Jeff asked.

"She arrived in 1942 when the Nazis occupied the Netherlands. A scant two years later she was discovered. She died in the Bergen-Belsen concentration camp in 1945."

Sven took them into the space of the Secret Annex where they climbed the steep steps up to the attic. Gracie's eyes filled with tears at the cramped quarters with renewed outrage at the racist attitudes of Germans against the Jews.

Jeff spotted the markings on the magazine wallpaper of the room. "What do these markings represent?"

Sven smiled. "Those are the growth charts for Anne and her sisters while in residence. They were safe until Tonny Ahlers betrayed their location to a detective."

“What a heartbreaking story,” lamented Gracie. “I’m glad we got a chance to see where she and her family spent those years.”

“How were her works spared?” Jeff softly asked.

“Following the arrest of the eight people hiding here, the helpers found Anne’s writings in the Secret Annex. Madam Miep Gies kept the diaries and her papers in the drawer of her desk. She’d hoped to return them to Anne, but of course that didn’t happen.”

They descended to the area that described the horrific persecution of the Jewish people in the Netherlands. The information was available to visitors, schools, and other groups. The atrocities would not be forgotten, Sven emphasized.

A couple of hours later, they thanked their guide and headed outside for a slow walk back to the hotel.

Gracie dabbed at her eyes. “I think Anne’s story and strength of survival should be remembered, but I wish she’d lived to tell her own story.”

Jeff hugged her close. “I agree. Thank you for bringing me along. I learned a great deal.”

“Me too. Let’s pick up a few gifts on the way back to the hotel. I need a bit of happy to round out our day.”

Jeff snatched her hand and started down the walkway with a silly two-step skip she adopted with a hint of laughter.

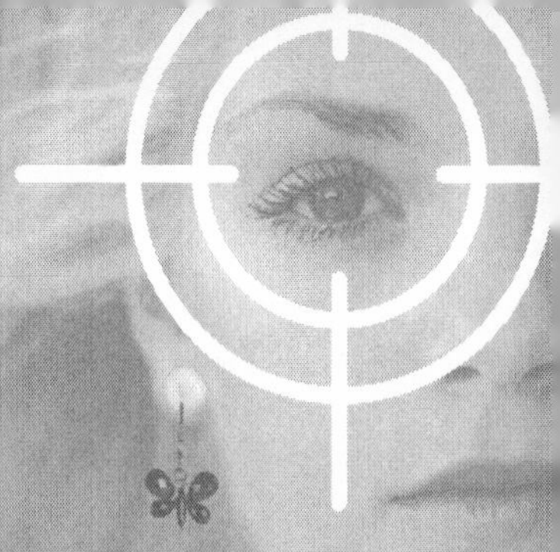

CHAPTER 4

Relaxation with a Bit of Fun

They returned to the hotel and took the open elevator to their floor. Jeff opened the door and motioned Gracie through then locked it. Gracie set the bag of souvenirs they'd acquired onto table by the entry. He spotted the plate of cheese and wine chilling in the silver ice bucket. "How 'bout I open the wine and take it to the patio along with the snacks? You can remove those shoes you've been complaining about and we can relax."

"A wonderful idea." She blew him a kiss before disappearing into the bedroom.

Jeff unlatched the glass doorway and set the plate on the table. He admired the view, satisfied it made a pretty backdrop for pleasant conversation. Returning inside to open the wine, he commented as they passed one another, "Great room, honey. The view's picturesque."

Gracie glided out and took a seat, gazing at the colors of the building, the flowers, the pedestrians, and the canal traffic. She smiled warmly as Jeff handed her a glass. "Thank you. If I'd realized this room contained a bird's eye view of the canal, I would have begged for it when the reservations were made."

"Have you always liked history?"

"I have. The story of Anne Frank was one I wanted to see firsthand. I couldn't help but admire the thoughtful discussion we had with our guide. Daan was right. Sven answered everything.

A remarkable, but tragic story. I'm appalled that racism and injustice against others still exists."

Raising his glass toward her, he said, "To Amsterdam—an amazing location. The Toren for the romantic room. And to you, Gracie, for your big heart and brilliant mind."

Warmly grinning, Gracie nodded. "Cheers, Jeff. So glad you're here."

The crystal note was perfect as they looked at one another then sipped. Gracie groaned her pleasure at the essence of the taste and almost-chocolate overtones of the wine. "This zinfandel is wonderful. Great choice."

"Thank you. I can't wait to go through the rest of what I have planned for this evening, including that foot massage I promised."

"Sounds perfect." Gracie's face glowed as she licked her lips. Then the ring of her phone paused the moment.

"It's Bailey. Fifteen minutes early. Sorry, I do have to take this."

Jeff's eyes twinkled. "I'll save your place. You aren't going that far."

Jeff's eyes followed Gracie inside. He noticed she didn't close the door. He watched her establish the security settings before answering, as usual. "Gracie Rodreguiz," he heard in her all-business tone from the activated speaker, so he could listen to both sides of the conversation. He mused, *her trust level of me must be growing.*

"Well, you sound official," Bailey's voice sounded clear. "Sorry, I know this is a bit early, but I figured since your presentation is tomorrow morning, you'd be turning in soon."

Grinning, she chuckled, "Bailey, my friend. Thank you for remembering my event, though I hope you're not stalking me. I'm a little nervous about how well I'll come across to this audience. By the way, our trophy is well shined, right? It's almost my turn to have it on display."

"I haven't forgotten. But stalking you? As if you don't know exactly where I am most of the time."

Despite the joke, it didn't escape Gracie's notice that Bailey sounded tense.

"Everything good in Amsterdam?" Bailey asked.

"Gorgeous. And even more so since Jeff's here with me."

"Oh, no! I've interrupted your evening, I—"

"No worries, he knew I was expecting your call. I read the high-level overview in the email you sent, but I sense you purposely left some stuff out, plus you seem a bit edgy. Catch me up?"

Jeff heard Bailey take a long breath. "Okay. You know we opened a case a while back involving the CEO of Pliant."

"Right. Huge fish in a dirty pond."

"Correct," Bailey groused. "The world might think of him as a whale—a huge, intelligent creature who deserves our support and protection. But we're now pretty sure he's more like a great white."

"Great white shark?"

"You got it. King predator of the sea, or in this case, of the ecology movement. As of yet, unproven though. Which is the problem."

"And the reason you're calling me. So, surveillance, right? Are we talking professionally, personally, or both?"

"Uh, well, that's among the many things on our list of tasks. And we're hoping to have a chance to find out a lot more about him up close and personal."

"Not sure I like the sound of that." Gracie turned to face Jeff for a moment, biting her lip.

"See if you like the sound of this. One week aboard a Monarch cruise, all expenses paid."

"Wow, I DO like the sound of that!"

"Thought you might. Hoping that would be your stance, our company booked two staterooms. One for me. One for you. Here's the thing. You're speaking at that conference, and then planning to enjoy the holidays in Europe, right? This cruise departs Miami in January, which might cut your vacation short. I know your passport's current, but how about your cruise wardrobe?"

"Ah." Gracie laughed uproariously. "That's a problem I know exactly how to fix. One question, though."

"Only one?" Bailey teased.

"Can I bring Jeff?"

Jeff noted the hopeful edge to Gracie's voice.

Bailey paused. "That solves one issue. Since Jeff is in your world, he knows some of your extra work capabilities and would pass our vetting protocols, right?"

"With flying colors," Gracie confirmed, "and then some. His area of specialization is a little different from mine, but he'd be an asset, whatever you have in mind, believe me."

With a sigh of relief, Bailey added, "Okay, full disclosure, my boyfriend is coming along too."

"Keith? Ah, he's graduated from being an occasional date to being an official boyfriend?"

"We'll see. He's due here in South City, and we, uh…we have issues to hammer out. Meanwhile, as far as this mission is concerned, our relationship's a cover. He'll be tracking the shipments while you and I keep an eye on our bad guy. But Keith and I can travel as a couple, holding hands, smooching, and, uh, well, whatever else."

"Sounds like real hardship duty," Gracie replied with a touch of irony in her tone.

Jeff inched forward, trying to catch Gracie's facial features.

Bailey laughed. Gracie appeared pleased to hear some of the tension leave her friend's voice.

"So," Gracie said, "we'll be two couples on a romantic holiday. Straw hats, string bikinis, slinky dresses, and too much food."

Bailey chuckled again. "You've got the picture. I take it I'm going to like Jeff personally, not just professionally?"

"You'll love him like a brother. Fair warning, he's been taking handsome-lessons, but he's all mine."

"Absolutely. I've always wanted a brother." Bailey took a breath. "Honestly, I'll be grateful for the help from both of you. If we're right about our bad guy, he's as dangerous as they come. It looks like prior snoopers are missing, presumed dead." Her tone abruptly shifted from concern to take-charge. "Listen, my friend, following our meeting, you'll receive the full itinerary, so you know which islands we're visiting. We think there'll be a transaction at or near every port, so we'll have to ramp up our faux tourist activities. All the T&C's will be captured in the contract I'll send over. I hope we'll get the friends and family discount, hmm?"

Gracie smirked and added, "I'm sure we can come to an equitable arrangement depending on the number of resource hours. Family discounts definitely apply for such sweet duty as a cruise ship in the Caribbean in January. But to your earlier point, I'll do a full background on each island stop, so we know what infrastructure's available locally. Fortunately, Jeff can help with that."

"One more thing. We'll want drones, but they'll have to be super-subtle. I know your team can come up with just about anything. And with our marketing brains, we're always thinking branding. So how about tiny drones made to look like—"

"Monarch butterflies?" Gracie interrupted.

"Took the words right out of my mouth," Bailey said with a chuckle.

"Agreed. That's a problem I'll tackle. I think possibilities might also include dragonflies, exotic birds, or even lizards. Perhaps something different for the island stops. But while onboard, yes, add the symbol for the ship. I'll send it to you."

"As usual, we're on the same page. Okay, I've kept you on the phone long enough," Bailey said. "Thanks. Enjoy your conference, and we'll see you on the conference call tomorrow night."

"Hey," Gracie put in. "If this Pliant CEO is misbehaving, I'll help you make him pay."

"Thanks. This cruise will be our best get-together since school! You're awesome."

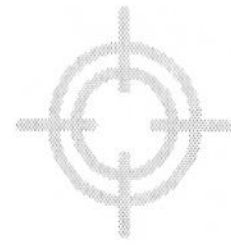

Gracie disconnected and sauntered back outside. "That was different, honey."

He refreshed her wine and grinned. "We're headed to Miami after Christmas? I'm glad you invited me."

Gracie leaned over and sweetly kissed him. "Me too."

They nearly finished the bottle of wine as they enjoyed the sounds of the city, a pleasant mixture of laughter, music from small groups lingering at outside tables, and conversations.

"Jeff, honey, I need to take care of a few things, if you don't mind."

"Sure, I'll jump in the shower and continue with my crime novel. Join me soon." He raised his eyebrows with a hint of future promises in his eyes, then gently kissed her, not nearly long enough.

Chuckling and even sparkling as her skin heated up, she smiled. "You sure know how to entice a girl to finish her chores. Be in soon."

Shaking off the thoughts of things to come, Gracie started up her laptop. She read a couple of emails, then sent her notes on her future time off. One email caught her eye for the conference tomorrow. It indicated where to arrive for a badge and possible follow-up events as options.

Using the special encryption enabled on her phone, Gracie placed a quick call to her twin.

He answered immediately. “Hey, Gracie. What’s up? When you didn’t call right after speaking with Bailey, I figured you were busy.”

“I’ll be busy after we outline ideas to help her. Sometimes it’s creepy when I realize you listen to most of my phone conversations.”

“I get it. But you do control the block sequence.”

“As long as you don’t spy on my choices of underwear and then tell me. Argh, you’re such a brat sometimes.”

“Back at ya, sis.” JJ, enjoying their favorite game of sibling taunting, sincerely added, “I told you I wouldn’t grade your choice of underwear ever again.”

“Regarding the earlier snoopers on Pliant activity ending up dead under suspicious circumstances, I’d say Bailey’s intel is good. Let’s decide what you need for the upcoming case with your college buddy.

“We’ll work together to make certain nothing bad happens to any of you. I’ll use our resources to protect the information-gathering process.”

Gracie smirked like she’d just won the lottery. “Oh, so you do care about Jeff and me? That’s so sweet, JJ. I know you’re the perfect mate for the dear Jo. You are so lucky that she wanted you.” Gracie chuckled and made kissing noises. “Back to the project. What kind of evidence-gathering can we engineer and not get caught? I like the idea of drones or digitally enabled insects, and we need a way to use them without alerting the cruise line security staff, even if we add cruise line branding to make it look official."

"Brayson and I spoke. He suggested a couple of things, then said he was going to go tinker in the back room. I suspect he wants a day or two to let his creative juices flow. He'll be your main backup contact." Then, snickering, JJ added, "Hey, where does Jeff go for his handsome-lessons? You can't seem to keep your hands off him. I don't want to fall behind in this category, ya know."

"JJ, you keep an eye on me, Bailey, and our team for this gig, and I'll make sure you get all the details for customized handsome-lessons. Don't get mad at me if they turn you down, and they only take cases where there is room for improvement."

"Ah, go on, you're killing me!" JJ chuckled. "I'll check back tomorrow after your presentation tomorrow to discuss our tactics. For now, say *goodnight, Gracie.*"

"Goodnight, Gracie."

CHAPTER 5

Price for Success

After a jam-packed conference, all Gracie wanted was to return to the hotel and unwind. The problem with newly earned notoriety is that everyone wanted to camp on.

Just as they crossed the threshold of the Hotel Toren, Daan Jensen, the concierge, called out, "Ms. Rodreguiz, a word please."

She looked quizzically at Jeff then back to the fast-approaching man. She shifted her weight from foot to foot, trying to hold on a little longer before the promised massage.

"The hotel wishes to extend our warmest congratulations on your outstanding presentation," Daan said. "We listened to the playback. You spoke with poise and authority. You've become something of a celebrity to the locals. Our staff is becoming overrun fielding requests for meetings, or at least introductions. I judge these requests as too intrusive and have alerted the staff to the proper responses. However, with your consent, we'd appreciate permission for our staff photographer to take shots of you with them. People like staying in places where famous people visited, so we'd use those publicity shots to boost our social media campaign. It would be a boon for the team at the hotel. To show our gratitude, I promise a free extra night stay, gourmet in-suite meals and wines at no cost to you for the remainder of your stay."

Maintaining her pleased expression while suppressing the urge to run screaming from the hotel, Gracie offered out of the side of her mouth to Jeff, "Holy crap, winged avenger! What do we do now?"

Jeff smiled as a professional, and promptly replied, "Daan, please forgive our reluctance to participate, but Ms. Rodreguiz is very conscious of her branding. This appears a little too commercial for her professional role representing World Bank."

Somewhat crestfallen, Daan pleaded, "Oh, is there no possibility of leveraging the moment for both of our situations?"

Gracie leaned forward as an idea formed. "My support could have a price, Daan. I'll agree to take part as described, but I want to see a worthy charity included. I would also like reassurances that this charity would receive any proceeds generated from the activity. Will that be agreeable?"

Gracie felt Jeff squeeze her hand like a gentle reassurance.

"Those terms are better than outstanding, madam. I'll provide you the details of what we consider a worthy charity. It's just down the street."

"If it is the continuing efforts to eradicate the injustices individuals like Anne Frank face in today's world, then we are aligned, Daan."

Jeff quietly offered, "Gracie, put on your dancing shoes 'cause the party isn't over."

Thankfully for Gracie's tired feet, two hours of meet-n-greet with photo ops passed in seeming seconds. At last, the pair headed to the elevators.

Jeff had barely opened their room door when Gracie slipped ahead, making a beeline for the sofa. She flumped down. "I'm exhausted! Not only a presentation, but panel discussions, and networking with financial leaders. I hadn't considered the committee to start serving wine just before noon, but someone mentioned it was tradition. And of course, the encore performance added here at the hotel. Heavens."

Jeff slid beside her on the couch and draped an arm over her shoulders. "Your speech was great. By all reports, you're a mind-blowing success, and clearly the global expert on the safe application of artificial intelligence in the financial marketplace. Before history rolls over it, what a nice gesture of the charity photo session for equal rights especially for displaced children."

Pulling her a little closer, he added, "For such a delicate lady—all five foot six, at a hundred-nineteen pounds soaking wet—from the opening line you commanded attention like Athena from the Acropolis."

They chuckled together.

"Thank you. It's good to know my boyfriend's got my back. I couldn't believe that annoying mister-endless-questions guy. I know he consumed too much of the fermented grape, yet his unappreciated advances were a total damper for everyone at the party. Thank you, my hero, for intercepting and encouraging him toward the buffet table."

Jeff snorted. "Even from where I watched, I saw that Dr. Grope was heading for personal space. You handled it most professionally. I got close enough just as you politely explained that you weren't part of the petting zoo. Hysterical, honey. And the look on his face, trust me…priceless. I think he memorized everything about you."

Gracie snuggled into Jeff's shoulder and rested her eyes. "I wanted to use the crushing high-heel stomp into his instep, or would the spin-kick to the side of his head have been better? I secretly hoped to see you standing on his hand while trying to help him up."

They laughed uproariously. Jeff pulled her a bit closer, distracting her with a passionate, probing kiss before releasing her lips. "Seriously, honey, your viewpoints on finances and investments, including properly leveraging technology without total dependency, put the crowd squarely in your hands. You did great."

Gracie's expression reflected her confidence. Then her phone registered an incoming call, and she promptly accepted with a smile. "Hi, JJ. We still on for tomorrow?... Great, we'll see you at ten…" Gracie's face immediately contorted into a frown, looking like a pin had just popped her bubble. "Well, I wanted to share good positive information. My face is everywhere as the next what?... But the charity photos were only for a good cause…JJ, we agreed this event might gain me some global notoriety and, yeah, I leaped on the hotel social media thing, especially after the tour with Sven, like listening to our family history lessons."

She frowned and shook her head, started pacing, but stopped as he announced one more problem. "Oh no! There's a video of the confrontation?…Only segments? Can you get it removed from social media? Call Mark, please, he owes me…" Glumly she added, "That many places already, huh? Well, that's just great. What? The charity social media has me being nominated for Sainthood? Thanks for the bad news. So, what's the good news? You said you had both."

Straightening and sitting at the edge of the couch, looking ready to launch into space, she roared, "You're only kidding about the little man with lewd intentions toward me, but Jeff did great. Oh, and I'm not nominated for Sainthood after all?... Ewww." She inhaled sharply and narrowed her eyes. "I'm so annoyed you yanked my chain. Good night, JJ. The handsome-lessons insider information is off the table, mister."

Gracie, with steam nearly pouring out of her ears, plotted her revenge tactic. She noted Jeff innocently looking around the room, phantom whistling in the air, and not daring to speak until she calmed down. Unfortunately, unable to contain it any longer, he chuckled, which threatened to send her into a category five-rage. But as his eyes met hers, she laughed along. "That annoying brother of mine sure knows how to get under my skin."

JJ nominated Gracie as host then opened the video bridge and granted access to those in the waiting area. The couples sitting side-by-side permitted a complete view of all the faces on the bridge. JJ grinned at his deputy. Brayson moved off camera and muted his microphone before Gracie began the briefing.

She looked at the guests and thought it interesting how uncomfortable Bailey and Keith appeared. She wondered if her friend would share details on their relationship.

"Before we get too far," Gracie suggested, "JJ needs to gather additional details for the contract he received. JJ, can you provide your concerns, please?"

"During our review, we identified an apparent problem created by Phillip Pliant, the CEO of Pliant Industries. He entered into a huge non-sustainable multi-year contract for recycling plastics. We found some evidence to suggest he's an ecological gangster of sorts. His connections continue to give him bidding advantages over other competitors, like Republic Services, for taking out the trash." JJ looked at the participants and back toward his notes then continued, "His biggest score to date is the New Jersey recyclables contract. Pliant cobbled together some shipping transport to export all the plastics from New Jersey and the New York metropolitan area to sell to the Chinese.

"The Chinese took the waste because they repurposed it into resalable products. It was profitable until the Chinese government halted all imported plastic trash and made their manufacturers buy Chinese and Russian leftovers. Waste from US-based companies is no longer accepted. It's a good guess that the Chinese made this change because they were ticked about their deteriorating trade relations with the U.S."

JJ cleared his throat and, with unwavering eyes wanting to convey his concern, he continued, "Overnight, Pliant's business model was gutted by the Chinese edict. No one else in Southeast Asia possesses the recycling capabilities to handle Pliant's contracted volume. The immediate problem his group needed to resolve centered around the excess supply. Based on the commitments he signed, to handle the plastic waste stockpile is growing at exponential rates with no outlet to accept that volume."

"Why didn't he just petition the state to let him out of the contract?" Jeff asked.

"We took the liberty of using the Freedom of Information Act to get a copy of the contract to review the terms and conditions," JJ said. "The Ts and Cs are quite clear that termination is only possible if the contractor declares bankruptcy."

Keith shook his tanned face and surmised, "Let me guess, Phillip Pliant didn't claw his way to his current status by folding up like a cheap lawn chair, so bankruptcy isn't an option."

JJ nodded. "Exactly. Enemies, and even friends, have mysteriously vanished, or simply outlived their usefulness after they've crossed Pliant. That about summarizes the current state."

Bailey jumped into the conversation. "So, if he is still accepting the money and recyclables from that east coast contract, but he has no large consumer for the plastics, where's it going?"

"That, Bailey, is an excellent question, and one we are working to track as rapidly as possible. His loading facilities are humming along, and his shipping contracts are in place. All we're seeing is the back end of the vessels leaving the harbor, and at various intervals, they return empty."

Gracie looked at Jeff, then toward the images of the others. "Is our role to find out the destination of these shipments and identify the buyers?"

"That is my team's hope." Bailey inclined her head.

Gracie shook her head. "Not much to go on. JJ, are there any other threads we can pull to discover possible avenues for the man to dispose of the plastics?"

JJ cocked his head, feeling hopeful. He added a tinge of confidence to his voice. "We have one interesting clue. It seems that Mr. Phillip Pliant likes Caribbean cruises, to the tune of one or more a month. We found that a bit odd as until recently, he never indulged in this pastime. Not to mention that, he could do something far more exclusive."

Bailey placed a finger on her chin and wrinkled her face before she asked, "The same routes or different?"

JJ nodded and smiled appreciatively at her thought process. "We don't know yet. I think this is what you'll need to explore and begin gathering hard evidence for a legal case. Your plans to get added to his cruise, Bailey, are perfect, but you may want to reconsider traveling as couples. That might limit your views and inroads to Pliant. You might want a serious what-if planning session to cover all the possibilities. Plaint loves pretty things. If we need to modify the reservations there's time for those types of changes."

Bailey nodded and said, "Jeff, Gracie mentioned you have a litigation background."

Gracie sensed Jeff's interest and squeezed his hand reassuringly. "I do, Bailey," Jeff said, "JJ, Gracie and I did some preliminary digging attacking different sources. We need a secure way to secure information as it is uncovered and share it without having repetitive meetings."

"JJ, can you establish a secure remote drop box for any and all related information," Gracie suggested. "Undoubtedly the proof will grow over time. It makes sense to have all facts with back-up accessible to the entire team. We don't want to lose our treasure trove of data for a potential trial with some error we might prevent."

"Great idea, Gracie. I'll set it up and text the link to your smartphones. I'd like to say that from our research to date, Phillip Pliant is not a nice individual, regardless of how the media portrays him. He is heavily guarded with what appears to be gangster types—armed and dangerous. He is rarely alone, except perhaps in heavily guarded quarters. We don't want to raise his suspicions in any way. We don't want to make the mistake of being observed tracking him. I suspect the results of such actions could prove fatal. He's been investigated before. The trackers we could identify, in most cases, ended up missing or infirmed. Bailey, I know your group wants the legal justification to prosecute, but only with significant security precautions."

Bailey set her jaw, then said, "Exactly right. Safety first."

Keith's dark eyes shifted to Bailey, followed by an endearing expression. "Yes, sir."

Gracie felt they'd made headway. "Bailey, I think JJ's idea about changing our approach is worth discussing. Let's think about it and meet up later. Considerations that popped to mind were getting additional rooms, with each of us having more flexibility, or rooming the guys in one suite and us in another. Either one of these might allow us an inroad to join Pliant's entourage. If that rich man is cruising, it's likely he's doing it in style with all the amenities money can buy."

Bailey nodded though the brightness vanished from her eyes. "Those might be good to consider. I'd like to talk with Keith, and then, as you suggested, get back together, Gracie. Maybe a call in the morning if you have time."

"Good idea, Bailey. That will give Jeff and me time to brainstorm as well."

"From the outside looking in," JJ suggested, "you would maintain your distances and give every appearance you are two girls relaxing. He might find one of you attractive."

The girls arched their eyebrows showing concern to their respective men.

"I can say the two suites initially reserved are next to each other with connecting balconies. Make certain you take that into account during your discussions."

Nods of understanding seemed to confirm that thought had crossed their minds.

"Let me know what you decide, Bailey. If we need to alter reservations, consider it easily done."

"Thanks," the group said in unison before JJ ended the call.

Gracie leaned back in her chair watching the moonlight flicker over the water in the canal. "Jeff, can I get more foot rub, please?"

"Of course, sweetheart."

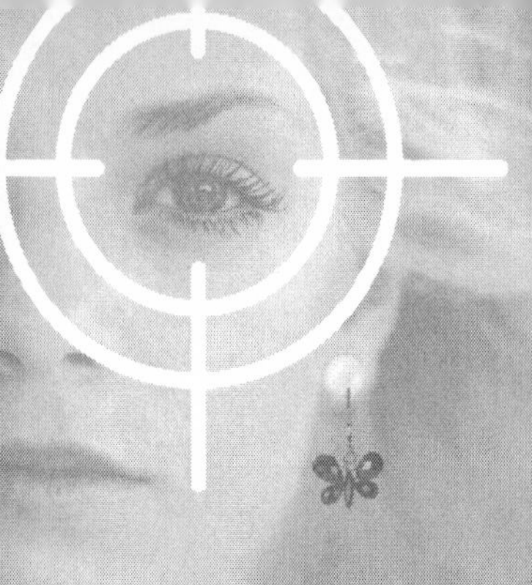

CHAPTER 6

Strategic Planning

Following the conference call with JJ, Gracie and Bailey's exchanged texts for a couple of hours. The girls decided on a virtual remote happy hour later that evening. Each couple made certain they had their choice of wine, beer, and assorted snacks to help everyone loosen up, allowing for a productive exchange. Gracie wanted to get everyone's opinion, and if possible, agreement on the plan before Bailey and Keith came to town. Boarding was coming up quick, especially if the reservations required a change. Other than the background checks completed several months ago, Gracie knew very little about Keith.

Months ago, Bailey cried to her about losing her heart to a man who'd gone on an unexplained absence for nearly a year. The details were vague and obscure hints implied gaps the size of the Grand Canyon existed in their relationship.

"Gracie," Jeff calmly stated. "Honey, I had my heart set on a vacation with you and me, but it seems from the discussion earlier, my dream could dissolve. I'll go with your decision, but I love spending time with you."

Gracie felt a bit sad with Jeff's direction of the discussion. "I know. But you've seen his background. Don't you want to help lock up Pliant if we find enough incriminating evidence?"

"Of course, I do. His deeds are likely worse than we are aware of at this point. But I want us both safe and happy."

She leaned into him with a hug. "We'll figure it out. I've got confidence in our abilities to pivot and adapt to meet any situation. To be honest, I've felt that way about you from the start, Jeff."

He pulled her closer and kissed the top of her head. "Hmm, nice. Open that bridge, Gracie. Let's do this."

Gracie launched the video call. Bailey and Keith immediately joined. Grinning at her friend, she said, "Hi, you two. Nice to see you again."

Bailey nodded and wiggled her fingers in response. "Gracie, thanks for putting this together. I thought we would try to accomplish a few things with this call. One, I'd like to have some introductions because we need to build confidence in our ability to work together. Two, I'd like to run through options like JJ mentioned, to position us for success. And three, discuss any extras we need to get before boarding. How does that sound?"

"I like your plan, girlfriend," said Gracie. "Bailey, would you please start?" Gracie liked the way Bailey leaned a bit into Keith. She hoped the romantic getaway they had would help overcome their problems. She'd find out on the ship.

Bailey nodded. "I grew up in California with doting parents who made certain I tried a variety of activities. I loved acting and journalism in high school, which I continued into college. When I got accepted to the Master's program in Ireland, I thought I'd discovered my pot of gold at the end of the rainbow, especially when I found a best friend, who is more like a sister. I never had a serious boyfriend until Keith. I work for an amazing ecology group, a job that encouraged me to pursue my education with the marketing program. I enjoy good food, water sports, and puppies. I've never met a stranger. I don't care to watch much TV unless it's curled up with popcorn and a glass of wine—a rare occurrence."

"Do you like dancing or mic night when you go out?" Jeff asked.

Bailey blushed and Keith grinned, giving her a raised eyebrow.

"Okay, okay," she admitted. "I love to dance and sing on karaoke night. I hope they have a contest on board because I plan to win."

Keith hooted. "She forgot to mention, she's very competitive too." He affectionately ruffled her hair and raised his hand to go next. "I spent six years in the Navy after attending the Naval Academy. I earned a spot to try out as a SEAL and earned a slot with the best team. Our team saw some pretty tough duty, but we all made it home. That experience allowed me to gain proficiency in scuba diving and planning escape routes when I'm in a contained space. If I appear to be AWOL, you'll find me exploring the nooks and crannies of the ship. Like a rabbit who wants to have more than one exit from his warren."

Gracie noticed his eyes light up when mentioning his training. She'd heard Navy SEALs were tight like other military elite groups.

"It also gave you a great, lean but muscular body," Bailey interjected, waggling her brows.

"You can get a room later. Please continue, Keith," Gracie added.

"I'm nearly as competitive as Bailey." She punched his shoulder, and he shrugged. "I like travel. I speak Italian and French in addition to English, because my parents insisted. I enjoy a good, rare steak, shot of whisky, and hot fudge sundaes on occasion. I'm up for trying new things. My tendency is to sit back and watch people, deciding if I want to interact with them, so…a bit more reticent." Keith looked toward an imaginary horizon beyond Gracie's head then said, "That's about it. Jeff how 'bout you, man? Bailey mentioned you're a lawyer."

Jeff eyed the two on video and Gracie patted his knee. "Keith, she's right in that I'm technically a lawyer, but I no longer practice law. Currently, I'm a consultant for legal provenances of property and high-end items like artwork. I did well in building evidence against the bad guys. I liked being in front of the judge and jury to put the case before them one layer at a time, like an artichoke with tasty outer petals, convincing inner petals, the choke where you realized the jury is buying the story, and the heart those folks never see."

Gracie laughed. "And a great storyteller, too. I've caught glimmers of his heart."

Jeff looked at her for a moment. "You aren't calling me an artichoke, are you?"

Gracie blinked eyes trying to convey innocence.

"But you are a distraction, Gracie. One of the few I indulge in. I routinely work out in a gym, play a decent game of handball and tennis. I like to dive off a board—no scuba like you, Keith—swim and snorkel. I enjoy a variety of music. I tend to effectively read people, which serves me in my profession. Gracie, I think that leaves you, honey."

Gracie's mind raced over how much she'd share. Most of her background Bailey and Jeff knew, but she wanted to add a few new tidbits. "I spent my youth traveling between Luxembourg and Switzerland. I was homeschooled by my family members and a couple of tutors. I have a twin brother who is seconds older and never lets me forget it. I speak Spanish, English, and French relatively fluently with a smattering of German, Polish, and Italian. Growing up, my best friend was my brother. We competed in everything. I hold a black belt in karate and tae kwon do, which is how I exercise. I am not a fan of running though I can if needed. I would rather swim and relax by a pool, which is why I wanted this cruise. I have only a few friends outside of my family. I work part time in our family consultant business, and as Director of Marketing at World Bank. I'm almost as good a storyteller as Jeff, but I giggle more. I'm bad at telling jokes as I end up laughing out the punchline and ruin it. I enjoy art galleries, travel, learning about different cultures, and helping people. Giving back is engrained in me, in my heart."

Keith said, "We are an impressive group. I had no idea you had so much self-defense experience, Gracie. Good to know. I think my strength is scouting the boat. Overall, the plan may be easier if we don't board as couples or like we know each other."

Jeff nodded. "The background on Pliant I've reviewed so far suggests he likes the ladies as pretty ornaments, especially at dinner. He's got a private room reserved for dinners with folks who might join the ship at one port and leave at another. The guy likes to schmooze and needs to feel important. Maybe, with Gracie making headlines around the world with her speech in Amsterdam, Pliant might recognize her."

"If that's the case," Bailey said, "then I'll be her publicist, and she can't go anywhere without me. Always travel together, just like at school. Right, girlfriend?"

Gracie tilted her head and looked at everyone. "I know I wanted a romantic get-away with my heart throb." She grinned and bumped shoulders with Jeff. "I suspect you wanted the same." Keith and Bailey both nodded. "If we keep the rooms we've booked and switch names on the reservations, we can travel between rooms via the balcony. If we have to, we can knock on the doors."

Keith leaned over delivering a less than innocent leer. "We can always try to pick you up and you can play hard to get."

Bailey pointedly looked at Keith and replied, "As long as we don't keep secrets from each other, I can do that." Keith leaned over, kissed her cheek and whispered something in her ear that broke the tension as a blush blossomed on her face.

"Sounds good," said Gracie. "JJ can fix the records. We'll see you in a few days at the hotel."

"Bye," they said in unison, and Gracie closed the call.

"Do you need to call JJ and let him know our decision?" Jeff asked.

"Nope, that's Bailey's job, and she'll do it. Plus, he'll listen to the call and get to work right away. We need a shower and time to enjoy the rest of our evening. I want to sightsee a bit in the morning, if it's okay with you. Then we can take the rental car Daan provided for our next destination."

"I like your planning." He pulled her into a strong embrace then carried her toward the shower.

CHAPTER 7

The Coolness Factor

Gracie felt energized when they woke. Jeff helped pack their bags, verifying nothing got missed.

"Jeff, this room and trip were worth it. Thank you for joining me." She set her purse on top of her jacket.

"I loved being with you. Memories need reinforcement," he added, as he waltzed her around the room and out to the balcony for last minute selfies."

"You're fun." Grabbing up her things, she continued, "I want to stop by a few of the spots for a few more special holiday gifts for family. Maybe go to the Van Gogh Museum for a short look around, then back here for our afternoon drive to Luxembourg."

"I like it. Even a short tour of the museum would be cool." Jeff collected the rest of the bags and followed her to the elevator.

"Good morning," Sophie greeted. "Daan has reserved the car, which will be here around noon. Leave your bags and I'll get them loaded for you."

"Sophie, you, Daan, and the entire staff are amazing." Gracie felt the lump in her throat as her eyes got a little misty. "Our trip here is one for the records. Thank you." She reached out both hands and enveloped Sophie's with a quick squeeze."

"Come on, Gracie. The bakery is calling to me."

"Yes." She looked at him and noticed the twinkle in his eyes. "We need to grab some road trip snacks too."

Jeff rubbed his hands together in anticipation.

"Place your order and I'll grab it then put it in the car for you. I'll add some waters as well," promised Sophie.

"Thank you." Gracie grabbed Jeff's hand. "Let's get some food and see some amazing things."

"Jeff, do you mind taking the wheel," Gracie asked in front of the hotel. "I love the route we're taking; it brings back memories."

"Suits me, honey. I like to drive, and as I recall they aren't too fussy about speed limits if one drives safe."

"Your call."

They maintained a running dialogue during the nearly five-hour drive to Luxembourg. The weather cooperated making the travel easy. She recalled a few of the paintings they'd been able to see and delighted that their taste seemed similar. Before realizing it, they approached their destination. Gracie's eyes misted when Jeff pulled the car into a space in front of the family offices, where she'd spent so much time as a child.

"Jeff, the trees and bushes are fuller than I remember. I liked in winter when snow highlighted the black shingled roof." The simple exterior had white painted walls offset by grey slate shutters over darkened windows. "Those windows on the side of the building double as video screens to a computer inside. One of the many security features we've come across."

Jeff walked around and opened her door, extending his hand to her. "Good to know. The place looks like a children's activity venue. I'd expect people to knock on the door."

"That's not common practice in this region of the world." Gracie felt nostalgic. "I remember asking my folks why the sign indicated Private Day Care and Dance Lessons, by appointment only, when it primarily did private investigations. Mom said the word private kept random visitors from knocking, and the answering service conveyed to every caller with regrets that classes were filled. Our CATS team base of operations remained closed to prying eyes. It was the first place outside of home where JJ and I played and slept while the folks worked."

Jeff squeezed her hand and smiled at her. "Did you enjoy a lot of time with your parents growing up?"

"We did. Dad loved to play and romp with us, both here and at home. Here we also trained in martial arts with them and, when we got older, with their team. Everyone was patient and supportive while we honed our skills. For many years we had no idea that all kids weren't raised that way."

"What way?" Jeff asked.

"Self-sufficient, self-reliant, and well-versed in a variety of subjects. We each have strong reading, writing, and verbal skills in three languages." She laughed. "Lucky for us, two of the dialects were already in use at home so we practiced with each other. Funny, it never felt like work, just extended playtime."

"I bet it was fun always having someone to play with. When did you learn that maybe your early years weren't like that of other children?"

"Honestly, it wasn't until I attended a university in Ireland. In our youth we were raised that normal meant we shared information within the family. During events when guests were invited to the house, we got coached on what to say and what to omit. One trick we learned from Mom was to listen with our ears not our mouths. It helped us gain clarity, plus we were rarely left unattended. When I met Bailey and we roomed together in the graduate programs, I spent a lot of time listening to her life story. It was so different even though we had similar values regarding friends and family. I think that's why we became so close. I think the world of her. I'd do anything to help her." She leaned over and kissed him. "Come on, let's go see what the guys in the back room cooked up."

Walking into the familiar doorway, Gracie used the automated retinal scan to gain access to the facility. Jeff followed on her heels. Suddenly, alarms blared and lights flashed a multitude of colors that Gracie realized would start a reaction of motion sickness if they persisted. She rapidly fingered a text to JJ to release them from the narrow holding area where they were trapped between two secure doors.

JJ appeared with an angry frown the moment the door released and blissful silence filled the softly lit space. "You know better than to try and let someone tailgate into this facility on your access, my adorable sister." He broke into a grin and stuck out his hand to Jeff. "Sorry about that, but we don't play fast and loose when it comes to security. Come on in. We've got a lot to show you two before it's time to go to the airport."

JJ led them to the spacious gym area where Brayson was tweaking an eighteen inch in diameter, quadcopter drone. Several other items, draped with a cover, were arranged on the table.

Gracie hip-bumped Jeff. "This place is bigger inside than you would suspect from outside."

He nodded. "No kidding."

Gracie smiled, spotting Brayson approaching. She considered him an attractive, though older man, with a square face, dark eyes, and dark hair still in a near-military cut. He equaled Jeff's height at six feet but maintained his distinctive stocky frame without an ounce of fat. "This is Brayson. He has worked in the organization for a long time. He has a special ops background and can communicate in several languages. So, if you think he's talking in tongues, he probably is." Gracie gave Brayson a quick hug.

"Does he teach dance lessons, or is that your brother?" Jeff said with a straight face.

She and JJ laughed and then Brayson joined in.

Brayson said, "Greetings. You two look good together, and he delivers fast comebacks." He extended his hand to Jeff. "Nice to meet you, man."

Leaning into Jeff, Gracie smiled sweetly. "Thanks, Brayson, we like each other."

JJ grinned, held up the aircraft, by-passed Gracie, and commented, "Ah, Jeff, glad you're here. Hope you can take instructions on how to use this drone." She bristled at being slighted as the drone operator. Jeff watched with raised eyebrows.

Gracie looked JJ square in the eye and huffed. "Hey, this is my gig. I'll manage the surveillance drone, thank you very much!" Grabbing the control appliance from him, Gracie powered up all four copter blades. She convinced herself it was simply as she launched it straight up. The whir of the blades practically soundless, until the noisy thud into the wall immediately followed by the sounds of pieces bouncing off the floor, shattering the copter blades. "Oh, crap!"

JJ frowned at Gracie and smacked his lips in disappointment. "Can we get another drone out here, please? My sister led with her ego rather than her brain."

Gracie stuck out her tongue at her brother. Then glanced at Jeff to see if he looked shocked. To her, he appeared torn, innocently looking at everything in the area to stay out of the fray, or he'd bust out laughing with the wrong eye contact. The stone-faced attorney persona won the battle.

Feeling negligent, Gracie quietly returned the joystick controller to Brayson. She watched him feign sorrow at pieces of the quadcopter drone he retrieved on the way to get the spare.

JJ snagged Gracie by the arm and directed her to a small office. He closed the door. They glared at each other nearly toe-to-toe, neither of them willing to give a fraction of an inch.

"Gracie, spill it. It's not like you to grab or show your ego."

Gracie planted her feet and jammed her hands on her hips. To offset having to look up at her twin, she added a defiant set to her chin. "Your mean teasing made me mad. Then you snub me for operating the drone in front of my boyfriend, in spite of the fact we were always equals here. What do you expect, JJ? We both run organizations that leverage cutting edge technology and cyber security, so it's inappropriate to tease like we're still adolescents. Besides, I can still kick your ass in the gym, and you know it."

JJ lowered his eyes, looking a bit remorseful then pulled her into a quick hug. "You're right. I'm sorry. I should not tease you about some things. Love you. Mean it. I do like Jeff. Glad you do as well."

Gracie punched his shoulder hard enough that JJ felt it. Then she pirouetted out the door.

Returning to the table with the new drone in place, Gracie felt a twinge of heat on her cheeks from embarrassment. She admitted, "Harder than it looks. My apologies, JJ. Brayson, I didn't mean to destroy it during the test flight."

Brayson nodded with a grim expression. "Butterflies due to your upcoming mission, I suspect, Gracie. I needed a fix 'em up project."

Gracie felt relieved. "Jeff, can you try next? We both need to learn how to handle the equipment."

"Okay, Gracie, but if it hits the wall, you do get to laugh."

"If it hits the wall," Brayson inserted, "you both get to build a couple from scratch to appreciate the intricacies."

Brayson explained the controls. Jeff listened intently. Taking the drone, he fired up the motors and, using the joystick, brought the craft to eye level. The sounds of the rotors seemed like a hum that ruffled his hair. He cautiously walked around the hovering ship, studying the angles. "What is my range for the drone? Height, distance… And what about the optics? How close or far away is the camera rated? Also, what happens to the unit if someone grabs it? I assume you have some built-in security protocols to prevent anyone from repurposing the device?"

Gracie saw JJ and Brayson exchanged silent glances. She smiled at Jeff's obvious familiarity with the machinery.

Jeff deadpanned, "As my good friends in Texas say, *this ain't my first rodeo*."

Brayson was the first to laugh. "You know what's funny? It's discovering that who we thought was a green bean around drones is a seasoned closet pro." Warming to the subject and the man, he continued, "This Quintana has a flying time of twelve minutes before she begins to power down. Her camera optics are more like a satellite than a smartphone. You can get up to 24 times the enhanced image of the target, letting you stay farther back." Brayson took a breath and inclined his head. "That's the good news. The bad news is, people caught videoing a private citizen, invading their personal space, or spying, can get tagged for invasion of privacy. There's almost no place you can run where they won't extradite you to face charges. Does that help?"

Jeff nodded then pushed the joystick controller to Gracie. "You take it."

Gracie carefully handed it back. "No, you take it."

JJ chuckled. "You sure you guys want to do this? I'm sensing hesitation. How about we drop in operatives into each suspect area to do the surveillance. You stick closer to the subjects. You'll be less constricted. Bailey won't need to know."

Gracie nodded in agreement.

Jeff handed back the joystick controller to Brayson. "Excellent handling air device, sir. I've only ever used them in videoing construction sites or the sunbathers on the roof next to my building who were determined not to have any tan lines."

Gracie turned her head with a look of astonishment. Jeff grinned as he hip-bumped her. "Made you look."

JJ grinned at the antics, liking Jeff better each time they interacted. "Alright, we'll schedule in resources to your target destinations. I can't tell you who they are yet. They'll know you and keep to the sidelines. You'll know them by the code word *swordfish*."

"Swordfish?" Gracie groaned. "How corny is that?"

"Corny?" Brayson complained. "How about asking me to drop the encrypted cell phone into your bag in New York as we pass on the street like two old-time secret agents in a movie?"

"But that was so cool." Gracie crunched her shoulders and ducked, acting the part.

The guys chuckled.

Brayson returned to the table and removed the drape with a flourish. "Let's talk about the other reconnaissance devices we have for you. A smartphone camera is way too obvious, so I've got two high-resolution Zeiss cameras built into this bag clip disguised to look like a flower. The wire that leads to the actual electronics looks like the flower stem, which should help cloak the electronics. The second unit is for Bailey's handbag or identification holder. It has photo recon capabilities. They each have modest GPS chips in case we need to locate you. We also have remote controlled shaped like insects for taking pictures or providing distractions."

JJ handed Gracie what appeared to be a professional makeup case.

"Thanks, JJ, but I have a full complement of cosmetics."

Ruffling her hair gently, he added, "I know, which is why you always look so put together. However, this Tumi bag is your backup case that holds some miniature drones disguised as a variety of insects. Instructions are inside. You and Jeff can play with these and speculate how they might be leveraged. I thought these critters would be useful, and the security case is impenetrable."

Jeff checked his collectible analog watch. "Gracie, we need to turn in the rental and catch that flight. Guys, are we done here?"

JJ nodded. "I think we're good." He hugged his sister and shook Jeff's hand as he escorted them to the security entrance.

They added the case to the car. Gracie turned for an additional embrace for Brayson and whispered, "Thank you."

They got in and waved as Jeff started the car. He leaned over and kissed her cheek, asking, "You had Brayson discreetly drop a burner cell phone into your bag like he was on a covert secret spy assignment?"

"It makes me all goose-pimply just thinking about being deep undercover."

"I didn't know that about you, Gracie. Another side. I mean, it's okay, but I didn't know that about you."

CHAPTER 8

Contentious Travel Experience

Gracie and Jeff's return trip to New York City proved uneventful. "Jeff, we can catch up on our work and still have time for a couple of parties, if you want to." Gracie suggested.

"That works. You decide which one you want. I have no preferences."

"Fair enough. I'm going to also set up the return travel to land us in Miami a couple of days ahead of boarding for the cruise."

"Let me know, honey, if I need to help with anything." Jeff insisted.

Friends welcomed them with open arms. Several people commented on Gracie's success in Amsterdam, stating many of the social media channels shared the highlights. Some asked if they were a serious couple. Each artfully sidestepped any commitment one way or the other, but their interactions when they were together sent a positive signal.

Jeff worked as a freelance consultant for the last year, so it was easy to pivot to support research on the cruise. Gracie insisted on a paid contract which JJ constructed. Jeff would subcontract through CATS, in case anyone checked. Gracie assigned tasks to her staff to help cover activities through January. She planned to do meetings remotely for World Bank from her family home.

Their flight from New York to *Zürich* to visit her family, including all the cousins, took off without a hitch Christmas Eve. They both enjoyed visiting with her relatives again and the seasonal traditions. Jeff got extra attention from the kids that made her happy. She watched him get mesmerized when Satya sat next to him and explained, out of the blue, her correlation of jet engines to peanut butter in a succinct manner. Gracie swooped her young cousin into a spin when she finished, and both of them tittered like they'd shared a private joke. A scant five days later, Gracie and Jeff rose early and said their goodbyes before heading to the airport for their flight toward Miami.

Once they settled into the ride share, Gracie commented, "I hope you had fun, honey. They all think you're a keeper." She petted his arm affectionately.

Jeff grinned. "I like all of them. But that Satya, what a pistol. She's brilliant."

"True, she's a lot of fun. Of course, they all are. I do love my family, and the holidays bring out the best."

"I like the way everyone pitches in to help. Lots of amusing banter."

"No one in my family is without a quick comeback to any subject."

He pulled her closer with his arm around her shoulder and sweetly kissed her cheek. "I get it. You looked especially pretty for the formal dinner. I enjoy spending time with you."

Gracie chuckled. "Back at you, handsome."

Excited to get going, Gracie and Jeff quickly entered the line and were giddy when they approached the ticket counter with their roller bags. The gate agent deflated their enthusiasm quicker than a pinprick in a balloon when she announced, "I'm sorry, Ms. Rodreguiz, but I don't show any first-class reservations for this flight in my system. In fact, I see no flights for your name at all. Do you have the date right? Are you sure you have the correct airline?"

Gracie's internal rage snapped her back to reality but she schooled her features. She produced the flight confirmation and record locator for Fast Fliers airline. The physical evidence made the gate agent swallow; tears filled her eyes as she avoided eye contact. The agent shook her head slightly and took a deep inhale before squeaking, "Fast Fliers recently finished the merger with Adios Airlines. All our IT systems, including the reservation system from both companies, were combined last week. It's been awful to discover at the last-minute tickets not properly moved. In some cases, not at all. I am sorry"

Gracie took a breath and looked toward Jeff, hoping he would get her silent plea for intervention before she lost her composure.

Jeff squeezed her hand and interjected with his calming demeanor, "Miss, you can see from our paperwork we're at the right airline." Pointing toward the top of the sheet, he continued, "The proof of the right date shows here. We are victims of a computer glitch."

He closed his eyes and grabbed his heart, feigning a jilted lover look that made Gracie want to snicker. Jeff smiled at the stressed agent who lifted her lips, her features easing.

"Can you find a way to get us on this flight so we can get to our destination? We're headed for a cruise that will leave without us if we aren't there.

"It's not fair," Gracie mumbled while the gate agent furiously typed on her keyboard. She kicked the edge of her suitcase. "I get angry when plans get messed up. Our travel has been perfect to date. Now this!" She looked at him and softened her features. "I had no idea of your acting ability, though. I'll keep it in mind."

After a final series of keystrokes, the gate agent smiled. "In answer to your first question, no, this is a fully booked flight as are the next two leaving for Miami. The good news is that I got two seats for you on a sister airline, Higher Fliers, which is scheduled to depart within the hour. I couldn't get you first class, though, and the gate is in the other terminal which requires you to get moving." She handed Jeff two vouchers. "Present these to the gate agent. I apologize but the seats are not together. You can work with the gate agent and, if needed, beg the other passengers." She pointed to her left. "Grab the rail to get to the terminal from there."

Jeff gratefully accepted the voucher and, turning around, saw a group of annoyed people who overheard the conversation and feared their flight getting messed up while the gate agent fixed their problem. Jeff raised his hands to sooth the travelers. "Folks, we're really sorry to have held up the line, but it wasn't our fault. This woman is the best, most understanding gate agent on the planet. She's going to help you too." Jeff looked over his shoulder to see her beaming as the crowd grudgingly clapped. He took a bow as Gracie shook her head.

With a minute to spare before the doors closed to the train, they jumped on and arrived at the other terminal in short order. They checked their bags with the counter agent then cleared customs and security in record time. Rushing to the gate, they had no time to revise their seat assignments before boarding.

Gracie's seat was the first one they located. It was on an aisle. The man in the middle looked at her with a grin. "Sir, this is my first time flying and the airlines messed up our seats. I need to sit next to my husband as he promised he'd hold my hand the whole time." She felt the tears trickled down her cheeks as she snuffled. "Please, if you'll switch seats, we'll cover your beverage costs on the flight."

Clearly a European gentleman, he rose. "Of course, my dear. Sir, please take my seat and hand me your seat card. I'd feel guilty if I didn't help you calm her nerves." He patted Gracie's shoulder.

Stowing their bags, they located their seats and buckled in. "Gracie, I had no idea of all your talents either." He grasped her hand, and she kissed him.

"Thank you, honey," she said, loudly enough for the neighboring passengers to hear.

Clapping ensued at the happy ending, then everyone almost paid attention to the safety speech of the crew.

"I sure hope we never have another near-death experience like that again," Jeff confessed. Leaning over, he whispered in her ear, "Your act to get our seats together deserves a Best Supporting Actor award."

Feeling bad, she batted her eyelashes. "I'm sorry, honey, at the mess up with our travel. Not how I hoped, but at least we get the two days in Miami to regroup. We got robbed of our first-class seating and relegated to the cattle section where we're charged for everything, including toilet paper. I almost wish we'd flown private. But at least we're together and learning new fun facts regarding our acting abilities."

Jeff smirked and added, "I'm glad the security people didn't hold us up too badly. Thankfully, they didn't run us through the delousing procedure like people had to do at the close of WWII."

"Eww." Gracie scrunched her face at the imagery her mind produced. "YOU didn't get subjected to the new hyper-invasive radar scan and receive the comment at the last security checkpoint *nice panties*."

"Wanna bet? However, I can't disagree with their assessment."

Gracie relaxed and started a laughing fit that Jeff quickly joined.

Gracie slyly grinned at Jeff as he held her hand. "I'll buy the drinks, honey."

They landed uneventfully on the ground in Miami. Jeff retrieved their bags then herded them through customs. He noticed with some dismay that a wheel on one of the roller-boards got crushed, forcing him to carry it. Sunshine greeted them as they wrangled their way to the area for ride-share pickups. Their HOMBRE ride service app showed five minutes to arrival.

"Jeff, I'll try not to let travel disruptions get to me. Thanks for helping me stay centered. I've got my happy feet back on." Gracie gave Jeff a sweet peck on the cheek.

Jeff returned a half-hearted smile and pointed to the annoying suitcase. "This is going to be trouble."

"That's a problem I can fix. I'll get a new piece delivered to the hotel. We have two nights to eliminate jet lag, so we're good."

Gracie scanned the area, looking for their ride. Her phone chirped with a text message from the driver.

> Your HOMBRE ride service is here, Ms. Rodreguiz.
> Please look for us on the West side of the terminal in the gray minivan.

Gracie's fingers jammed the letters on her phone as if her fingers screamed. Frustration frazzled her at the text. She stomped her foot and responded to the message. She turned her phone toward Jeff.

> Listen, HOMBRE, WE are on the East side of the terminal.
> Please move to where we are on the East side by the ride share sign.

Minutes later, a late model minivan, covered in layers of gray dirt and dust, screeched to a halt in front of Gracie. A Middle Eastern driver leaped from the car, flustered. The robes of his attire swirled around in the Florida breeze while he straightened the keffiyeh on his head. He gestured with his hands in the air, mumbling something. In faulty, broken English, he pleaded,

"No anger with me, please. Today is day two as an HOMBRE driver, and the app sent me to the wrong side of airport. Please do not give me a poor rating. Five-star ratings are critical for advancement. I need to earn enough to buy a driver's license and insurance. Punish me with fewer tips, but if it is poor, your rating will cost me my job. I beg you." Then the man earnestly held one hand to his chest while he knelt.

Jeff and Gracie looked at each other, exchanging sad looks, and she felt her cheeks glow with embarrassment. She looked at the prone HOMBRE driver. Lookie-loos gathered. Gracie extended a hand. "You got a name?"

The man lifted his head and wiped an invisible tear from his eye. "My name is Khalid Effendi."

Not looking to collect any more spectators, Gracie asked, "Khalid, can we go now, please? Get us to the Aloft Hotel I put into the application, and we'll see about your rating."

Khalid brightened. He promptly loaded both her and Jeff, but struggled with the bags.

As they pushed through the airport gate and onto the highway, Gracie smirked. "Quite a performance, Khalid. The robes, the keffiyeh perfectly arranged, the broken English, the pleading with the tears. I wish we'd passed the hat around to the bystanders for gratuities. Couldn't my brother have arranged normal transport rather than create a sideshow?"

"A guy has to find fun where he can, especially on this uh… team." With perfect English, he continued, "JJ asked me to update you." He took a deep breath. "Pliant hasn't landed. His forward team arrived an hour ago and went directly to the Mandarin Oriental Miami to secure the top two floors. Plaint has a meeting with businessmen scheduled for tonight and tomorrow, by invitation only. I just sent you a video of Pliant's team so you can familiarize yourself with their faces. I'll snag Pliant's when he arrives and send photos along.

"Can you stop at a store so I can get a new roller bag?" asked Jeff.

"Yes, of course. We're actually close."

Gracie spotted his eyes looking back via the rearview mirror. "Thank you, Khalid."

"I heard your flight plans got jacked. I hate when that happens. As far as the display picking you up; it makes people laugh and remember me, not you. Hiding in plain sight."

"Thank you, again."

Jeff looked at Gracie and then the driver. "We've got no worries, right?"

Gracie inclined her head to Khalid for the details.

"Jeff, from your briefing, you know the history on this guy is bad at best. He's a big dog and he's not hiding under the porch. Gracie, JJ deposited the additional research we uncovered into the secure drop box. We removed the information sources to allow you to share the data with Bailey. She won't be able to see how the *information magnets* are delivering intel on her Pliant executive. At first glance, he's stinky but careful. You'll have your hands full proving it."

Gracie wormed her hand into Jeff's and beamed. "Thank you, Khalid. When do we get contact with the *drone hunter*?"

"We're still working that angle. The contact password is unchanged. Do you remember the challenge-response?"

Gracie, weary with the travel and the exchange, deadpanned, "Shaken not stirred."

Khalid cleared his throat.

She harrumphed. "Alright, yes, *is that canned or fresh* is my response. Do you know if Bailey's arrival is unchanged?"

"She'll be here tomorrow."

"I hope her romantic weekend with Keith worked out."

"Gracie, please explain our support details to Jeff so he'll relax. Pliant has defeated others who tried to build a case, so we want everyone to stay safe."

Jeff fidgeted. Gracie stroked her thumb over his hand and gave him a look of confidence; it had a calming effect. He nodded his commitment to her project.

Gracie noticed Khalid looked pleased with their silent exchange.

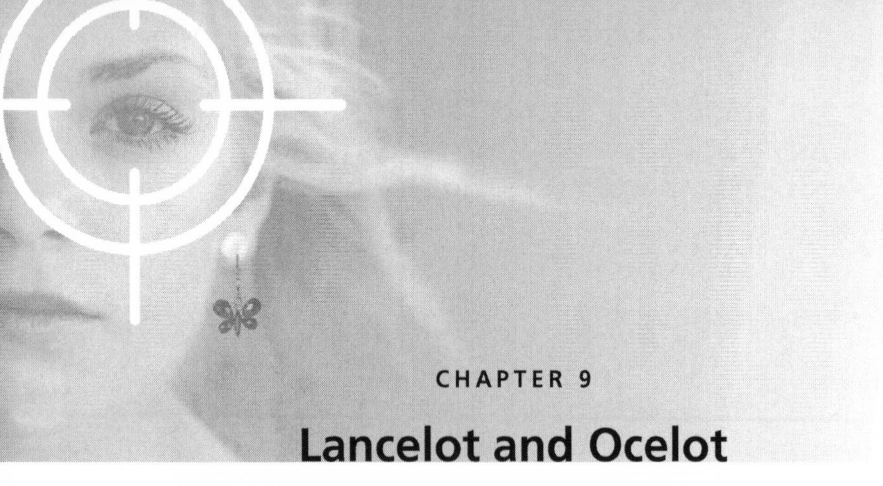

CHAPTER 9

Lancelot and Ocelot

After securing a new bag to replace the damaged piece of luggage, Khalid delivered Gracie and Jeff to the Aloft without incident. Walking inside, Gracie commented at the mass of people vying for check-in. "Wow, it looks like everyone else had the same idea about early arrival."

"Gracie, let me leave the bags with the bellman. Maybe we can grab some coffee and relax in the café until the line thins out. Standing in line has no appeal for me."

Gracie delivered a sly smile and nodded, watching him saunter to the bell-cap podium. She went through the sliding glass door to the café. The blue and green interior gave her a sense of relaxation amplified by the gurgling water cascading over the tiers of the fountain set to the far side. Approaching the counter, she placed an order for coffee for Jeff and Earl Grey for herself, and then secured a table. Jeff approached, glanced at the fountain, and his shoulders visibly relaxed.

"Nice, huh?" She inclined her head toward the water tripping over the colorful rocks.

"Yep, and so much better than the squabbling din from the guests growing impatient out there."

Her name was called. Gracie rushed over to grab their orders. As she turned, she noticed Jeff squinting in the direction of a man at the far end of the café. He shook his head as if he was trying to bring up a memory.

"What's up with that guy, Jeff? Are you okay?"

Jeff faced her, blinked, and stated in a tone of disbelief, "That guy on the phone is really railing at someone. I swear I know him from somewhere."

"You mean the highly animated one, irked about a paperwork snafu, who's infringing on the Zen calm in this area? If he gets much louder, I'm going to reinsert my flying earplugs to dampen his decibel level."

Jeff abruptly slapped the tabletop, nearly disrupting their drinks. "That's Lance Pope! I haven't seen him since, well… years. Wonder what he's doing here."

"How do you know him, Jeff?"

"I did some work with him and we became friends. He tells great stories and loves to embellish."

Gracie smiled and waved at the man, prompting him to stop in mid-sentence.

Taken aback and then roving his eyes over them both, the man wrinkled his brow. He disconnected his call. Grabbing his cup, the man with sandy hair on the longish side, lightweight slacks and a tropical shirt with imprinted tigers, stood and headed their way.

By the time he reached the table, his agitated features had been replaced with warm recognition. "Jeff, dude. What the heck are you doing here?" Smiling at Gracie, he suggested, "I see your taste in women is still at the unobtainable edge for most of us normal guys." Adding an attractive, mischievous smile, he uttered, "Miss, if you find yourself, like all the others, no longer in his orbit, I'll sign up as your escort."

Gracie rotated her head to cast a feigned look of outrage and rolled her eyes at Jeff. Jeff, in turn, straightening out the imagined kinks in his neck, swallowed hard and turned toward the man. "Lance, allow me to introduce Gracie Rodreguiz. Gracie, may I present Lance Pope, a man of some high ambition in the Haunted House trade. Whatcha doing in Miami?"

Gracie extended a hand. "Nice to meet you, Lance."

He shook her hand and she felt the slight texture of calluses. "I'm here to pick up my newest acquisition, a baby ocelot," he clarified. "Since our time together in the Haunted House business, I've developed a passion for the big cats. I am trying to get an orphaned ocelot through customs, but the officials are yanking my chain about the paperwork. The baby needs feeding and attention, not paperwork."

Gracie furrowed her brow. "I didn't think people could import exotic wildlife into the United States anymore."

Lance proudly proclaimed, "I'm the last person to be granted a license. I've been slowly acquiring orphaned big cats to save them from being paraded at circuses or zoos. I've set up a modest preserve in central Florida so they can grow and roam free. I focus on animals that, for one reason or another, can't return to the wild. I hate seeing these beautiful cats caged."

"That sounds so noble." Gracie pulled out her phone and started texting while the men talked.

Jeff asked, "Hey, the Haunted House business is that good? These animals can't be cheap, and they certainly don't live on Cheerios."

Lance puffed up a little with pride. "I've earned several awards for the annual haunted houses I've established around the country. My team gets called in as consultants to help those companies struggling to survive so, yes, business is good. I could use some of your legal advice, though, Jeff."

"Lance, how about we discuss work after I return from vacation? However, to your earlier comment, what kind of creatures do you have at this refuge? Are they just big cats?"

"Here in Florida we don't just have lions and tigers. Someone called us one time and asked if we would take their pet wolves. It's a familiar story. Since they wouldn't do well in our humidity, I ended up shipping them to our Colorado refuge. What begins as a cuddly fur-ball at a few weeks old often becomes a miscast giant in a suburban neighborhood. The owners typically are confronted with either having the animal destroyed or giving it away. Most owners cry when they give them up. We think our sanctuary is a far better option for the animal." Lance cleared his throat, warming to the subject. "People think it's neat to have a wild animal as a pet, but they forget it doesn't fit into everyday domestic situations. We do have several wild birds—you know, the kind where they cut their wings to prevent them escaping—which thrive in our aviary."

Gracie's attention was divided between texting and listening to his impassioned conversation. Her phone chirped several times during the exchange. At the last chirp, she read the text and asked, "Lance, would you please try the import customs folks again?"

Lance's brow furrowed, but he moved to make the call as directed. The ringing, loud enough for them all to hear, seemed endless before someone answered. He stood and walked a few steps away. "Hello, I am Lance Pope, I spoke to you earlier and…" His eyes widened. "Uh, pardon me? Are you saying she's ready for pick up? What? I don't understand. Oh, the World Bank representative provided the needed clarification. I see." Lance cut his eyes to Gracie, who remained poised. After disconnecting from the call, Lance offered, "Gracie, I don't know how to thank you. I'm in your debt. When you need any help, I'll grant you a boon." He leaned a bit closer to Gracie and commented with his eyebrows waggling, "One last thing, I've never seen Jeff with any other girl, let alone a charming lady of good breeding such as yourself. I was teasing him, but the offer to escort you anytime stands."

After a round of chuckling by all, Gracie said, "I might take you up on that, Lance, if you're serious about granting a boon. Let's exchange numbers, then you go retrieve the poor baby and keep it safe."

Lance pushed his contact information to Gracie and Jeff's cell phones. They shook hands and he vanished out the back door, making a hasty retreat to his vehicle.

Jeff offered a high-five, which she returned. "That, my sweet, was a very nice thing you did for him. Thank you. He's a generous man with a great heart."

They sipped their beverages until Jeff asked, "About this favor, what do you have in mind?"

Gracie, feeling like the cat that swallowed the canary, drummed her fingers together with her elbows on the table. "I've got an idea."

Jeff noticeably blanched. "These are now the four most terrifying words in your vocabulary."

CHAPTER 10

The Practiced Touch

Finally, the Aloft check-in mob vanished. Gracie motioned to the lull, so they collected their belongings and approached the reception desk to secure their room. Just after the clerk handed their keys across the long counter, the assistant hotel manager came forward and pulled them aside.

He handed Gracie a package covered in brown paper, roughly two-foot square by three feet high. "Ms. Rodreguiz, this arrived by special delivery this morning. Would you like to take it with you or have the bellman bring it up? It's not heavy at all."

Gracie squealed and clapped her hands, hoping to convey her overwhelming delight. "Perfect. My earrings made it. Thank the maker. I'll have choices for every outfit, every time of day. You know, wearing the same earrings all day long…it just isn't done."

The manager cast her an uneasy eye and extended the package for one of them to carry. "Honey, aren't you glad these arrived?" Gracie gleefully added looking toward Jeff, hoping he wouldn't totally lose it.

Jeff lowered his head and then brushed at a speck of dust on his shoes. He mumbled, "Yes of course, darling. I know you'll be happy." Swallowing, he looked up and winked at the gentleman. "We'd better take them now so she won't lose a moment picking out earrings."

Nodding with a perplexed expression, the manager asked, "You had twelve cubic feet of earrings sent special delivery for your cruise? I'm a little confused."

Gracie raising a hand and flicking her fingers in dismissal, replied, "Not to worry. It's a girl thing." She picked up her carryon, and added, "Sweetheart, can you bring them, please?"

Jeff nodded politely, securing the package under his arm. They made a beeline for the elevators. On the ride up, Gracie chuckled. Jeff only studied her from the side but decided not to ask. Once inside their room, she went right to work opening the package to peek at the contents JJ sent. After a quick inventory of the mini aerial surveillance drones, she grabbed one of the smallest units. "This so cool. We have the collection of wearables to track our location stashed in my makeup case. Here we have mini-flyers we can split between us all for times we are sitting in outside venues where flying critters are expected."

Jeff nodded an appreciative wink.

She was about to fire it up in their room but caught herself. Smiling, sweetly Gracie turned to Jeff. "Can you teach me, please?"

Appearing pleased, he nuzzled her, accepted the control unit, and began the lessons. After half an hour or so of testing each unit, Gracie was promoted to drone pilot *ordinaire*.

"Babe, it might be best if I do our micro- and mini-drone surveillance while you deal with Mr. Pliant. I think we need to divide and conquer. JJ's team can manage the big drones we tested in his shop. Initially, I'd be better in the background with the cameras."

Gracie sighed and looked a bit disappointed. "I think you're right. I'll need an angle to get in close, though. Bailey and Keith may think of something. Maybe JJ has some ideas to share on our joint call later. Just don't tell him how many drones are left after our training exercise. We both know how he pouts when I break his toys."

Jeff nodded with a smile. "Based on their limited range except in specific areas, I don't see us doing a lot with these units. Most of what we need to plan on is the ol' gumshoe efforts of asking questions and doing follow-up research. Aerial surveillance isn't our main play, but it is good for close call intel and these units are remarkable."

"Jeff, let's pack up our toys and enjoy dinner before our conference call with JJ."

"Splendid."

CHAPTER 11

It Begins This Way

After ordering dinner room service, Jeff asked, "What time is our call?"

"We've half an hour," Gracie mentioned. "After that, remind me to call Bailey to update her and Keith. I texted JJ earlier about our roles on this gig, and he said he had an idea but needed to finish up some research."

"Is this the way you guys always operate?" He drew her attention so he could see her eyes. "You thrive on riding at the tip of the spear; it seems risky. I'm here to help but want to make certain you don't court unnecessary trouble. I don't want to over step but shouldn't this point person be a little more…you know—"

She interrupted with a groan. "Please tell me you weren't going to say male? I would hate for you to seriously think, with my training and experience that I couldn't take care of myself. My mom was on a dark ops mission when she was carrying my brother and me. I've learned from the best and am trained to beat adversaries twice my size. Numerous times I've even flattened JJ in our martial arts exercises. Please don't think I can't take care of myself because I can, honey. Besides, Mr. Wood, if anything happens to me, I'll miss holding and loving you."

Jeff stared unflinchingly at this Amazon Warrior of a woman, and politely asked, "Did you tell JJ about our drone casualties? Or that you let the assistant hotel manager think you have an earring fetish? Or that you sometimes wander into traffic while absorbed looking at your smartphone?"

Gracie became silent momentarily, then she chuckled. "Point taken. You're worried. I think I like having someone unrelated to me care what happens to me. Yes, at times I do need to be more situationally aware. Perhaps, Jeff, that's your role in my life."

Jeff smiled broadly and pulled her close. "As a show of my acceptance to a dangerous but exciting protection assignment, would you prefer a chivalrous and delicate kiss to your slender hand, or a big sloppy wet and unending passionate kiss?"

The amorous question had the desired effect of leaving her speechless. A knock on the door sealed the delay in pursuit of romance for the moment. "Let's eat, do the conference call, and then debate the options. We could decide over a quick rock, paper, scissors competition."

Jeff groaned. "No fair. You always win."

JJ opened the bridge. "Good afternoon. You both look refreshed. I trust your accommodations are to your liking."

Gracie replied with a smile at the camera and grabbed Jeff's hand below viewing. "Yep, it's great. I swept the room and found no eavesdropping or surveillance units."

"Good, girl. Did you like the package, and did you let Jeff try any of them?"

Gracie frowned and groused, "Of course, Jeff tested them, and trained me too, smarty pants."

"And how many do I need to replace in the shipment scheduled for tomorrow?" he pointedly questioned. "Brayson and I have got a bet going."

Jeff laughed, then Gracie joined in. "JJ, we only found five of the thirty drones non-operational after our testing."

JJ smirked. "Jostled in transport—easily replaced. I still win; Brayson said they'd all be toast. Did you like the insects, Gracie?"

"I did, especially the butterflies. Thank you. What did you come up with after your research?"

Gracie spotted uneasiness pass across Jeff's eyes.

JJ smugly grinned. "We discovered our target is a social media junkie, particularly in the finance arena where artificial intelligence is in the mix. We'll highlight your Amsterdam keynote so that your lovely face shows up on his phone alerts before he first spots you on the boat. We want your face top of his mind. The extra time you spent at the hotel for charity will also come in handy to salt several of the other social media sights he prowls, though it's doubtful he would understand what suffering the Jews endured. You have a memorable face, especially with that smile like Mom's."

"Oh, thank goodness the Amsterdam debacle perhaps wasn't such a mess. Cool. Nice touch, JJ."

"Once he notices you, use your feminine charms. I know you hate that idea, but it'll work."

Gracie chuckled. "It is what it is. Go on."

"That should get you noticed as a celeb, and with any luck, you can use your wiles to wangle an invite to his private parties. He hosts lots of events when he cruises. And for some reason, Gracie, they are bigger after a port stop. Don't understand why that's the case. Still working on that aspect."

Gracie nodded her head, and touched her hand to her chin tapping slightly, thinking. "In all seriousness, what exactly do you want me to do with my feminine wiles?"

Jeff suppressed a smirk as JJ clucked his tongue. "Gee, let's ask Jeff if he can give you some tutoring on this aspect. Sometimes you are so unaware, Gracie."

Trying to defuse this avenue of discussion, Jeff asked, "JJ, we noticed you only sent the small, short-range drones. That suggests you have someone in mind to handle the long-range ones."

JJ, back on track, stated, "Yep, Brayson is scheduled as an eccentric guest photographer. He'll have all the proper access to fly and record for the cruise line. The smaller drones are for close proximity situations that require discretion and maneuverability with limited risk to you four. Some of the insects can sit in plants or flower arrangements. I really liked the ones for Gracie and Bailey's hair. We'll see how each of them work on the first day."

"If I can get into Pliant's parties," Gracie stated, "then I will pull Bailey in as a buddy. That leaves Jeff and Keith on the periphery in case of any trouble."

JJ reminded, "Brayson will be onboard in case things go sideways. You may see a few other people you know, Gracie. Jeff, we purposely left their faces off the briefings to avoid giving their cover away. Now all that has to happen is to have Jeff teach you some feminine wiles so you'll be invited to the table with Pliant."

"JJ, I have high confidence that my Gracie has all the necessities for an operation like this."

"That's all I had from this end. Recommend you meet with Bailey and Keith, discuss the particulars, and rehearse the plan. Jeff, give them hands-on with the drones in case they have an opportunity or need to use them."

Gracie smiled affectionately. "Send a few extra then, JJ. I'm not the only one who flies poorly. I roomed with Bailey in school, and I doubt her eye-hand coordination has improved much." Cutting her eyes to Jeff, she added, "That statement is between us, honey."

After disconnecting, Jeff wrapped his arm around her shoulders and hugged her. "He knows you pretty well, doesn't he?"

Gracie sulked. "Yes, dammit."

CHAPTER 12

Let's Talk, but not here...

Gracie's phone chirped and she answered it on the first ring. "Hi, Bailey, did you and Keith check in yet?"

"Yep. We just got unpacked," Bailey replied, cheerfully. "We're starving. How about we meet you downstairs in the dining area to discuss our final plans?

"Gee, Bailey, we've already eaten and, well...frankly discussing our plan in an open venue isn't smart. You never know who's listening. I recommend you and Keith grab some dinner then come up here so we can have a private conversation. We have some things to show you."

"Oh, yeah, you're right. I forgot you are already on assignment," whispered Bailey. "Give me that room number and we'll be there as soon as we grab our food."

"Deal."

Gracie rushed to the door at the sound of knocking. Only a moment was lost until she and Bailey warmly embraced each other, squealing with delight. She turned toward Keith and smiled.

He raised an eyebrow at the touchy scene. "I'm just a handshake kind of guy, so...."

Gracie made a face of disbelief as she provided an enthusiastic hug. "Nice to meet you, Keith."

Bailey grinned and embraced Jeff. "You're right, Gracie, like a brother. Cool."

"Keith, I'm with you concerning handshakes," said Jeff. Each smiled, with neither of them doing the macho strong hand thing.

Setting their food on the table on the patio, Keith and Bailey refilled their plates with the remaining meats and salad. Jeff poured wine while their guests attacked their tasty morsels.

Gracie exclaimed, "I'm excited to think we're going to nail this shark."

"Bailey, this is your gig and we had the discussion the other night, but how do you envision it?" Jeff asked. "I'd like your thoughts as I'm kind of the new guy and don't have your background, Keith. I'm happy to get plugged into the right areas. Whatever helps."

"Great idea," Gracie agreed. "Bailey, we each want to add value the right way. What's the current rundown?"

"Gracie," Bailey said, "you haven't changed a bit, ideas aplenty. I loved that video clip of Pliant at the airport. We have current photos to work from. Keith pointed out the heavies in Plaint's entourage. They look similar: tall with broad shoulders, and close-cropped hair. Even their clothing appears almost like a uniform."

"Likely with shoulder holsters under those jackets," commented Keith.

"Gracie," suggested Bailey, "you and I need to look for an opening to get invited as part of his orbit, which hopefully will include his parties and dining."

Gracie bubbled with excitement to share JJ's thoughts on the subject. "Call on me, teacher. I have an idea."

Jeff and Keith assessed each other but remained silent.

Bailey comically surveyed the audience. "Hmm, no swell ideas for getting into his in crowd?"

Gracie, not to be denied, added, "I know something we might try."

Bailey tapped her pen on the tabletop. "You in the front row, the over-achiever. What's your idea?"

"My source thinks we might leverage Pliant's thirst for artificial intelligence in finance. He routinely prowls social media and has a considerable presence across several platforms. If he gets enough photos and comments from my Amsterdam presentation, he might approach me. Then it's his ballgame." Gracie, with a look like the cat that swallowed the canary, continued, "I'll insist my dinner companion and publicist join me. Bailey, we sit at the same table in his private dining area."

Jeff motioned for Keith to join him at the inside table for a sidebar chat. They recognized that the girls' conversation was escalating into high-speed exchanges that hovered at two hundred words per minute with gusts exceeding six hundred. They were aware of these women and their vast capabilities. Gracie slightly nodded and wiggled her fingers Jeff's way at their departure.

Seated with a view of the girls, he lowered his shoulders in resolution and nodded toward Keith. "It's a shame those two don't get along better. Anyway, how about I show you some of the support gear we got for operations?"

Keith grinned. "Excellent suggestion, Dr. Wood. I'm no more thrilled than you about the rooming arrangements. I also worry that they may take risks. We need to insist they stick close together."

"I couldn't agree more."

CHAPTER 13

Checking In...Check it Out

The ride-share arrived right on time, and the girls loaded up in minutes. The guys took a subsequent ride share vehicle. The navigation to the destination was smooth, but as they got closer to the pier where several cruise lines berthed, the traffic slowed to a crawl. It didn't help that the girls had no idea which terminal provided access to their cruise line.

"I figured we'd be able to read the ship's name and start up the gangway," Gracie grumbled. "I didn't count on tracking a terminal number because you can't see the ships from this angle." A quick text to JJ resulted in the response of their target terminal number.

Their driver delivered them promptly to the location once she conveyed the information.

They navigated the various security checkpoints with the correct documentation and arrived at the desk of the concierge/boarding agent. The girls held back—letting several groups go ahead of them to clear the first step to boarding—until no one was behind them. By design, the guys were outside the terminal waiting for the signal to follow Pliant and his entourage to the next security point.

Finally, the text Gracie received indicated it was time to move. She put her arm through Bailey's. "Let's board this vessel and start relaxing after the Paparazzi hounding me in Europe.

Argh! I enjoyed the attention, but there is a point where it becomes intrusive."

"I agree, Gracie," sympathized Bailey. "I'll help you avoid unwanted attention so you can get some sun, sip some drinks, and do that people-watching thing you adore."

Gracie heard the noise of travelers with deep, impatient voices filing in behind them.

Looking toward the ship's representative, Gracie quietly implored, "Ma'am, there's a slight misunderstanding. Bailey and I are in the same cabin, but we'd like two charge cards, one assigned to each of us. Can you make that change, please?" She presented her card then added, "Bailey, give your card to the nice lady to use for your purchases."

"This a bit unusual for the check-in process." Flustered, the clerk added, "Let me see if I can make the change. If I can't you'll need to board and check with the customer services area. I also need your passports." The clerk tapped her ear bud and made a few inaudible comments to someone on the other end. She looked at Bailey then Gracie as if verifying the identifications. She delivered their key cards with a satisfied expression. "Easier to change than I expected. Enjoy your cruise." A crewmember hoisted the girls' bags onto the conveyor belt.

Gracie panicked and called, "Wait, I need to grab my sun-glasses from the blue bag. I forgot to take them out. I know it'll be hours before our things reach the cabin."

Gracie pulled out her glasses and held them up in triumph. Turning toward the next point of embarkation, Bailey caught Gracie's arm. "Gracie, your makeup is smudged. Touch it up before we get our photos taken by that hottie with the camera up ahead. This trip is going to be packed with memories of relaxing fun."

Without moving away from the counter, Gracie quickly produced her compact and peered at her reflection. She panned it left over her shoulder and caught Pliant's image. She snapped a quick shot and touched her cheek with the brush. Satisfied with the touch-up, she turned to her friend. "All better." She twisted and deliberately bumped into Pliant. "Oh, my goodness! My apologies. Are you okay?"

Pliant studied her a moment and frowned. "Are you finished holding up the line? The wretched traffic I got stuck behind made me miss my priority check-in status. Here I am, boarding with everyone else, and, as my luck would have it, I got in line behind you. If your makeup is satisfactorily restored, may I have a turn at checking in?"

Bailey tugged on Gracie's arm. "Come on, Gracie, Mr. Grumpy Britches is feeling inconvenienced. I don't want him to take it out on us. Let's get our welcome aboard photo and then head to a quiet bar. We can review your next speech like we planned."

The girls sauntered over for photos with the two backgrounds. The photographer grinned and suggested extra shots, which invoked squeals of silliness before the girls took off in search of that bar.

Jeff and Keith kept on the heels of Pliant and his group to complete the check-in process. Jeff grinned hearing Pliant's comment. "I think I've seen that troublesome girl before. Remind me to check the social feeds after we board, Max."

Keith and Jeff sailed through the check-in process, joking with each other and flirting with the clerk. A crewmember loaded their bags, tagged with their room number, onto the conveyor belt. With hardly a glance at the girls, they headed off to the next checkpoint for photos and safety check.

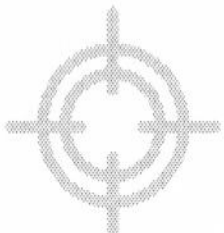

Jeff and Keith located a table at the edge of the bar. It provided the perfect observation spot for all the passengers seated at the tables around them. They made mental notes and then talked about some of the more colorful characters.

"Keith, this ship has a cornucopia of guests. A good division of older travelers and younger successful professionals. Not many children."

Keith smirked. "Exactly. When school is in session, family travel gets reduced, but older cruisers increase. It'll minimize the squealing at the pool for sure. Our partners are making noise and attracting attention with their vivacious conversations." They admired the girls' antics with their wait-staff and nearby passengers.

"Do you think we're noticing them more because we love them, or because they're just trying to get attention?" asked Jeff.

Keith shook his head. "That's a tough one, bud. I think I'd have to go with both reasons. Because of your second comment, they're going to attract a lot of attention, but your first comment means we need to keep an eye on who notices them."

Jeff laughed aloud. Then, setting down his menu and looking forward to dinner, he added, "Good thing those two aren't shy." He sighed and added, "I'm a little let down that we can't all sit together and cut up. I suspect this being out of reach will be more of a challenge than I imagined."

Keith tilted his head and rolled his eyes. "It's the first time I've seen them in action together. They're having fun, even if they are focused on getting this guy. I think we'll have our work cut out for us. But, yeah, I know how you feel." Pushing past his feelings, Keith continued, "I'm going to see if I can access the cargo holds early tomorrow morning before everyone is awake. Might find something that interests our efforts. With this being the first night, I suspect the hangovers will keep folks in their cabins until late morning."

"I agree. The couple to your left has two drinks on the table and walked in with one in-hand. I'm thinking they'll be a part of the late riser group. I'll check out the gym and walking track to see what's available, and who might be staying sober."

Their drinks arrived and they toasted. Jeff raised his glass. "*Salude*!" Then he leaned closer as their glasses met, and quietly added, "Thanks, Keith, for unlocking the balcony gate. At least we can move between cabins after dark."

"I agree. Bailey established schedules to keep us in place until Pliant takes Gracie's bait. Do you really think that plan's going to succeed?"

"Knowing Gracie—" Jeff shrugged agreement— "it'll work."

Keith scowled as Bailey inclined her head with a flirty flip of her hair to a comment from the guy adjacent to her table. "Jeff, I think, to maintain the deception, we need to be hitting on some of these ladies. The girls shouldn't get all the fun."

Jeff took a sip of his drink and leaned back, relaxed. "We clean up good, and this is a target-rich environment. Let's not create a problem. She'll be in your cabin later. It's just an act. Bringing back an eager someone to the room so she can show off her tattoos and check out yours, is definitely out of bounds."

Keith looked chagrined and cocked his head as if considering alternatives.

Jeff laughed. "Nope, I don't have any tattoos, but I'm told it's a great pickup line."

They ordered bar snacks and resumed people-watching. "Hopefully this plan works well, so we can keep an eye on them," said Keith.

At a nearby table, Jeff acknowledged an elderly lady sizing him up, then replied, "We'll know soon enough." He shifted uncomfortably at the visual inventory she was taking of him.

Keith, amused by the scene, smirked. "The target-rich environment statement you made does seem to be the case. I didn't expect us to be targets. The silver hair at the next table is staring at you. Are you going to use the tattoo pick-up line on her, or should I?"

CHAPTER 14
Table for Two?

The morning alarm on Gracie's phone sounded for rise and shine. Jeff delivered another heartfelt, fun smooch before she texted Bailey she was headed over. She appeared sad as she waited to hear the gentle tapping on the patio door before moving onto the balcony to the adjacent cabin. Gracie turned to gaze at Jeff one more time, then disappeared. Jeff sighed with an ache in his heart. He mumbled, "We'll get past this, if I don't let it get me down."

True to their distancing arrangement, the guys donned swim trunks and headed to the water slides near the big pool. It offered a great view of the water attractions on the deck and sun chairs. By mid-morning, Keith and Jeff enjoyed cutting up with wrung-out looking people edging their way to the bar begging for remedies for their morning headaches. Several moms, with pasted-on smiles, passed with kids in tow, headed toward the water park.

A little before noon, Bailey and Gracie showed up in string bikinis and bright cover-ups. They parked themselves and their accouterments outside the wet area on two loungers. Gracie moved a table on either side and spread out her towel. Bailey signaled a waiter and ordered two fruity chic drinks. With their wide hats and large sunglasses, they settled in for serious people-watching.

By early afternoon, the deck chair real estate became scarce as more people packed into play in the water attractions. Though removed from the activity, the human traffic and noise made conversation between Gracie and Bailey rise in volume.

Bailey pushed her glass to Gracie. "Your turn."

Gracie returned with their drinks just as the hottie photographer appeared. "Hey girls, my name's Brayson. I took a couple of shots yesterday when you boarded. The camera loves you both. When I noticed you here relaxing, I thought I might ask if you'd consider taking some shots to help advertise the cruise line. I'll need a signed release, but, of course, we won't reveal your names in ads."

Bailey sat up and beamed at the nice-looking man. "Gracie, this might give us that extra push we talked about."

Gracie chewed her lip a bit as she ran through the possibilities. "Alright, Bailey, if you want to. It shouldn't hurt anything." Gracie shyly smiled at the cameraman. "Brayson, you said, right? Sure, we'll sign your forms, but is this for just now or on and off during the cruise?"

"Here on deck today for sure," Brayson said, "then we'll see if another venue looks promising. Your photos will be no cost as well. I have the authority of the cruise ship to provide coupons for free drinks, discounts on purchases in the shops, and custom coffees on demand for the entire cruise. Nothing offshore however." He handed them each a piece of paper and a pen. They scribbled and handed the papers back to Brayson, exchanging conquering hero expressions.

"Now don't change anything since I want you to look unrehearsed," said Brayson. "I need to do a little gear setup for lighting and height with my drone camera."

The activity became interesting for the idle passersby including the person of interest for Bailey and Gracie. Pliant, and one associate, lingered longer than the other casual observers and even sported a puzzled look. Gracie noticed Plaint flipping through what she suspected were apps on his cell, then pausing to type as if in a search bar. She watched Pliant's expression brighten. He leaned over close to say something into his associate's ear, who then nodded.

Bailey and Gracie hammed it up for the photographer, encouraged by the comments of folks walking by. The photoshoot continued until Pliant moved out of the area. The drone bobbed and weaved to make digital records. Brayson slyly winked at Gracie who inclined in private recognition.

By late afternoon the girls were tired of the sun and needed to rest before dinner. After a fast shower, they headed for a snack in the open seating area looking fresh and relaxed in sexy sundresses. Each of them sported rosy skin from a bit too much sun.

Keith and Jeff stepped into line with trays in-hand, offering their best pickup lines as dinner companions. Gracie cut her eyes to Bailey who, out the corner of her eye, spotted Pliant's associate watching the exchange. Gracie shook her head, and Bailey said, "We're not looking for dinner companions tonight. We've work to catch up on, and a speech to rewrite."

Both guys scrunched their faces at what they must have thought was a poor brushoff. Keith rebuked, "Perhaps next time, ladies."

The girls took their trays and sashayed to an open table by the window. Their bubbliness was Yang to dejected Ying withdrawal of Keith and Jeff.

Gracie hoped Jeff realized it was a part of the act. When he turned with his back to Pliant and snuck a wink, she relaxed.

Gracie and Bailey returned to their room delighted to find a message from Pliant clipped to the door. Gracie fingered the embossed invitation, which conveyed the same level of printed prestige as being invited to the captain's table. It read…

Phillip Pliant cordially invites you
to join his dinner party tonight

Deck 12 forward private dining.
Cocktails served at six.

"We're in, Bailey."

They walked into the cabin and hip-bumped after the door clicked shut, then texted the boys about the perfect turn of events.

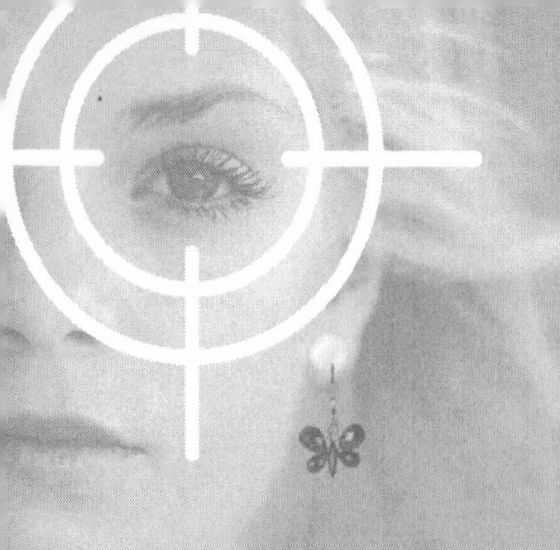

CHAPTER 15

Cat and Mouse

Gracie reviewed their outfits with a critical eye. "I think we are setting the right tone. Simple cocktail dresses. Not flashy or revealing."

"Agree, you look put together, but not like a showoff."

Gracie turned Bailey around then cocked her head. "Yep, but switch the dangle earrings with the studs. And, add that pretty hair clip I bought you. It'll go great with that dress." She mentally ran down the check list. "He's seen us before but likely doesn't think we make the connection. Let me break the ice."

"Good, I'm your press coordinator so talking to other people collecting names and backgrounds is my focus."

Gracie opened her clutch and added two small butterfly drones. "We'll see how private this room is and if we can we'll add these fellows to stick around like garden artwork."

"I like that. I'll take one too." Bailey added it and set her jaw. "We're ready. Let's do this."

They chatted quietly until they reached the location. Gracie recognized the man outside the door from the photos of the Pliant's advance group. She presented their invitation. "Good evening, sir. I believe we're expected."

The man spoke into his watch while he opened the door. "Yes, ma'am. You're expected."

The room had a garden on the window side with a view of the calm ocean. Rounded tables set to accommodate six people each had low flower arrangements in a variety of tropical colors. "Bailey, this is nice. We might be able to leverage the garden to our benefit."

"I think you're right about the flowers. I also think I recognize the lady in the ice-blue dress, but I can't recall her name."

Gracie mentally counted roughly a dozen people in similar attire, and drinks in-hand. The mix of perfumes from the ladies was mild, but not overpowering. Conversation sounded friendly as she caught comments about shopping and excursions. Pliant approached them, tanned against his off-white linen suit, a wavy cut to his black hair with dark piercing eyes. She categorized him as refined yet with an aura of danger and an agenda.

"Ladies, so delighted that you accepted my invitation."

Gracie feigned a shocked expression. "Oh dear." She raised her hand to her mouth. "We met you at check in and delayed you. I want to apologize and—"

"Tsk, tsk. That's old news, Ms. Rodreguiz." He extended a hand. "My name is Phillip Pliant." He shifted his focus. "It's nice to meet you too, Ms. Smith. What would you ladies like to drink? The bar is open. Miguel," he called, "get these guests their drinks. Please mingle. With your finance background, this group might interest you. I need to finish a conversation with someone before dinner."

His expression reminded Gracie of someone a step above used-car salesman. "Bailey, I think we should divide and gather as much background as we can on this group."

Miguel approached with a friendly smile. "What sort of cocktail would you like? We have a Lavender Daiquiri as the ship cocktail of the night."

"I'd like to try one," Bailey said.

"Miguel, may I have a crisp white wine, please?"

They followed him to the bar to retrieve their drinks, and set about their mission, meeting several guests.

Dinner service began roughly forty minutes after their arrival. The girls ended up at different tables, between them meeting most of the guests. A brief exchange in the restroom confirmed the people at this party were wealthy and connected. Gracie discovered two were investors in Pliant Industries. Bailey confirmed the lady dressed in blue was an upcoming star in a recent streaming series.

Even when dinner ended, the bar remained open. "Gracie, I'm having a blast. That Miguel is great at keeping the glasses full."

"I noticed," she chuckled. "I've had some interesting conversations and set one butterfly after I finished my meal."

"Nice, I found a spot to set a dragonfly behind a pretty flower I bent to smell. The garden area makes you feel like you're in a person's backyard."

"With the ocean in the background. Does that remind you of home, Bailey?"

"I wish."

Pliant tapped Gracie on the shoulder. "Ms. Rodreguiz, I've not had a minute until now to visit with you. Ms. Smith, if you'll excuse us, I'd like to hear more about your thought on world economic projections."

"Please call me, Gracie."

"Only if you'll address me as Phillip. Miguel, Ms. Smith needs a refill." He turned and, with his hand on the small of Gracie's back, shepherded her toward an isolated area at the edge of the garden.

CHAPTER 16

The Stalk

Bailey wove through the hallways of the boat. She'd found it challenging to locate the correct floor and direction to safely navigate to her room. Steadying herself against the walls and, struggling to read the numbers, she muttered, "Note to self—practice finding your way back to the room *before* getting half-crocked at a party."

After several wrong turns and near wrong choice cabin numbers, she finally arrived at the cabin with the same number as the electronic key. She noted with some dismay the late hour on the bedside clock in the cabin. Bailey strove for stealth in getting ready for bed but still managed to stub her toe that ordinarily would have produced several expletives at high decibel levels. When the figure under the covers made no sound, she thought her stealthy entrance succeeded.

The triumphant smugness she felt at her deception was extinguished like a quick puff to a match when she slipped under the covers and Keith tersely snarled in the darkened room. "Kinda late for a first date, honey."

Annoyed at the less-than-subtle rebuke, Bailey argued, "For the record, I'm getting under the covers with only you, in case that's your real question. Gracie's still at the after-party, chatting up a storm. I got tired and want to rest up for the early shore shopping. I begged off. She said that was fine."

"Great, so when she finishes, she'll be back through here to get to bed with Jeff." He rolled away and mumbled, "Nothing like sleeping in the lobby to cool the mood."

She snuggled up to his back. "I already thought of that and gave her the key. It should be too late for anyone to notice what door she enters. Plus, she's cautious. Are you tired or not really?"

He rolled back and his lips felt happy. He rearranged the covers a bit. "I'm fine. How 'bout you?"

"Suddenly I'm not sleepy anymore."

The curtains to the sliding patio door had been left open just enough to allow the light from the rising sun to slice into the cabin room. This natural alarm gently woke Jeff ahead of the clock on his phone. He grabbed the device and disabled it before it launched into a tone of Wagner's *Flight of the Valkyries.*

Jeff finished dressing and bent toward Gracie's beautiful form, which hadn't budged since he got up. "Honey," he whispered, "we're docked. I need to get off as close to first as possible to select the best target to follow. I suspect you might want to sleep in after you got in so late. I will set the DND tag on the door."

She popped open an eye that immediately closed, then reached up to hug him. "Wow, I'm not quite awake. Thanks for saying something. I had way too much root beer last night, but I learned about Pliant's scheduled meetings with some local officials. I'm going to try and crash those events."

He lifted an eyebrow as his brow furrowed. "Did he invite you or is this something you're trying to engineer? This is not my field of expertise, sweetie, but how much time can you spend with this guy before it looks like you're too chummy?"

She opened her lovely eyes and gave him a quick kiss. "Point taken. He invited us to join the party again tonight, so backing off makes sense. Thanks. If I act too eager, then it looks like I'm trying to seduce him—which is disgusting—rather than being a chatty finance quant. I'll grab Bailey for breakfast, letting you and Keith stick to your plan. We'll keep our distance."

Reasoning through their options and tasks, Jeff confessed, "Keith wants to get a closer look at the entourage and what they do away from the boss. I plan to do some on-shore research if I can get access to recent transactional records. Is Brayson doing photo shoots everywhere? Based on what I reviewed so far, he secured amazing access."

Sitting up, she grabbed the coffee, still piping hot, from the side table, patting his arm in appreciation. "Yes, I need to review the shots too and add missing commentary. What kind of research did you have in mind?"

"We know Pliant has no place to drop his contracted volume of recyclable materials. But adding the pristine islands of the Caribbean as a sanctioned dumping ground doesn't make sense. I suspect we're missing something, so I'm looking for the possibilities. I thought I would speak to the locals, especially if they fawn over Pliant."

"You've got great hunches, darling. I'll phone next door so we can seamlessly room shift." She gave him another quick kiss, then secured her robe from the adjacent chair as she headed toward the room's phone.

Jeff's mobile buzzed, and he looked at the screen. His shoulders slumped as he thumbed through the pictures, frowned, and turned the screen toward her. "Seriously, Gracie, this is you at the Pliant table long after Bailey left? At least that seems to be the case based on Brayson's notations. Is he wrong?"

Jeff watched as Gracie's face fell, and her eyes looked guilty as she nodded. "She tried asking me to walk with her, but I was in my element with Pliant. I said I'd be there soon. I didn't realize how long I stayed after she left."

Jeff set down the cell. He gently held her shoulders and looked into her eyes. "Gracie, I thought we agreed to stay in teams for our best security. I get that I'm not your escort for this show, but you can't be going it alone without backup."

"Brayson sent them to you, or was it JJ?" she mumbled, with fear streaking across her face.

"JJ. He dressed me down in the text, then sent the photos with the notations. Remember the briefing JJ started with? We're hunting something that knows how to hunt as well. A false move, a simple suspicion—a lone female surrounded by vile eco-gangster and his heavies creates a recipe for disaster. I know you feel overprotected, but he's right. You shouldn't be flying faster than your guardian angels. We all know how good you are and how self-reliant. But let's be safer, smarter. Please?" His honest petition drove home a heartfelt point.

Gracie pouted. "I apologize for disregarding our rules. I'm glad we're a team and grateful that Brayson's close. Honestly. Thank you, sweetheart. It won't happen again."

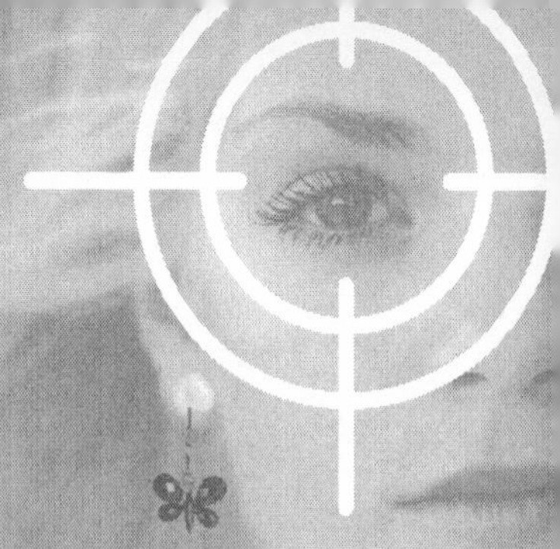

CHAPTER 17

Evidence and Information

Excited chattering emanated from the passengers as they moved through the badge scanning toward the security exit. The efficient crew frequently repeated for guests to board before five that afternoon, ship's time. A fatherly voice that boomed out over the wharf—*remember where we're parked*—had everyone chuckling. Jeff overheard several conversations on the best shopping and stops for rum in the San Juan port. With no paid excursions available for the passengers, Jeff suspected the goal was to shop 'til they dropped, then crawl back. Smiling at individual's greetings without engaging in any long discourse, Jeff maintained a healthy distance from the target. Pliant and his entourage headed down the pier with purpose. Jeff marked the boarding time on his mobile device and verified the time to his self-winding watch.

He noticed several black limos parked near the end of the pier, reflecting the sunshine in flawless, gleaming exteriors. A bodyguard type, dressed in a linen suit, exited each vehicle as Pliant's group approached. Phillip and his backup split between the waiting vehicles and then departed. Jeff approached the closest souvenir stand and opened his eyes wide as he commented, "Wow! What was that all about? I didn't know we had visiting dignitaries on board."

The aged lady's welcoming smile vanished as she spat on the ground in contempt. "They fawn all over that man every time he arrives. The way they treat him you'd think the governor worked for him."

Jeff sensed the woman needed to vent her unhappiness. "Oh. What makes this character so important, if I might ask?"

"He promises to bring new business to San Juan. We need the revenue flowing to recover from the last hurricane," she sneered. "With new jobs, people won't have to beg for money from the tourists getting off the boats in stalls like this one."

"Help me understand. I'd think that would be good news. New businesses and industry for the locals would help your economy or am I missing something?" he innocently asked.

The older woman scrunched up her face, increasing her weathered wrinkle lines, and shook her head, with her lips thinning. "Ha! You sound like them. You people from another place believe it when someone says they're ready to bring positive change to our way of life. Then we can live like you." She snorted. "But it never happens that way. The construction contracts go to family members who only hire their friends. The rich get richer. I may only be a stall retailer hawking my goods to tourists, but I'm my own boss. I bow and scrape with dignity to my customers. Him, we don't trust."

Jeff suppressed a smile, feeling a deep appreciation in his heart for wise women everywhere. He selected several t-shirts, a couple of island specific souvenirs, and handed her a hundred-dollar bill.

Flustered, she frowned. "I can't make change for that. Don't you have something smaller? Or are you trying to get it for free??"

Pleased at her surprise, he calmly stated, "Ma'am, I like your stand, your products, and your independence. Even if I had a smaller bill, I wouldn't change it out. Keep the difference and get something for yourself."

She bagged his goods with care, smoothing extra tissue paper between the items. She rose to her full height and straightened her shoulders when handing him the bag.

As an afterthought he asked, "Ma'am, I could use a small favor if you don't mind. Where could I look up official contracts for buying and selling land on this or neighboring islands? Being a foreigner, I'd like to see if buying here would be a good investment, particularly with honorable citizens like you."

The matron tucked the bill under her blouse then provided directions to the library and recorder's office six blocks over. She gave him a quick hug. "My daughter, Mia, works for the controller in the office. Tell her Maria sent you."

Jeff mused as he walked away. *That exchange saved me two wasted hours of hunting for the records office.*

Keith reconnoitered the empty passages and meeting rooms of the deserted ship, peeking in doorways and doing a mental inventory of where items were located. Now and again, stewards tried to assist him, but he politely declined, claiming to be wandering. One event caught his interest when a Pliant guard, escorted by a crewmember, approached a secured door which the crewmember unlocked. Both men entered and Keith heard the lock engage from the inside as he approached. On a whim, Keith moved past the door to an alcove and leaned against it with a phone device to his ear in case anyone else wandered the halls.

Fifteen minutes later, the men exited with Pliant's guy carrying a modest sized gym bag bulging at the seams. The man's strained forearm alerted Keith that it was heavy. Keith hugged the hallway recess as the man scanned in both directions.

The crewmember locked the door. "I'll take you down the internal elevator through the crew-only door to deck one so you can depart."

Blast it! I'll never get down and through departure before they're gone, Keith thought. "Since I can't tail them, maybe I can check out what's behind door number one."

He verified the hallway was deserted and moved to the door-knob with his lock-pick tools in-hand. A few careful twists in the keyhole gained access. Slipping in, he closed and locked the handle lock. Dimly lit from ceiling lights, the large windowless storage area had random pathways making movement difficult. Stacks of boxes, some with company names of retailers, with various tags appeared undisturbed. The scent of mustiness complemented the dust particles he aroused as he walked through. Nothing in his indeterminate search appeared open…until he bumped into the shrink-wrapped pallet he recalled seeing loaded under the close supervision of Pliant's lieutenants in Miami. He moved around to the back side, cut open a small section of the wrap and reached in to inspect the contents.

He pulled out a series of plastic, molded items that appeared more like products than waste cargo. Somewhat confused, he wondered if perhaps these items were samples intended for a buyer's inspection. The initial items were mostly toys, like Lego bricks and bath toys. Then he retrieved house-sized bricks with the interlocking notches. One more reach into the interior of the pallet yielded a surprise. Keith pulled the item free, turned on the light of his cell phone, and frowned. "Now isn't that special?"

Snapping a photo, he cocked his head at voices coming from a different area of the cargo hold. He turned off the light and shoved the items back under the shrink-wrap, pulling it tight to make it look undisturbed. Then he ducked behind a pallet.

"Hey, let's start our count at the far area and work our way back here."

"Sure."

The footfalls moved to the far side with no further discussion. Keith soundlessly emerged from his hiding spot and headed for the door. Under his breath he groused, "Dammit, not enough time to take photos until I can map the rounds by the crew. I'll return in off hours."

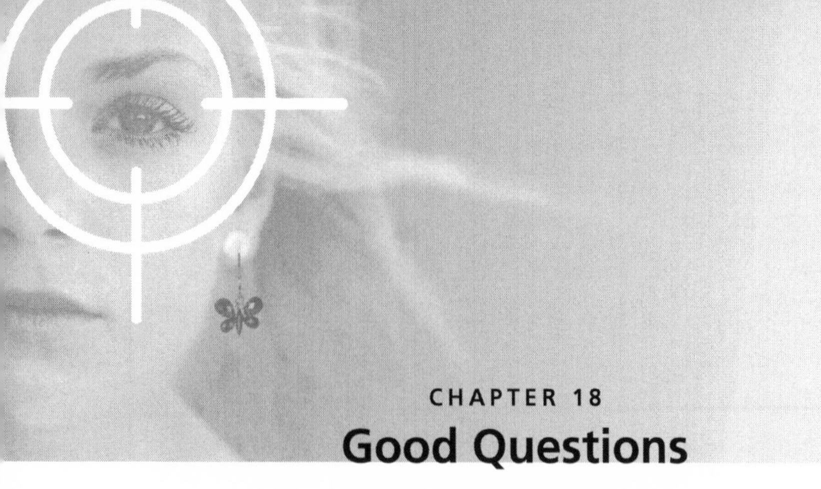

CHAPTER 18
Good Questions

The hours flew by as Jeff pored through all the paper record books that covered the most recent six months. As various documents caught his attention, he'd note the item number and take it to Mia to print. Then he reviewed the next journal.

Finally, Jeff checked his watch. "Oops," he groaned. He rushed the latest ledger back to Mia. "Mia, thank you for letting me use your microfiche resources."

She smiled, taking the ledger and handing him the printed copies from behind the counter. "Did you find what you needed?"

Somewhat disappointed, Jeff half-heartedly offered, "I found some interesting things to keep myself busy for a while. I spent too much time reading the contracts before sending them to print. I'd better head back so I don't miss the ship, forcing me to rent a cigarette boat to get to the next port of call. What do I owe you, ma'am?"

"That'll be forty dollars cash or sixty dollars with a credit card. The fees we get tagged for make cash the best value."

He handed her a fifty-dollar bill and winked. "Get yourself a snack with the change. I really appreciate your printing suggestion. I'm investigating whether your delightful island paradise might support a manufacturing facility that my bosses are considering locating in this region. Someplace to work and play, you know.

It's a shame I didn't find any evidence to suggest the island's infrastructure will support what we have in mind. Thanks again."

"No. Wait," she said with a hint of panic crossing her face. "I have signed contracts, but they are set for restricted viewing. I think these documents might prove our island can support manufacturing. We could use the industry, if our people get to work there."

She opened a locked cabinet drawer and lifted out a hefty folder, placing it on the desk. "I really can't make copies of these as they aren't on microfiche yet."

Jeff grinned at his ruse and pulled out his cell. "If you'll turn pages, I'll take a few shots to look at during my travels." Then he added with a nod of appreciation, "Our little secret."

Mia nodded and smiled as she flipped pages.

Jeff captured dozens of images, including one signed by Pliant. He stopped and returned his cell to his pocket. "You've been helpful. May I have your phone number so if the details check out, I can let you know?"

Mia jotted her number and added, "My husband could use the work. He was a supervisor before the last hurricane flattened the storage depot."

Outside, he breathed a sigh of relief and checked the time. Tucking his souvenir bag close, he scrunched his eyes and picked up his pace. As he retraced his route to the pier, he spotted a landmark and sign that read *Bitcoin ATM* here. Curious, Jeff altered his course but stopped short as several of Pliant's men parked themselves around the terminal. Two of them stood with their backs to the third who was busy with a transaction. Jeff watched casually via the storefront window's reflection as they placed several bricks of currency into a moderate-sized briefcase and then departed.

Jeff lost sight of them in the growing throng of passengers headed toward the gangway. He noted the collective sigh of the people in line to board as *last call* boomed across the pier. As he waited in line for the ID check-in and package inspections for contraband liquor, with the island carrier connection still active, Jeff pushed the images on his cell phone to the team drop box. Jeff smiled to himself at it having been a good day as a gumshoe.

The giant vessel, with five thousand or so souls, eased away from the pier and gracefully headed out of the harbor. After the ship was underway, Jeff and Keith met up in one of the quieter bars. Each ordered a drink. Once secured, they retreated to a secluded table in a dark corner. They sat and toasted.

"Keith, there's definitely something going on with that island. I snagged copies of several examples of contracts, but there wasn't much in the way of building permits. I suspect things are moving cautiously in the negotiations for processing the plastics, or the contracts are a cover for bribes to officials. I found nothing so far on Pliant's trash barges being received or unloaded, even though I spotted their clear marking on two boats in the harbor."

Keith cocked his head to the side. "You may not have found the details yet, but I located some interesting inventory in the hold. I got a chance to inspect that pallet of Pliant's and it looks to be a salesman's product samples. Several commercial grade items made from type-one plastics. The Lego-like building bricks for building construction seemed quite promising."

Jeff opened his eyes feeling disbelief. "You mean Pliant might actually be a good guy trying to launch a legitimate recycling business? That's disappointing."

Keith smirked. "Yeah, that's what I thought. Everything in this pallet was unpackaged, like one-offs like samples. I flashed on a traveling salesmen gig. Until I reached in a last time and extracted something far more complex from plastic. An item created using a 3D printer. I found a single-use weapon. These are the kind you shoot once then throw away. His inventory of manufactured plastics, isn't squeaky clean." Keith pressed his cell phone into Jeff's hand so he could see the photos taken in the cargo hold.

"The updated documents JJ sent illustrated a couple of companies who have developed advanced technology slotted for deployment on the island. Type-one plastic repurposing has been at the top of the desired list for a long time. But certainly not the volume exported by Pliant."

Keith sipped his cocktail and closed his eyes as if searching his mind. "It seems Pliant is trying to build a market for these recycled materials, but not all of it can be used with conventional processes. That begs the question of: what's happening to the unusable plastic? Buddy, it looks like we need more clues."

"Agreed. The Gemini Corporation and Eastman Chemical are two of the leading plastic recycling companies. They are making huge inroads on ways to reprocess the lower grade types. But I was unable to locate Pliant's contact licensing their technologies. The questions are: where's he getting the technology from, and who does he expect to sell disposable weapons to?"

"Good inquiries."

They sat deep in thought sipping their drinks, watching the crowd of people move in and out of the bar like schools of fish on their way to something else.

CHAPTER 19

Surprises and Shockers

Bailey hooked her arm into her friend's and insisted, "Gracie, come on. We've got shopping to do tomorrow and you promised to help me find that special gift. I'm sure these charming folks will invite us back again. However, if we stay much longer, it'll be tomorrow." Gracie leaned into Bailey for balance, rising from the chair.

Gracie smiled graciously at her tablemates, like an afterthought of too much alcohol. Following an acknowledging nod to the host, they weaved their way to the elevators.

"Brother! I never thought I'd admit it, but every night parties are a pain. Bailey, thanks for helping us leave at a decent time."

"And, thank you, Gracie, for ensuring we got club sodas after our first glass of sparkling wine. Let's make sure that our considerate bartender Marian keeps getting nice tips for not revealing our virgin drinks. I am so glad she replaced Miguel."

"I agree we lucked out, that she realizes we are lightweights. She is tiny and unassuming with a twinkle in her eye. I like her."

"Yep. I don't know how that bunch goes at it every night. Do you think we can tail Pliant tomorrow in port? After the information our guys uncovered and our insects transmitted, I'm anxious to see what they're up to on this island."

"One hundred percent with you. It'll be fun to enjoy the guys awake so we can talk, after multiple nights of *last call ladies and gentlemen* at the Pliant party binges. We get two days in St. Kitts, but back on board at sundown each day. Fun for extra exploring and shopping."

"Me too. An early evening will certainly help things. Keith and I are arguing more since we boarded."

Arching her eyebrows and frowning, she gently placed a hand on her friend's shoulder, and inquired, "Oh, dear. No huggy-bear, kissy-face?"

"I could ask you the same thing, but I won't. To be honest, I've got to figure out a way to deal with the pent-up tension and short, crisp responses. A chill in the warm air when the sun's shining is annoying."

"Deal with the pent-up tension," she chuckled. "I like the sound of that. But in answer to your question, the timing hasn't worked well for us either. But at least we aren't arguing."

Bailey grinned and looped her arm through her bestie's and skip-stepped. "Then perhaps Jeff might enjoy a second surprise with the early evening."

Gracie frowned, even as she kept up with the silly steps Bailey did to the hallway's jazz beat. "The only issue there is that they'll come through our cabin before Keith gets to you. I can't put too much on the visual buffet for Jeff until Keith exits for the night."

Snickering, Bailey suggested, "If nice visuals are on display, you might alert Keith that his main course is just through the balcony." They chuckled and hummed along to the saxophone wafting through the overhead speakers.

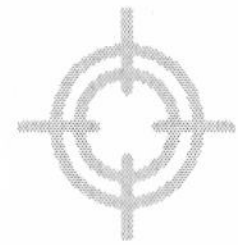

After watching the girls join the Pliant partygoers to the private room for drinks and dining, the guys grew quiet. Keith focused on the assignment, referring to his notepad. Jeff appeared distracted. The food arrived at their table. Keith ordered a nice bottle of wine to enjoy with their meals and both relaxed, though they declined dessert.

Their table waiter alerted them to the next shift of diners en route, so the guys conveyed their thanks for the meal and left. They meandered to their favorite bar glancing in some of the shop windows with no comments. Keith snagged a secluded table while Jeff picked up their orders from the bartender, who recognized them by recalling their beverage preferences. Jeff slid into the empty chair and set the glasses on the table.

"Thanks for grabbing these." He raised a glass. "Cheers. What're your plans for tomorrow?" Keith asked.

"I'll hit the records office first thing. We've got more time in St. Kitts, so I need to dig into the tax records for land purchases and transfers. I want to crosscheck some names. What about you?"

Keith started to respond and raised his eyes. Jeff followed his gaze, then glanced over as a well-tailored blond-haired man with a slight tan approached them. "May I join you, gents?" He didn't make eye contact. His stance came off as guarded, wary.

Jeff sensed something off. Inclining his head toward Keith, he turned toward the gentleman. "Sure, pull up a chair. My colleague and friend gripes about my repetitive storytelling. Perhaps you can insert some variety."

"My name's Jonas," he volunteered, extending his hand. "And you are?"

Each in turn introduced themself. Jonas pulled over a chair and sat. After a few minutes of idle conversation, they all fell silent. Jeff felt the man had an agenda but decided to let things evolve without rushing.

After the waitress delivered another round of drinks, Jonas leaned in. "My treat." He lifted his glass. "Cheers!" He waggled his eyebrows, and conspiratorially observed, "I couldn't help but notice you boys are missing female company. You seem eligible and not really a couple. Are you looking for the right sort of ladies to round out your evening?"

Keith looked down then sheepishly replied, "Okay, so we haven't exactly found, to use your terminology, suitable feminine companionship. Are you part of the ship's guest services rounding up the losers who strike out?"

Jonas laughed. "No." He caught his breath. "Let me walk it back. My role here is to match resources to help the party atmosphere. I'm for happy guys. I am happy to make introductions. These are unique possibilities for the right sort of men who can treat ladies with appropriate decorum, but only with verified credentials." Jonas reached into his pocket and pulled out a small stack of photos. He handed Jeff pictures of several attractive and nicely dressed girls, provocatively posed. Jeff concealed his contempt for the intruder with his distasteful line of business. What was his angle?

Jeff passed the photos to Keith, then commented, "I don't recall escort services as a part of the onboard activities. Is this a free service?"

Both watched in disbelief as Jonas pulled out a mobile credit card reader and launched into his pitch. "I can take cash or credit cards for a $200 introduction fee. I'll need a room number. Your choice will arrive in twenty minutes for an hour of enjoyable, fulfilling socialization. Please let me know if you need any special paraphernalia to enhance the encounter."

Keith sarcastically asked, "Only young girls like these?" handing back the advertisements. "Don't you have someone a little bit more mature and experienced?"

"Gentlemen, these women are quite seasoned in their enthusiasm for entertaining, if that's your concern. If you wish to take advantage of several nightly sessions and prepay, I can offer a good discount, although you'll likely get someone different each evening. Variety is the spice and keeps things exciting. I recommend you mention preference in hair color, size, and clothing requirements when placing your orders."

Keeping his astonishment inside, Jeff set his hand to his chin as if considering. "Wow, such a nice selection and reasonable rates. However, I'm a little uncomfortable with this type of transaction. Let me think about it. I'll get back with you tomorrow."

Keith nodded his agreement. "If that's alright with you, Jonas?"

"Perhaps I misjudged you. We're gender agnostic, if that is a problem."

Jeff felt stunned and was glad Keith remained speechless with an expression that resembled that of the sphinx. The lack of agreement and prolonged silence finally alerted Jonas that this was a no sale table.

He gathered up his pictures and drink. As he turned to leave, he said, "It gets lonely on a long voyage like this. I'll be around."

For several minutes after the man vanished, Jeff finally swallowed. "A call girl enterprise on a cruise ship. Quite the business model. Since we are outside the 12-mile limit of United States' jurisdiction, I'm not even sure you could classify it as illegal. I mean they don't fire up the casinos until we are in international waters, why not this too?"

Keith shook his head. "We could bring it to the attention of a crew member, but we have no proof."

Jeff sighed.

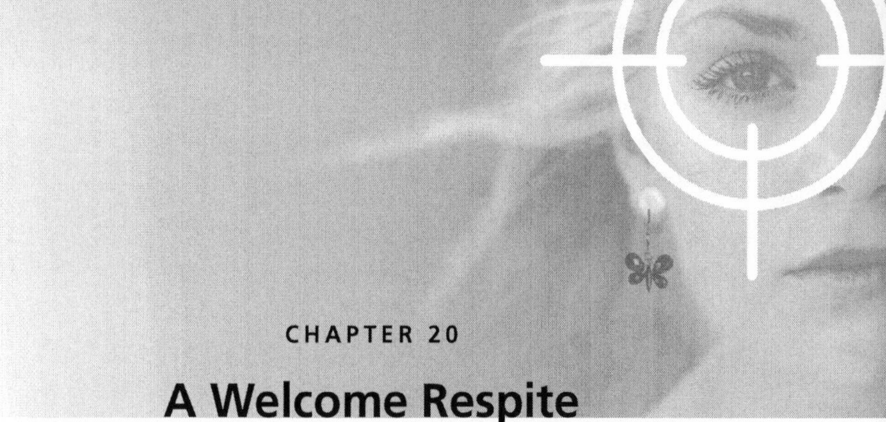

CHAPTER 20

A Welcome Respite

Gracie and Bailey arrived at their cabin thinking of the romance planned for this evening. The turned-down bed, chocolates on the pillow, and adorable towel duck wearing Gracie's sunglasses and sipping a large drink from a plastic coconut, had both girls cracking up so hard tears trailed down Bailey's cheeks.

"Hey, girl, I'm gonna take a fast shower and lather myself with that luxurious lavender lotion. Then it's your turn. I want to be fresh when Jeff knocks on the door to shift."

"Great idea. Hurry. I'll lay out your silk robe and heeled sandals. I'll be right back."

Bailey vanished into the bathroom and Gracie smiled as the shower started. Checking to make certain the hallway door was deadbolted, she opened the balcony door. She slid the outdoor patio partition to the side to open up the area. The guys replaced it each morning to avoid maid service curiosity or gossip. Smiling that the room was dark, meaning they'd beat the guys back, she turned and felt the ocean breeze on her face. Lights reflected on the waves far below. There were two levels above them. Sounds of laughter, singing, and music from deck activities intermittently floated on the wind. Exhilarated, she inhaled deeply the clean smells as they raced across the calm seas. Gracie returned to their cabin but left the door ajar to fill the cabin with fresh ocean air.

Bailey emerged from the bathroom; her sweet lavender scent was perfect. "Gracie, it's all yours. I'm so glad you opened the door."

"There is something about the sea that feels freeing, don't you think?"

"I agree. The weather day and night…perfect with waters so calm the movement is a gentle rhythm like a slow samba." Bailey did the motions of a samba in the open space before grabbing her robe, then sliding into it in harmony with losing her towel in a fluid, practiced motion.

Gracie laughed as she snagged the towel and entered the bathroom for her shower. She called out, "Knock three times on the door if Jeff arrives before I finish, please."

"Gotcha covered."

Gracie finished her shower and decided the lavender lotion worked so she added a fine layer. Then scrubbed her teeth and brushed her shiny hair. She checked each side of her face and shoulders in the mirror, verifying the sun caused a golden glow rather than heated radiance. Her silky purple robe cinched tight at her waist complemented the lingering fragrance. She made a mental note to wear a wide brim hat in the sun tomorrow. She exited the bathroom and spotted Bailey sitting outside on the patio sipping something. The room looked perfect with clothes stowed, bed turned down, and pillows fluffed.

She stepped on the deck and deeply inhaled. "Wow, that shower was exactly what I needed to refresh and relax. Whatcha drinking?"

"I grabbed a fuzzy water from the refrigerator for each of us." Handing one to her friend, Bailey added, "I figured we'd just lounge out here until the boys arrive. They'll be surprised we escaped early. I've been mulling over all the fun Keith and I will have tonight."

Gracie sat and blinked with mock exaggeration, tapping the side of her glass. "Do you want to share details?"

Bailey laughed. "Nah, you have your imagination and I have mine. But I doubt the thoughts are wildly different."

Gracie cocked her head toward the adjacent balcony door and whispered, "I think I heard their door open."

Bailey turned toward the door, softly squealing as the light shone through the filmy curtains. Rubbing her hands together, Gracie caught the glint in her friend's eyes when she looked over. "Since they don't know we're out here, perhaps we'll catch a free show."

Gracie scooted her chair around for a better view. They heard muffled conversation, but nothing specific. They couldn't see all the interior and were hoping for reflections in the mirror. Gracie grinned when she saw Jeff, naked from the waist up and held her breath when he approached the glass door and flung back the curtains.

Bailey spotted the lightweight lounge pants. "Darn it." The comment caused Gracie to hysterically giggle. Jeff opened the door, surprised to see the girls.

"Hi there. You look like you're enjoying yourselves," he commented, raising an eyebrow and adding a grin. He leaned against their balcony wall with his eyes focused on Gracie, obviously taking inventory.

"We finished showers and thought we'd sit outside and await our knights in shining armor," offered Bailey. "Speaking of which, where's my knight, Jeff?"

"He's showering off the memories of a strange conversation from the bar," Jeff stated with a shake of his head. "So, odd. We hoped you two would return before the witching hour."

Gracie said, "Did you want to wait outside, Bailey, or enact your planned surprise on your man?"

Just then Keith emerged from the bath area and was taken aback by the sight of the girls. He said nothing but extended his hand to collect Bailey's and moved them towards the girls' room.

Bailey sauntered to the door as Keith led and turned looking over her shoulder with a gleam in her eye. "I think I'll wait inside where it'll be warmer. You two have a fun night, we'll try to keep the noise down." With that she opened the door, shutting it behind her and pulling the heavier drape across the opening.

"Jeff, did you want to sit out here and relax or head inside?"

He approached her and extended his hand. "Come on, let's go in. I'd like what you're having and I need to fill you in on the bar scene from earlier."

"Okay," she agreed and took his hand.

He got a cold soda from the refrigerator and poured it into his tumbler. "Let's sit, honey."

The sofa was an ideal cuddle spot. "Did you get a chance to look at the photos Keith added from his visit to the cargo area?"

"I did and asked JJ to research specifications for these across the internet. I thought the weapons were a creative recycling effort and wonder if there is a high demand for such products. Perhaps JJ can determine the possible ammunition grade they could utilize. I'll let you know when he shares anything on the subject." Gracie hugged him for a long minute. "Finish your drink and help me actualize my thoughts and ideas. She kissed him sweetly on the lips and stood. "I'll be under the covers reading or something until you want to tell me about the bar thing." As she slipped under the covers, the rustle of her robe resulted in him quickly following suit. He draped an arm over her and she scooched closer.

"So, what happened?" Gracie asked.

"A guy approached us, name of Jonas. Don't have the last name but I suspect it's on the passenger manifest. He showed us glossies of what I classify as underage girls. Pretty…and posed for appeal."

Gracie turned toward him, screwed up her face, and narrowed her eyes. "Why?"

"He offered select evening entertainment for a fee, the boat being a lonely place and all. We looked unattached and he thought we needed on-demand options."

"Other than pretty and young, any other characteristics you care to share?"

"Honey, we didn't meet any of them, but they appeared of Hispanic or Caribbean heritage. It just felt odd. I think that's why Keith needed a long shower to remove that image. Jonas was visibly disappointed that we didn't bite down for his deals and then offered us boys in case that was the reason we rejected his offer."

Gracie pulled her phone and sent a quick message to JJ. She received an immediate acknowledgement. "He'll look into it. Is that all, honey?"

"That's all I wanted to tell you about the bar." He looked at her with heat in his eyes.

"Good." Gracie reached over and pressed off the light. Then slid out of her silk robe. "I was hoping we could move on to an evening exploring my creative thought process." Her arms reached around him under the covers.

Jeff switched off his light, which allowed a soft reflection of the moon-glow to further set the mood. He encircled his arms around her and murmured, "That sounds like a perfect way to learn more about you, sweetheart."

Jonas knocked on the door three times, paused, then twice more. The door yielded after it was unlocked and he harshly forced his way inside. The teens faced him with anxious looks on their faces but remained silent. Jonas, still stewing over the missed sale to the marks, snarled, "No sale tonight. Maybe I'll have better luck with the drunk, late-night crowd. I know Mateo wants results." He went on, mumbling to himself, "I should know better than to target boy scouts for adult entertainment."

These teens had pretty features, plump kissable lips, and curved bodies with brown skin that hid any bruises. Their long, dark wavy hair cascaded nicely over their shoulders nearly to their waists. He knew they were friends and spoke limited English. Mateo had taught them the words they needed and when to use them. Fear flashed in their faces, huddled together in the corner. The tone of their soft Spanish words conveyed fear and resignation. He noticed since Mateo told him to market them that their tears increased if he raised his voice or lifted a hand in anger. The dimly lit room added to their panicked expressions.

Jonas, his anger simmering, strolled to the open bar and poured a drink. He plopped into the chair and studied the two girls he knew were no longer close to being virgins—Mateo's property. Taking a few sips, his evil lascivious smile translated to the pair as no words could. Tears rolled down their cheeks as they silently clung to one another. He stood and whipped off his belt then motioned to them. He bellowed, "On second thought, you two are not taking the evening off." He motioned with his hand. "Get over here, now."

All too clearly, they understood their terror was not yet over today and reluctantly removed their clothes.

CHAPTER 21

Hide and Seek

Respective alarms interrupted the comfortable slumber of intertwined bodies. Bailey crawled out from under Keith's arm and mumbled, "That alarm came sooner than I expected."

Keith moved, shifted to his side, and whispered, "We could ignore the time and go back to sleep for a while. Or we could…" He swooped her into his arms and kissed her neck.

Bailey reluctantly rejected the enticing suggestion and slipped out of the covers, racing to the bathroom door. Before closing it, she sent him a perfect smile. "No more of that pulling me in for one more smooch. You are my kryptonite."

Keith pushed himself to a sitting position grinning at her comment. Reflecting on the evening's playtime as the nicest part of the trip so far, he heard the speedboats from the shore reminding him they'd be docking soon. He got up and looked through his notes for the day's plan. He heard a gentle tapping on the door and looked to see Jeff. Stepping outside, he motioned Jeff to have a seat.

"Bailey will be finished in a second. We had a nice evening, how 'bout you two?"

"We had a wonderful evening. I told Gracie about Jonas. She put in a request with her contacts to check on him, if that's his real name. I wish we could have fun on this trip rather than feel like we're walking on a tightrope."

“I’m sure once we bust this guy, we can take a look at another trip, though we may have to save some time off. When Bailey comes out, let’s go grab food and review our itinerary for the day.”

The balcony door slid open and Bailey appeared. “Good morning, again, honey,” she said, and added a kiss. “Wow, look at the breathtaking shoreline. Those houses on the side of the cliffs have a marvelous ocean view, but must be scary during hurricanes.” Inhaling she added, “It smells like breakfast cooking somewhere. Jeff, is Gracie up? We need to dress for shore so we can leave with the first wave.”

“Yep. She’s up and getting ready. Keith and I were just discussing going to the buffet for breakfast. We need to plan our day too. Thanks, Bailey, for helping Gracie retire early last night.”

“No problem. Talk later.” She wiggled her fingers at Keith in a final see ya later motion before she slipped inside her cabin.

Keith moved the balcony divider back into position with a little more force than necessary. “Another long day,” he grumbled.

Jeff noticed the staff bustled during the breakfast buffet, filling cups, clearing tables, and helping answer guest’s questions about destinations on shore.

“It definitely smells like breakfast of champions. So many choices. Today I feel like buffet with the spicey Mexican burrito with chorizo.”

“It appears everyone’s tastes are covered. I think I’ll head over to the omelet maker for a fresh creation.” Keith pressed a hand to his heart then lumbered toward the chef managing two pans at a time.

With a generously filled plate in one hand and coffee in the other, Jeff hunted an open table. He enjoyed hearing the delightful mixture of languages conversing and carefree laughter from those seated. He secured the vacant spot by a window facing the bay. He felt the ship slow, maneuvering its way to the pier. He speared his selections reading the text delivered while he was in the food line.

"Hmm…Gracie liked your photo of the single purpose pistol you forwarded to JJ." Jeff remarked when Keith joined him. "She also sent it along to an arms expert. They asked for more pictures of the inventory and wanted us to check for ammo."

Keith looked out the window with a scowl. He fidgeted with his mobile app, deliberately pushing his selections around the plate. "We're docking soon and should hear the announcement on the loudspeakers. According to the daily activity list, we get twelve hours in paradise. I don't expect the local records office to open before ten. With passengers wanting to get on the morning excursions to beat the heat, the halls might be reasonably empty. Let's snoop the storeroom with the pallets. I bet there's more to see."

"I like your plan, then we can go ashore. I see another Pliant cargo ship docking at what seems like the supply piers behind your line of sight."

They signaled for an additional cup of coffee from the steward, who grabbed their empty plates.

The speaker erupted with the captain's voice. "Good morning and welcome to a beautiful day to go ashore. The crew is busy securing the gangplank. Our schedule is to open the doors in half an hour. Crew members are available to help direct you if needed. Set your watches to ship time, have a nice day."

"Do you want to grab any more food and head back to the cabin after we get that coffee?" asked Jeff. "We have a reasonable view of the dock area. If we see mass exodus, then I agree it's a good time to go nose around."

Keith rose. "Yep, and the remaining crew will stay busy cleaning. I'm full but we might grab a few apples and bananas for snacks later."

The coffee arrived. The aroma suggested a fresh pot as the source. Jeff's sip verified near perfection. "Ambrosia. Are you and Bailey still sparring about the party hours?"

"No, we didn't argue. I worry she only brought me back for this assignment, but I'd like a bit more couples-time. Especially when I look out at paradise," he added with a sweep of his arm toward the shoreline. "Wishful thinking, I guess."

"You're not alone. Here we are. I hope if we finish this up, the rest will work out."

"To be honest, Jeff, I'm not much of a party animal. I worry should we agree to move forward with our relationship, it'll never be as exciting as these parties."

Jeff turned slightly and glanced absentmindedly toward shore. "Worried about competing against a man we're going to help put behind bars? Hmm. I don't think these parties are impressing them. Gracie thinks Pliant's a prig."

"Maybe I should ask Bailey her thoughts."

"Good idea."

They exited the food court and found the closest stairs to walk up to their deck. At the top of each floor, they noted elevators crammed full of noisy people excited about their upcoming adventures. Only a few crewmembers were encountered during their trek. Empty hallways and stairwells echoed their footfalls as they bounded up the stairs.

"Let's grab a few of the toys Gracie brought," suggested Jeff. "She told me they'd placed a few of the mini drones in the garden area of Pliant's dining room and that the information traveled to JJ."

Inside the cabin they were like kids in a toy shop opening and inspecting the miniatures. They activated an application on their phones to control the devices and ran a few tests, like kids playing with action figures. Each of them pocketed a couple of their favorites.

"You're right, Jeff. These are very cool toys. Let's head toward the stern and take those stairs down."

No other person crossed their path as they meandered toward their destination.

"Keith, I think most folks left the ship early."

"I am glad we haven't seen anyone. We're almost there." Keith grabbed the storage door handle and deftly opened it, faster than before."

"Good job," acknowledged Jeff as they slipped inside and closed the door, locking it from the inside.

Keith led the way.

"Are you part homing pigeon? How are you seeing with the dim lighting?"

"I have a knack. I'm good at spelunking, too," whispered Keith.

Keith led the way through the tight walkways with the loom of shadows making the path uncertain.

Jeff mused how people loaded this confined area, when the sounds of a crackle, like paper being wadded, then soft footfalls ahead and to the right. He latched onto Keith's shoulder, halting his progression. A muffled conversation seemed to come from the direction they were headed. Keith nodded he'd heard. Jeff motioned for quiet and strained to hear the words. Keith maneuvered around other obstacles, gaining ground toward their goal.

Keith peeked slowly around the stack, stopped, crouched, and faced Jeff. The look of dismay was reflected from the dim shadows highlighting his features. Using hand signals to indicate clothing and shape, he indicated it was one of Pliant's guys, likely on guard duty.

Jeff nodded, then pulled out one of the miniatures and sneered.

The small insect drone powered up with miniscule sound. Using the app on his cell, he gave the control to Keith to make certain it aligned to the correct target. Keith advanced it erratically hugged to the line of the stacked cargo toward the target. The screen protector prevented the light shining past the two of them, but Keith kept his back to the drone as a precaution.

Jeff estimated the guard was maybe fifteen feet away behind two stacked rows of pallets. Too awkward to get the guy in sight.

The man groused, "I hate this stupid task of guarding boxes. Max already took the samples this morning. Now's he's in the sun and I'm stuck in this deary hold for another thirty minutes. Why do I get the shit duty every time?"

Keith pointed directions and Jeff navigated the drone, allowing it to approach the backside close to the floor. Once at the edge, it ascended with the active camera seeking the opening Keith previously created. A panoramic shot appeared on the phone's screen showing the goon leaning on a shorter pallet with his back to the one Keith previously investigated. Keith watched the screen and pointed toward the opening in the shrink wrap.

Jeff flipped through the options, selecting the drone to transform into a crawler just at the right position for entry. He felt beads of sweat popping out on his brow as his heart raced. The small but powerful camera captured a few valuable images before power levels indicated it was time to retrieve the device. Hearing the guard cough caused his heart to race.

Keith pointed to his watch and signaled it was time to extract the drone before the end of the time mentioned by the guard.

Jeff nodded and began the exit process. He directed the drone to the opening. Invoking a key stroke, transformed the crawler to fly just as the far cargo door banged open. The momentary extra light illuminated the far end of the area.

Sounds of discussion and footfalls rapidly increased. Silently the drone launched as two new men reached the guard.

"Hey," called out the guard.

"What is it, George?" asked the man.

The gravelly voice with an eastern accent, maybe New York, registered with Jeff. He'd think about it later.

"I saw something fly past. Probably a shadow of a dust mote, but I gotta check. The captain hates insects in the cargo areas. Sometimes they get into food. Give me a second."

"I'm ready to go, Fred. You need help swatting the fly?" the guard chuckled.

Jeff, focused on maneuvering the drone, grabbed it then shrank further back into the shadows and cover. Keith pitched a plastic water bug replica close to the crewmember who promptly crushed it with a resounding pop. Jeff and Keith released their breath.

Turning back toward the other men, he said, "I found a fat insect. Dead now. Let's get going before anyone spots another one and I'm stuck cleaning them out."

Keith and Jeff grinned at each other, then did a noiseless high five. They waited a few minutes in silence, then each took a deep breath and found the cargo hold exit.

Jeff thought, *this cloak and dagger stuff sure gives me the willies.*

CHAPTER 22

Caught in the Act

The mid-morning sun just cleared the taller buildings on St. Kitt's. Thankfully the modest breeze from the ocean made for a perfect temperature to sit outside. Gracie nearly crowed when she captured two seats in the open-air coffee shop with the perfect view of the gangway exit of their ship.

"Bailey, can you please grab breakfast while I hold this spot? From here we can see everyone who exits." Gracie liked the little establishment. It was quaint, weatherworn, and the rich coffee aroma filled the area.

Bailey returned looking pleased. "I found two coffees and grabbed several scrumptious looking biscuits—freshly baked, I was informed."

"Don't you just love this coffee shop, Bailey?"

"I do. I had no idea that a treasure like this was close to the pier. I am glad I asked customer services last night for their recommendation. This was number one if we arrived early. Another suggestion was further into town."

Gracie sipped her beverage. "Hey, it's my favorite latte. I find it fascinating to watch the tourists. I wonder how many packages they'll carry back to the ship when they finish a full day's shopping."

"I hope we'll win our bet on spotting our fish from this plum position. You've seemed to gain inroads to Mr. Pliant. He brought you to his table for the dessert course."

"I agree, but I don't know why. He's got something in mind, and he's waiting for the exact right time to broach the subject. In this type of waiting game, I have patience."

Perched on the pier-side stools, Gracie and Bailey sipped their beverages, watching people of all shapes and sizes enter the square, and decide which direction to proceed to their planned activity.

"I'll grab us a refill on the lattes. We've been here nearly an hour and this place is crowded. The noon meeting arrangement I overheard was to finalize some type of contract. I'd expect to see Pliant soon if he's getting together with local leaders."

Gracie set down the fresh cups and pushed her sunglasses up on her nose. The warm, moist air felt wonderful, and she knew it added a glow to her skin. She gestured with her hand. "Here we go."

Like a well-oiled amusement ride, Gracie watched two black stretch limos pull up and two guards in suits exited. They remained close to the passenger doors. One man held his hand to his ear and she saw his lips move. Seconds later Pliant's team emerged from the port checkpoint.

"Bingo. Well-rehearsed and specifically timed." Bailey tapped her watch. "You were right, they were planning to meet someone around noon time."

Gracie's response was interrupted by the chirp of her phone with a text. It was from Jeff.

Made it to the clerk's office. Keith and I shot more pictures.
Need help. Can you two join me?

"Jeff says he needs us at the records office. It sounds like the guys also did some additional snooping. We know Pliant is meeting someone, but not who so we'd waste our time sitting here. Come on, let's head over there and walk off the sweets we indulged in while waiting."

"Why don't you go? I'll shadow Pliant and company. That way Jeff gets extra hands, but we keep eyes on our target."

Gracie blanched, feeling uneasy at the offer. She studied Bailey's expression along with the glint in her eye. "You do recall the guys getting mad that we split up?"

"That was more about you in a space Pliant controlled. Not out in public like we are here on St. Kitts." Bailey swept her hand across the expanse to emphasize her point. "You'll be with Jeff. I'll be fine mixing in with the herds of tourists. I need everything we can get on this man, so we'll divide and conquer. Besides, Pliant barely knows my name. I'm just Gracie's buddy."

Gracie thought, *what a nice juicy rationalization for us to separate*. "I don't like it, but I think you're right. We need to maintain surveillance for all the proof points before we run out of time. Please play it safe."

"I will. This isn't my first rodeo. I know how to take care of myself. Be back in time for dinner. No worries."

With Bailey's promise, Gracie warmed to the separate assignments, and they exchanged a quick hug.

Smiling, she added, "I know you can. We just worry about each other. Good habits are hard to break. Now scoot. I'll get the bill so you can do your discreet monitoring. Happy hunting."

Gracie watched Bailey adjust her sunhat to look like all the other tourists. Gracie kept her in sight until the crowd swallowed her image. Turning to the barista, she paid the bill after securing another coffee and a couple of biscuits for Jeff.

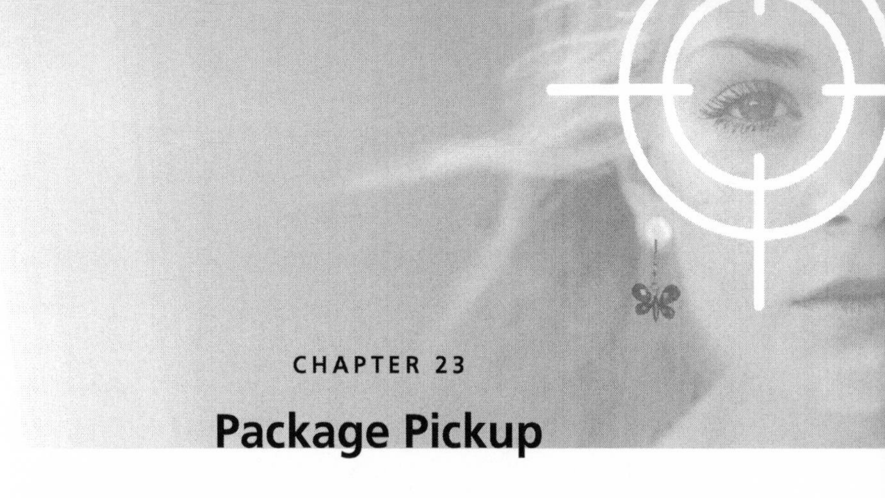

CHAPTER 23

Package Pickup

Gracie entered the quiet records office. The lazy fan rotated that included a mild random squeak. She gave Jeff a quick peck on the cheek trying to erase his frown after she handed him the coffee. "I thought you could use some coffee and a snack. It seems empty in here." She wrinkled her nose. "Though it has the musty scent of old paper. This is why I like digital document storage."

"But these old papers talk to you, where bits and bytes don't." He took a sip. "Thank you for the coffee, sweetie." Jeff smacked his lips a couple of times, shook his head and questioned, "Let me guess, Bailey didn't want to do the records thing in favor of following Pliant, right?"

Gracie nodded, looking at the records books on the table. "We talked about being separated, but she made a good point. She's a big girl and we do need to gather as much intel as possible. She promised to stay around other tourists. Honestly, I don't think she's at risk." Gracie pointed to the books. "Now show me how I can help."

Gracie and Jeff stood at the table in the rear of the records office where the mustiness of the room seemed stronger. The clerk indicated that everything concerning island properties was processed. They worked like a production line as they photographed the permits and contracts in rapid succession.

The pert clerk inclined her head with the file exchange that Jeff just acquired. "Sir, we're closing in ten minutes for lunch. I'll need all the files back before I leave."

"Yes, ma'am." He gave her a wink and hurried back to review the new materials. "Gracie, I know we don't have it all, but we've got enough at this point." Glancing at the clock, he added, "Two more minutes and we'll have just enough time to return the folders. The clerk has provided us with the right sort of files. Very helpful."

"I agree. We don't want to create an issue or gain unwanted attention. From what I've read on the fly, we've a treasure trove of materials."

They gathered the files and their personal belongings then proceeded to the counter. They set down the files, and Jeff asked, "Is there a restroom I can use?"

The clerk pointed toward the hallway. "Yes, sir, and you can exit out the rear door. Take two right turns and you'll be on the main street."

Turning to Gracie, Jeff grinned and kissed her cheek. "Thanks for your help, honey. We can split up here, babe. I'll return to the ship winding around the side streets so we aren't spotted together."

Gracie nodded and left out the front door, merging into the torrent of tourists.

Jeff exited through the employee entrance and located an outdoor café of sorts featuring local coffee. He ordered a dark roast and a pastry with spicy baked apples drizzled with chocolate. Finding a spot at a table in the shade, he took out his notebook then hunted for an available Wi-Fi connection.

Jeff's order number was called. He approached the counter and grabbed the tray. "Thanks, man. The tartlet smells spicy sweet. I am a sucker for fresh bakeshop goods any time of day."

"My wife is the best baker on the island. I can sell you a box if you want to take a few back onto the ship."

"That'd be great, thanks. Hey, is there an ATM anywhere close by?"

"Yes, sir. The only one on this side of the city is three blocks over. Let me draw you a map."

"Perfect." Jeff took a sip of the coffee and nibbled the flakey crust, which melted on his tongue. He sighed with contentment. "And, please, let me have six of these delicious pastries to go. My compliments to the chef."

Jeff sat to enjoy his snacks and people-watch. *If my hunch is correct, I might spot the currency exchange of Pliant's men. All the records I reviewed and not one cashier's check or wire transfer. Cash is nearly untraceable so an ATM from an offshore account is a possibility. Gracie said they are using limos, which should be easy to see if they are in the area.* He gathered up his to-go order, secured a refill on the coffee, and took off toward the ATM. The machine was surrounded by several local merchants using tempting taunts to snag business from the midday tourists. Jeff moved between vendors, staying in the shade, keeping a sharp eye on the ATM.

Thirty minutes later, his patience got rewarded. Jeff spotted four men exiting the limo, two holding standard briefcases. The face inside the vehicle looked like Pliant, but he couldn't testify to that. They approached the machine with the watchdogs keeping guard. Jeff grinned as he noted the cash exchanged at the ATM. Holding up a local vendor's tee-shirt as if to admire the screen print, Jeff watched as they retreated to the limo. He was stunned to see Bailey on the other side of the limo, taking selfies, and talking into her phone. A tourist bus stopped for jaywalkers temporarily blocking his view of her. The patient bus driver picked up a few stragglers begging for a ride. Finally, the street cleared, but both the limo and Bailey had vanished. A feeling of uneasiness settled on him as he stood to scan the area looking for her distinctive sunhat.

Back on board, Gracie uploaded all her photos and information to the team's secure weblink, with her notes. She spotted materials from Jeff on the drop box and alerted JJ to grab copies of everything.

Jeff knocked softly on the balcony door. Gracie grinned and let him in. Jeff looked around then asked, "Bailey's not here? I expected her to beat me back to the ship."

"There is no evidence that she came back here, even to drop off souvenirs." Gracie scrunched up her features, looking confused. "Why would you expect her back? She wanted to stay with Pliant while I came to help you. That was the only reason we weren't both there."

"I spotted her near the ATM when Pliant's guys were doing the exchange. The last time I saw her she was near his limo taking selfies."

Gracie shrugged. "Even though we are supposed to return at dark, the ship's not departing for another day. I bet she's following a hunch. Bailey's smart and has great instincts. She'll come back all bubbly and with new photos to discuss. No worries. Speaking of missing teammates, was Keith next door when you went through?"

"No. We split up too. I went record searching and he wanted to checkout a flatbed barge wearing a Pliant logo docked at the end of the pier. I did send a message to Brayson in case he wanted to grab some aerial shots of the cargo on it."

Jeff ran his fingers through his hair and stroked his chin. He opened his phone and scanned a few of the shots from earlier. "Just as I thought. I want to go look at that transporter too. I expect we'll see a hoard of workers unloading materials into trucks for hauling. Keith's probably still there. He might need a second pair of eyes." Jeff gave her a quick kiss goodbye. "Babe, let me know when Bailey returns. I'll feel better knowing she's back on board."

Gracie added a hug and additional smooch. "Thanks for worrying. We work well together, don't we? I'll see you later."

Jeff held her tight, then released her. "I forgot to mention, I brought back some amazing snacks to munch on in the morning." Putting the ends of his fingers to his lips, he made a kissing sound. "Sweet and delicious, just like you." He stared into her eyes, offering promises for later, which she acknowledged with a flirty hip-bump then fanny-pat as he opened the balcony door. Gracie sent a quick text to JJ on the current state of the team. If he had any news, he'd let her know.

CHAPTER 24
Simply Ask

Jeff sidled up to Keith who leaned against the corner of a weatherworn building about the color of vanilla bean ice cream, observing the activity on the cargo pier. "Hey, how's it going? This area is a lot quieter than the cruise ship pier, but about the same length. Not nearly the tourists traveling to and from the gangway."

Keith shrugged. "Agreed. I spotted less than a hundred or so locals in dockworker garb, not tourists. The stink of diesel floats in the air as the mild breeze shifts. Based on the storage buildings, I'm betting this is for cargo holding. There is a smaller dock used by fisherman. Size and call of the seagulls help identify that location."

He pointed past the colored buildings where Jeff caught the gulls dancing in the wind to an unheard symphony, undulating on the air current. "How many workers and trucks have received goods from the vessels?"

"None. And I've watched for the last hour or so," replied Keith. "Oddly enough, it looks like a lot of activity bringing small loads of provisions, but no unloading. Shortly after I arrived, the tugboat brought the barge from Pliant's mother ship in the harbor to unload based on how it sits in the water. No one approached it. I can't figure out what is going on. Workers drive pallet movers up and down. They're hidden part time by the boat, but even so, never reappear loaded. I considered moving closer; however, in these touristy clothes, I'd stick out like a sore thumb. Those guys have steel-toed shoes. I did venture far enough to see trucks lined up on the back streets out of sight. I can't identify the holdup to unloading. There seem to be enough local workers for the physical labor part. It might be a timing issue or local bureaucracy."

Jeff blinked a few times. "Why don't I go ask?"

Keith crossed his arms and shook his head while rolling his eyes. "Now I know why junior detectives were once called *gumshoes*. Way too direct."

Ignoring the rebuke, Jeff started toward the hive of activity at the shore end of the pier. Closing in on his destination, he noticed an aerial drone doing lazy circles around the area. Scanning, he spotted Brayson with the controller box at a rooftop table. Jeff noticed the faded lettering bar and grill on the wall. It seemed quieter than he expected with no music or chatter of guests, so likely not a tourist spot. He moseyed up the worn stairs that hugged the outer wall of the once-blue painted building and waited for Brayson to spot him. When Brayson gave a subtle nod, he sat next to him. Jeff felt relieved that the island breeze carried the trash-induced stench away from the bar rooftop.

"Hey, Jeff. You come to watch Clarence and me?"

"Uh…Clarence?" Jeff looked around for someone he had missed.

"That's Clarence up there. The quadcopter," chuckled Brayson. "The ship's captain gave me a commission to film the recycling efforts for assembly into an infomercial. The ambition is to bring more industry to the island and more tourists cruising. A win-win, my ship boss said. No one seems to have noticed it or so much as pointed to Clarence."

"How come nothing's going on? No visible frontend loaders or carrier trucks to help transport the stuff? It'll be dark soon. We'll be leaving port tomorrow with no evidence of cargo transfer, or a chance to look at the contents."

"Yes, I asked the same question," Brayson said. "I was told these crews work at night to minimize the truck traffic while tourists do their sightseeing in port. It seems someone decided moving trash from port and dodging visitors was problematic. The workers are happy as it's cooler at night." With a wink and nod, he quietly finished, "Fewer outsider witnesses to what is really going on."

"Anything else?"

"Yep. The entire operation is under contract and control of an island leader who goes by the name Julian. The workers I spoke to fear him. Even after discrete bribes, no one would offer information on his location. I'll share my shots to the drop box to help strengthen our case. I spotted Bailey's reconnaissance; she's making good inroads including the photo of Julian. It seems she's a bit over her skis and needs to slow her role as the Lone Ranger."

"I'll pass it along to Gracie. I was worried she was missing. Thanks."

"Don't forget, Keith has no idea I'm the help for you guys. Unless something goes south, he won't," assured Brayson.

Jeff nodded and left the rooftop to wander back to fill Keith in on his conversations with locals. "Maybe, we can get a look in the warehouse tomorrow…if I can locate an address."

Gracie breathed a sigh of relief as the cabin door opened and Bailey breezed in, tossing a few parcels onto the closest bed.

"Where've ya been, Bailey? They called *all aboard* a while ago. It's almost time for our Pliant show."

"Spent the day hanging out with Pliant." Bailey smugly grinned.

Stunned, Gracie's heart skipped some beats. She narrowed her eyes with concern. "What? Jeff said he last saw you taking selfies near the man's limo, but then you vanished. I told him not to worry. But I was a bit concerned. What gives?"

"Pliant called out to me while I was taking pictures, which, by the way, he was in the background of my shots along with his men. I thought he was going to tag me for taking his photo. Instead, he offered me a ride back to the ship. After some additional conversation and persuasion, I decided it was a perfect opportunity, so I accepted."

"What?" Gracie walked right up to her friend. "You promised me you'd stick to the crowded places with tourists, not go off and about in a car, in a town where he has connections. What would you do if he decided to take you somewhere and tie you up?"

Bailey's face turned red. "I know and I was scared. But before I got in, he asked me questions about me and my work for you. I told him you hired me for PR support just before Amsterdam. You said my background and relationship with you couldn't be traced so I made stuff up." Bailey stuck out her tongue as if to say *so there* before resuming her confession. "I told him I was fawning over you to get a bonus, but in reality, couldn't until the end of the trip because you are so high-maintenance and difficult. He thought about my comments for a few, then admitted he wanted to convince you to offer your endorsement on a loan from World Bank. I said I'd help get him on your good side as well as provide him additional contact information. He's going to pay me a bonus if he gets the loan."

Bailey shimmied out of her outfit. She opened the closet, selected a seafoam green cocktail dress, and grabbed the strappy sandals that matched. She snatched her cosmetic bag then sat in front of the mirror to continue her tale. "Once we shook on that, I decided to ask him for information on the ATM signage. He seemed put off until I asked if Bitcoin was a local currency. He laughed at that, then became animated in a detailed explanation. He told me about the different types of cryptocurrencies from ATMs becoming more popular everywhere and how people can scan in the QR code of their Bitcoin wallet to run a transaction. He said it was as easy as a bank card."

"Goodness." Gracie frowned with concern. "Did you ask him why his team was doing routine withdrawals, or why they're illegally dumping plastics too?"

From the way she eyed her friend through the mirror while dusting her eyelids with shadow then applying a couple of quick mascara swipes, Gracie sensed Bailey was moderately amused. "I did ask him why he needed that much cash, but I wasn't so direct. I got a laugh when I asked if he was subsidizing the on-board casino."

"Genius, my friend." Gracie tilted her head with a smile and sense of admiration. "You played dumb, asked him questions about decentralized finances built on blockchain technologies, and he blathered on. Makes sense, since that was his initial line of questioning during that first cocktail hour."

Bailey brushed her hair, added some creative fluffing to accentuate her waves, sprayed it quick, then stood. Pleased with the results, she slid into her dress and turned so Gracie could secure the fastening. "He took me to lunch. While we ate, a man with a French accent joined us to chitchat. Intros were made, and this Julian bowed slightly, lightly kissed my hand, and said, *enchantée.* Ah me, the old world manners of a nicely dressed guy. Then they both dismissively ignored me." Bailey added with a mischievous cat-swallowed-the-canary look, "With so much charm, I gushed about wanting a photo with him for my scrapbook. He obliged. While took one, I noticed one of Pliant's men made a discreet briefcase exchange with Julian's associate. I uploaded the photos and video of his offer to me in case you want to look at them."

Gracie thumbed her phone with her graceful fingers, rapidly alerting JJ and Brayson with a text. With a tone on the edge of annoyance, Gracie asked, "Are you about ready, Sherlock?"

Bailey nodded. Both girls retrieved their purses and pasted on irresistible smiles.

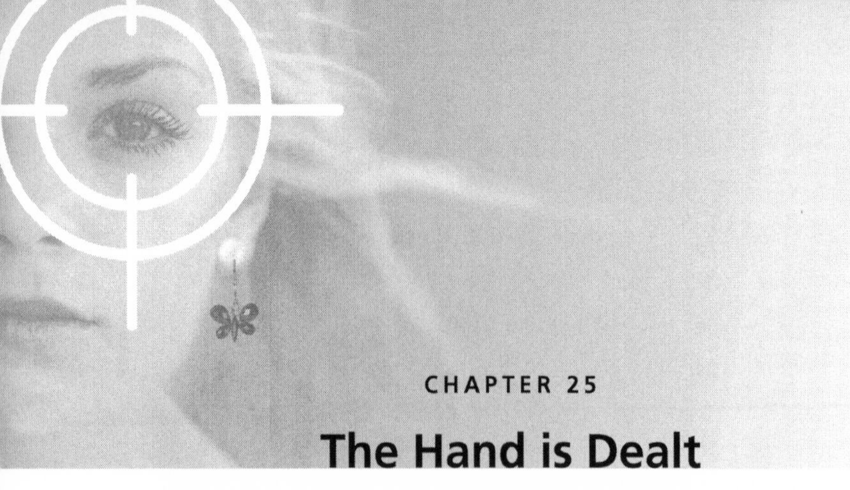

CHAPTER 25

The Hand is Dealt

Gracie strutted to the door and looked at tonight's guard with wide eyes. "I do apologize for our tardiness. I hope cocktail hour isn't over."

The guard tapped his mic, mumbled and opened the door. "You're at Mr. Pliant's table tonight. Name tags are at the place settings."

Cocktail hour was at an end and other diners hastily moved toward their seats. Two additional six tops were configured tonight. Gracie noted new faces in the crowd with three of them at Pliant's table. Gracie and Bailey had seats together at the host table. Two fresh-scrubbed female faces sat next to another new man who seemed more guard than escort. He had broad shoulders, nearly black hair, espresso-colored eyes and brown skin tone like her father.

Gracie remarked, "My name is Gracie and this is my colleague, Bailey. You are both lovely. Did you board today?"

The man's smile failed to reach his eyes as he intercepted the direct question to his young charges. "Good evening, ladies. May I introduce our two newest students, Sofia and Elena. They don't speak much English, yet. But they're quick to learn. We believe in this controlled environment they can observe and learn new social skills they will be able to use when they graduate."

Gracie picked up on his Spanish accent and took a chance. "Qué estás estudiando?" Gracie quietly translated to Bailey, "I asked what they're studying."

Pliant slid his chair too hard, banging the edge of the table leg. His eyes widened, imitating a stunned deer in the headlight's expression. Gracie watched him glance at the escort with concern. Elena bubbled, "*Estamos estudiando el comportamiento social y la interacción. Queremos aprender a ...*"

Pliant motioned for silence to the students and turned toward Gracie. "I had no idea you were fluent in Spanish, Gracie. How many languages do you speak?"

The distraction was enough. All at once the table was a flurry of activity. In an instant Sofia and Elena vanished along with the man.

Gracie noted the abruptness of the departure. While Bailey appeared speechless, Gracie asked, "Was it something we said? Or rather, that I said? I'm sorry if I alarmed them. I was only…"

"Forgive me, ladies. My brother is overindulgent with his exchange students. Tutoring young people is an inexact science with mixed consequences if the process is interrupted. You must forgive their hasty departure, but he tries to maintain a rigid, controlled study schedule."

Gracie wrinkled her nose and tilted her head as if confused. "They claimed to be studying social behavior and interaction but didn't get to finish. Are you running a boarding school in addition to your other ventures?"

Pliant ignored Gracie and turned to Bailey. "Did I answer all your earlier questions concerning Bitcoin, Bailey?"

Gracie felt the sting of his snub. She also sensed something else was wrong and flashed on her prior discussion with Jeff from the bar scene he'd related. The man that just left wasn't the man Jeff described as Jonas who propositioned them. Even so, the girls seemed out of place.

“All except one. What happens with the exchanged funds? You laughed at my naive ship casino question.”

“Ah, your lovely inquisitive mind. I have a soft spot in my heart for our Caribbean neighbors. The funds are to help them establish island industries to bring work, and eventually prosperity, to these people. My successes allow me to help underwrite new industries. In doing so, I gain new markets and the cycle continues. It’s exciting to uncover the possibilities and gratifying to help their economy.”

Gracie noticed his confidence returning with his fervent monologue. Believing the situation under his control, Pliant shifted the conversation with the comment, “Ms. Rodreguiz, I’ve done my homework on you. Based on your knowledge of international finance and your position within the field, I’d like to understand your World Banks’ lending policy to jumpstart new businesses in evolving markets like the Caribbean.”

Gracie felt the social gears shifting to cover something, but this was exactly the opportunity they wanted. Bailey might have uncovered a way to accomplish their goals with her risky stunt.

She flashed a Cheshire cat grin. “Ah, I now understand the generous dinner invitations. You want introductions to my international finance team to help fund business development. Here I thought it was my dancing eyes and persistent smiles, coupled with Bailey’s and my wit and charm that allowed us to enjoy your lavish hospitality.” She glanced at Bailey and patted her forearm. “Bailey, should we be offended?” She pouted prettily. “Or are you going to break out the negotiations tablet to outline the deal?” Gracie smiled and took a bite of her meal. “Phillip, er, Mr. Pliant, if it’s funding you seek, I’m happy to look at your business model and the associated accounting books. I’m sure it’ll just be a formality.”

Gracie struggled to remain calm as the smiling Pliant placed his icy hand on hers. He boasted, "I'm confident that all your concerns can be dispelled with this accounting review."

The after-dinner entertainment included a jazz trivia contest. Pliant insisted all the guests remain to play. Servers cleared the remnants of dining and passed out tablets and styluses to everyone.

"I promise this game is entertaining. Everyone has chances to score points," insisted Pliant. "There are questions on the history of jazz, common dance moves created during the jazz era which can be illustrated, popular singers, and more. This subject is one of my favorites."

The first question appeared on all the tablets. *What city is considered the birthplace of jazz?*

Gracie called, "New Orleans," a nanosecond ahead of Plaint, snagging the point.

The questions continued and the wins rotated between Gracie, Pliant, and Mrs. Robson to whom Bailey had spoken at length the first night. Pliant pulled Bailey from her chair and demonstrated the popular Latino-Jazz dance moves, evoking applause from everyone.

Gracie stood and delivered a perfect rendition of an Ella Fitzgerald number that brought tears to Plaint's eyes. He conceded the win with a short clap of his hands.

She admitted to herself that jazz must have influenced his childhood, especially when he played a surprisingly good saxophone jazz solo.

Gracie was delighted with her third-place. Mrs. Robson nailed second by a point. Plaint, leading by five for first, bowed to the applause. Gracie shared her prize with Bailey: an extra dessert with cognac. The bartender offered a discreet wink as she set down the amber ambrosia. Bailey added a couple of selfies highlighting their winners' status and other partygoers. To the casual observer, Bailey and Gracie wove out of the room grinning and hanging onto each other's arms, trying to maintain their balance.

"I love our bartender. Marian can create any drink non-alcoholic," Gracie commented.

"I'm glad we have a guardian angel." Pulling Gracie into a private alcove, Bailey added in a serious tone that made her flinch, "Gracie, you might-a missed it, but I caught the forlorn look on Sofia's and Elena's faces as their caretaker spirited them away. They don't appear blood related to me; however, one never knows."

"First, they were there, then they weren't. I wish we could have taken a picture. Maybe one of the critters caught them, we'll need to check the video feeds." She arched her eyebrows, facing Bailey. "What'd you, see?"

"Fear and helplessness."

"You got all that from a few seconds with no real conversation? No embellishment or…"

Bailey shook her head. "Sophia gave the universal hand sign for help where the man couldn't observe. You know the one all over social media, especially TikTok, of curled fingers, holding her thumb inside. The sign came to me coupled with fearful eyes. They were unceremoniously removed from the table as soon as they spoke. Their guardian doesn't seem like much of a parent. Something's wrong."

Gracie furrowed her brow recalling recent posts and warnings. "We've had a couple odd events. Jonas's proposition in the bar. These young women flashing you a help sign. Human trafficking all over social media.

"I recall reading a post on an airline crewmember who saw an older man escorting a young girl. When the man wasn't looking, she flashed the *help-me* hand sign and pleaded with her eyes. She was being abducted but got rescued. I cried for the child and cheered the flight attendant." Gracie ground her teeth. "Jeff didn't describe Jonas as Hispanic, which this guy clearly appeared to have somewhere in his DNA. Did Keith share any other details of Jonas's appearance?"

"Well-dressed, thin and light hair as I recall. But I could be wrong."

"Regardless, it's a great catch, Bailey. Let's add this to the drop box site along with the newest selfies. You're quite the tourist."

Bailey nodded as they got onto the elevator and headed to their deck. She moaned, "Looks like one more nasty piece of business that Pliant is involved in."

Uneasiness blanketed Gracie's mood.

CHAPTER 26

Deeper and More Dangerous

At first Keith tried to be quiet while readying himself but soon became annoyed that Bailey wasn't waking up before his departure. A little extra noise and a slight whistle had the desired effect. Finally, she burrowed under the covers, revealed her open eye visible at the top edge.

She groused, "Perky people like you this early in the morning are a real burden to the rest of us, ya know."

Keith smiled at the gentle teasing. "I told you the only scuba outing on the far side of St. Kitts starts thirty minutes after docking. This means we're off first rather than the fashionable eleven or so timeframe you favor. You and Gracie still planning to do the St. Kitts scenic tour?"

Shrugging off her sleep, she sat up and grinned. "As it turns out, we need to be moving in the same direction since we will be on tour right behind you. Of course, we won't get forced to pull on a wetsuit with flippers or fight with the barracudas like you."

"There're barracuda here?" Keith was barely able to maintain his mock alarm.

Not taking the bait, Bailey reached for the bedside phone. "I'll let Gracie know Captain Nemo is headed her way."

Keith gathered Bailey up and gave her a quick smooch and nuzzle that yielded a delighted giggle. "I'll go through the cabin door so you don't disturb them. It's early enough and hardly anyone up and out and about. This is the earliest event, and they haven't called the gangway open yet."

She looped an arm around his neck to complete a hasty hug. "See you later, Keith. Please be careful."

Keith quietly opened the cabin door and checked the hallway. Satisfied it was devoid of people, he signaled Bailey their hand sign of affection, but before closing the door he argued with himself. *You know Keith, you're squandering a romantic setting that promises amorous consequences in favor of your responsibilities to this assignment.* He sighed, and after looking both ways again, closed the door quiet as a mouse. He took comfort holding her smile in his heart.

Gracie grumbled at her poor time management that resulted in them arriving later to their shopping tour group than she wanted. The overweight tour guide glared at them for cutting it to the last minute but didn't comment. The annoyance was etched on her face. The silent chastising was emphasized by her tight lips curled into a snarl. Each girl made quiet apologies to the other members of the walking tour, ignoring the sideways looks from the guide as she delivered the rules. Gracie became immediately tired of the tour.

"Stick together as we go. I'll try to make certain you get enough time at each vendor. We can also decide a few options as a group. For example, rum sampling is a favorite along the way or you might prefer watching the pottery painters. Don't forget, buy what you can carry. You're responsible for holding onto any purchases. If you don't want to stay with the group, fine, but I won't hunt you down when it's time to go. Ship departs at six o'clock this evening. That's ship time."

The girls stayed to the back of the group as the walk began. They sized up the points of interest. After the first stop at the potter's shop, they looked to escape to find more on their own. They stayed on the edge of the group near the leader, who paused at the intersection waiting for the rest of the folks to assemble. Everyone chattered like magpies about the terrific bargains they secured. Gracie innocently asked, "What's down that road?"

The guide sniffed, curling her nose in disgust, and replied, "That takes you to the industrial district. Lots of bad smells, noise, and truck traffic. We're not going into that area, ladies and gentlemen." The guide turned and mentally counted the group. "Let's head this way for some scrumptious samples of local cuisine, including rum."

Gracie looked toward Bailey and received the inaudible *high sign* with eyebrows indicating this was their jump-off point. As the group departed, Bailey broke out her map to take notes and allow them to pretend to be lost in a self-made excursion.

After trooping down the road a while, Gracie complained, "Sheesh, these narrow streets make dodging this truck traffic challenging."

"I agree they could use some road repair crews. But I haven't seen a lot of pedestrians."

"You are right, Bailey, this is an industrial area not residential. I see a lot of trash on the sides of the roads. Maybe they need to add trash cans."

"No kidding. These potholes are making it hard for me to keep from stumbling. I wish I'd worn different shoes for our tour excursion."

"Your boots are more stylish, but my tennis shoes are gold."

"Even Jeff's research efforts seem more attractive than this staggering, stumbling walk. My feet are going to need— Hey,

Bailey, look." Gracie pointed ahead to a driveway now visible in the curve. "This looks like the destination for the trucks we've been dodging." She waved off the dust kicked up by yet another passing vehicle.

"Let's go in and ask for directions. Maybe we can see what kind of manufacturing they do."

A burly man in well-worn jeans stained with oil or grease strode up to the girls as they passed through the gate on the side of the driveway. His hat sported a logo that Gracie quickly captured. "Hey, you ladies don't belong here. This is a high-traffic manufacturing facility. You could be hurt. Especially wearing those boots." He screwed up his features, pointing at Gracie's feet.

Gracie muttered, "Trust me, I totally agree."

Bailey launched into her frantic lost tourist routine. "Sir, can you tell us where we are? I can't find this place on the map." Tears welled up in her eyes as she added, "We got separated from our tour group. Now we're terrified the ship will depart without us. Please, help us!"

Gracie mirrored the panicked features of her friend. The lost, pleading female routine had the desired effect. The burly man in charge transformed into a doting father figure, gently patting Bailey's shoulder. "It'll be alright."

"Where are we in relationship to this map?" Gracie showed him the map provided by the tour group.

The man looked it. "Calm down. I think I can help. We're a fairly new plastics recycling plant, so not yet on the existing tourist maps. Plastics are delivered to our sorters and processors. Once the plastics are chopped, they get conveyed into the furnace area. The material is transformed into bricks. Another manufacturer takes the usable materials and applies 3-D printing technology. This creates a variety of useful items that are then sold." He appeared a bit sheepish as he added after rolling his shirtsleeve, "Let me draw you a map back to your ship."

Just as a blast of beep, beep, beep sounded. The man shouted, "Look out!"

Gracie jumped as he grabbed her arm then Bailey's and yanked them to the side.

The movement took Gracie out of the way of the truck backing up, but she stumbled on the uneven ground.

"Ow! I've twisted my ankle." Tears welled in her eyes once again. She looked up toward Bailey and admitted, "We'll never make it back in time." Surveying the situation from the new vantage point, she added. "Thank you for saving us. You're right, a high traffic manufacturing facility is dangerous."

Gracie watched concern flash across the man's face as he helped her rise and stomp to the driver side of the truck. Gracie listened to the dress down of the driver in Spanish. She grinned at where the conversation was headed. After a few heated words, he motioned to them. "Hop in. Carlos will take you to the pier so you won't have to walk. Once there, ask the crew for a wheel-chair or crutches. I'm sorry for your injury, but this is a restricted area." He pointed to the *Adviso Prohibido el Paso* sign. "Good luck, ladies."

Bailey helped Gracie into the cab and climbed in after her. In Spanish, Gracie announced, "Thank you for helping us. Sorry to get you in trouble. I'm Gracie and this is Bailey. What do you do for the company?" She added softened facial features for effect. "We'd love to know more. For instance, you just entered the center to unload a bunch of plastics for reprocessing. Do you also take finished goods out?" Bailey smiled invitingly to add charm to the situation.

Gracie thrived on the one-two punch combination they were delivering to get information. The driver chatted with them the whole way back to the ship filling in several details about the recycling operation.

CHAPTER 27

Twilight Planning

Brayson rolled over wrapping his arm around the familiar form. He relaxed feeling the rhythmic rising and fall of her breathing. Without looking at the time, his internal clock suggested close to half past four in the morning. He inhaled her fresh scent and felt the tickle of her hair on his check. "Good morning, sweetheart," he whispered. "What time did you get in?"

Marian yawned and scootched her backside closer to him. "After midnight. I thought they had enough alcohol to retire earlier. I may have to change the portions for Pliant and his men. I'm beginning to feel like I'm back on assignment from my black ops days with two to five hours of sleep at the norm. After this gig, I'm looking forward to a week off."

Brayson softly chuckled. "Me too, honey." He wished they could simply go back to sleep and enjoy the gentle motion of the ship in port. "Did Gracie and Bailey duck out early or stay to the last hurrah?"

Marian stretched and shifted onto her back. She grasped his hand. "No, they left, but something odd occurred during dinner. It's been nagging me, even in my sleep. Yuck."

Awake now, he asked, "It must be pretty odd to creep into your dreams. Usually, you tell me all the saucy things you dream then we try to act them out."

"Not this one. A man joined Pliant at his table and brought a couple of girls. Pure eye-candy types who were told to watch and listen. I was instructed to give them club soda. I heard them whisper to one another in Spanish, saying they loved dressing up and eating good food."

"Do you feel they were threatened by the guy with them?"

She expelled a breath. "Nothing specific, but he was controlling and spoke sharply when they spoke up to Gracie's questions. Almost like they desired an interaction and he didn't. His tone was not kind nor gentle. They're young, impressionable and at that anxious to please age."

Brayson slid up the headboard into a sitting position, pulling the covers over her shoulder. "Pliant's guest list shifts in different ports. JJ is trying to find advanced copies of onboard roster changes. Seems odd for a ship to have changing guest lists, though. Plus, I proved at least one crewmember is in Pliant's pocket. JJ's investigating and I added the information to the drop box."

"Pliant's a piece of work. What an enormous ego. This man, however, seemed oddly familiar. Phillip introduced him to Gracie as his brother. The girls and their guardian vanished so fast. I was serving so I couldn't follow or even alert you. I don't recall anything in our files for this case suggesting Pliant had a brother, do you?"

Brayson reached over and flicked on the nightlight, bringing a glow into the cabin. He stroked his chin in thought. "Nope. I'll see if JJ can get the hallway film from that area. Maybe a bit of facial recognition will give us more information. I'll let you know."

Marian yawned again. "Darling, I would love to keep talking…and more, but I need to catch another hour of zzzz's before I do my morning stint. And, you need to go meet with your contact on your infomercial film."

Brayson let out a long sigh of regret. Leaning down, he kissed her sweetly. "Vacation soon for us. Love you."

He swiftly dressed, turned off the light, vanished through the balcony door and up the railing to the floor above.

CHAPTER 28

My Way or the Highway

The members of the scuba dive tour were all alpha personality types so there was no problem getting them assembled and over to the expert. The check-in process with the dive operator came to a halt when Keith presented his license.

Grinning like he had found a long lost relative, the tour guide returned Keith's identification and PADI license. "Impressive. I'm ex-military myself. The only people I've met with those diver credentials were Navy—"

Smiling, Keith cut him off. "The demolitions-enabled reference does that." He rolled his eyes. "I'm ex-Navy, thank you very much. However, I'm not on this excursion to blow things up. I want to see some choice underwater flora and fauna. Maybe a second stop to do some marine biology examination."

Red and black ink peeked out from under the captain's tee shirt sleeve as he adjusted his hat, sizing Keith up. "I'm not sure I quite understand, Mr. Griffin. I can take you to see anything you want. I know the waters. What're you interested in exploring?"

Trying to get his way without telling too much, Keith petitioned, "Mr. Drescher, you strike me as a man who knows all the best places to dive and which to avoid. As an ex-Marine," Keith added as he pointed toward the man's thick bicep, "it would be your recon efforts that seem the most intriguing. I'd like to see the good, bad, and forbidden."

A knife could cut the tension until Drescher spoke. "We'll need to pass some of the disappointing dive areas to reach the prime locations that I have in mind. Let me get to the ideal spots for the other guests first. On the way back, I'll have to stop to repair the engines. We'll be lined up with what I think you want. I'll make certain the repairs take long enough for you to prowl. I only have one tank for you, so on the initial dive, you stick to snorkeling."

Keith confidently replied, "Drescher, I see a great tip in your future."

The man's smile disappeared as he became quite serious. "The target I'm thinking of is routinely patrolled. Don't be gone too long or argue with anyone that shows up with a spear gun."

Amused, Keith held up his underwater camera. "I'm just here filming the biology and how it's dealing with mankind's trash disposal around islands in this region."

"Hope your camera has ample memory. You'll need it."

Jeff's morning had been textbook perfect. Light nuzzling on Gracie before she left, a perfect goat cheese omelet for his breakfast, and a short walk to the records department from the ship. The morning weather was Caribbean-perfect and the slight wind kept the temperature comfortable.

Jeff bounded up the stairs to the courthouse, as recommended by the clerk in the tax office. Certain types of building permits and contracts needing judges' signatures were stored here. The lazy fans whined making the air smell less musty. He advanced in the silent cavern to the wall sign listing names of the various offices, as well as the associated room numbers. Reading the list, he found the records clerk's office room number indicating the second floor. He walked up the stairs, hearing his footfalls echoing off the walls. He shrugged his shoulders thinking this must be a quiet court day. He rounded the corner at the top of the second floor and stepped right into two men. Too late, he recognized them as Pliant associates as they roughly manhandled him into the men's room gripping his arms making his muscles ache. He noticed the men were big, dressed in black trousers and wearing white short sleeved shirts. The man with brown hair held Jeff, maneuvering the two of them further into the lavatory. He wasn't sure what would happen but he realized it would hurt. The man with longer coal-black hair tied in the back, turned and locked the door from the inside. Jeff's fear ratcheted up and sweat beaded onto his forehead and armpits.

He squeezed Jeff's shoulder, tighter than necessary. Jeff flinched.

"You seem too interested in my boss's business," he announced. "We're a private organization. We get annoyed when we see anyone poking around looking for information or copying documents. We want to know why all the interest."

Jeff stood defiantly in silence. The interrogator slammed his fist into Jeff's stomach. He felt pain and nausea and swallowed hard. Jeff fell onto his knees trying to catch his breath gasping for air.

The man leaned over close to Jeff's ear. "Why?"

Jeff felt the man's spittle on his ear with the request echoing in his mind. He swallowed needed air along with his temper and sputtered, "Since you asked so nicely, I was hired to understand your business model so it could be used in another market. It's no secret that Pliant Industries is successful. Competitors want to emulate that success. All that takes is understanding the formula an organization uses. That's what I do."

"Then that's a grave mistake, mister."

Jeff curled into his mind trying to mentally hide from the pain caused by the men alternating strikes to his body. He wanted to escape and watch like a spectator rather than the victim. He nearly cried at the relentless blows until he was numb inside and out.

After the last rib punch, the man growled, "We think you need a new line of work, starting now. This is your only warning." The henchmen dropped him carelessly to the floor that let his head bounce off the hard tile.

Jeff groaned as the last kick landed in his abdomen. He heard the henchmen unlock the restroom door and beat a hasty exit.

Sprawled out on the floor and still trying to regain his senses, Jeff barely heard his phone chirp. Using great effort to retrieve it, he read the message:

Hang in there, I'm on the way

Jeff closed his eyes and pondered, *maybe they're right. Perhaps I do need a new line of work*. He spit out some blood. *Just wish they'd used fewer teaching aids.*

CHAPTER 29

The Show Must Go On

From an early age, Gracie focused on tasks at hand and worked in deliberate steps with action or purpose. She proved herself a skilled leader for the R-Group team and provided a solid sounding board to JJ, the lead of the CATS team for cyber-attack support to customers. The casual observer would see an alpha female in her dealings with the responsibilities she faced. For an unknown reason Gracie felt distracted and worried. Something nagged her mind. Unfocused, she put the finishing touches to her makeup, then looked at the cabin phone, trying to decide if she should call Jeff before she and Bailey left for dinner with the Pliant group.

Bailey watched her with amusement. Before she could comment, Gracie's phone chirped a text from JJ.

Gracie, call me after your dinner with Pliant. We need to talk.

Gracie couldn't withhold the concern that she knew as it showed in her eyes.

Bailey opted for a conversation shift. "Come on, let's go to dinner. After a great meal, you can sort things out. I sense something's off. However, it's nearly showtime."

Gracie glanced at her text again then at her friend as she stood. "I'm used to hearing something from Jeff. Since he left this morning, not even a text or photo. Now I get an obscure note from JJ. At least it's not flagged like an emergency." Gracie checked the lines of her cocktail dress in the mirror and smiled. "We look pretty good, don't you think?" She had trouble shaking off the uneasiness and hoped a subject change would do the trick.

"He's probably head-down at the hall of records and lost track of time. Boarding time is late today so he's fine. Fuss at him after dinner. We'll try to come back early again and surprise the guys. But we need to go for the cocktail hour and check out any new arrivals."

"You're right. Sorry for dawdling." Gracie grinned. She grabbed their evening bags and hip-bumped her friend on the way to the door.

Bailey laughed as they scampered down the hallway with Gracie doing some fancy footwork.

Gracie added, "...and the brother said, 'Your IQ tests results just got back. They were negative.'"

They howled rounding the corner to the reserved dining area. Pliant, pacing outside the door, abruptly stopping when he saw them. They stopped laughing. Gracie noticed the frown on Pliant's face outlined with genuine concern. She upped her mental awareness to high alert.

He unexpectedly reached for Gracie's hand and raised it carefully to his mouth for a brief brush of his lips. "How are you feeling, my dear?" He tucked her hand gently into the crook of his arm, and added, "Let me assist you to your seat." He took measured steps rather than strides toward their table.

Gracie, felt confused, but replied, "I'm fine. How kind of you to greet us at the door."

Pliant pulled out the chair with one hand and ushered her into her seat, scooting the chair closer. Bailey took the open seat next to Pliant. He sat close to Gracie and looked her in the eye. "I was informed you twisted your ankle. I hope you aren't planning a lawsuit."

"Lawsuit?" Shaking her head. "Mr. Pliant, I'm missing something and don't understand why you're discussing a lawsuit."

"My yard foreman contacted me to advise me of the incident while you were ashore." He cleared his throat and patted her arm. "I became concerned when the photo he attached was you. Then I got worried you would want to sue."

Gracie and Bailey exchanged bemused looks then chuckled. Gracie elaborated with mirth in her tone. "Oh dear. Twisted ankle routine number three. Ladies sometimes use this excuse when they're too tired to run back to a boat after getting hopelessly lost, missing the streets with the tour group, and ending up away from the shopping. Mobile transport is faster when someone knows the roads." She scooted back her chair and stood, demonstrating a lovely pirouette. Other guests clapped so she smiled prettily and bowed. "Because of my poor choice of footwear, I did hurt my ankle slightly in the fall but I must confess, I milked it a little more than I should have to secure a ride back to the pier. All better, I promise. I'm so sorry I worried your foreman."

Gracie could tell he bought the fairy tale. Nodding his head, he acknowledged the deception with a bit relief on his face. "Good to hear. I'll call my attorney later and let him know all is well." He patted Bailey's arm like one would an ally. "What would you ladies like to drink this evening?"

Bailey leaned a bit forward and flashed her eyes at Gracie with a look of relief. "Please. You choose, Mr. Pliant."

Gracie took note of the subtle change in Pliant's deference to Bailey as he signaled to the bartender Marian for drinks. Moments later she placed the drinks on the table, and Pliant raised his glass toward Bailey. "You two have been generous with your time at my table, but I don't feel I know everything about you. During our luncheon, Bailey, you illustrated your curiosity. I noticed you kept quiet when Gracie and I discussed finance or Third World business models. I enjoyed our discussion on cryptocurrency and want to explore more topics you might enjoy."

Pliant leaned over, possessively placed his hand on Bailey's arm, and inhaled her scent, resulting in his displaying a brief smile.

Gracie watched the hair on Bailey's arms erupt along with visible goosebumps on her bare arms. She suspected the discomfort ricocheted across Bailey's arms and shoulders, like flippers perfectly powering a pinball across the playing field.

"Why…uh," stuttered Bailey with a grin. "How sweet of you, Mr. Pliant."

"Tut-tut, Bailey, please call me Phillip. All my close friends do. I would very much like us to be friends." His fingertips danced across her skin as if playing the valves of his saxophone to a tune in his mind. "I have some information on your friend, Gracie. But I found little background info on you, my dear Bailey. Tell me some things you're passionate about to see if that is what I discovered."

Bailey stilled at the unexpected advance from her target and paled. Tension dissipated when the bartender delivered a fresh round of drinks. Bailey hastily pulled back her arm to pick up the glass with a nod of thanks. Pliant retreated into his own space at the table, but the apprehension shadowed her expression.

Bailey's smile was wide but didn't reach her eyes when she rose. "I look forward to hearing the details. Please excuse me for a moment as I need to visit the ladies' room. Won't be but a moment."

Gracie stood. "Great idea. Gentlemen, we'll be right back."

Inside the room, Bailey leaned over, peeking under the stalls. Standing, she stomped her feet. "Can you believe that jerk putting his oily, slimy hand on me!? Ick, ick, ick! I feel like running back to the cabin for a shower scrub, and then throwing up. Eww."

"He definitely has designs. But you're a beautiful woman." Chuckling, Gracie added, "Don't think this is what you meant by handling him yourself. We want to maintain distance but remain engaged. Tightrope walking is our specialty. Just make small talk about shopping and things we want to see so he doesn't think we're blowing him off."

Bailey steeled her eyes at her friend then raised her chin. "I don't like how his attitude changed. He's making me nervous. Gracie, we're in this for the end game. No more separation for ANY reason."

Gracie paused before leaving the washroom, and reminded, "Put your game face back on. Remember we're just a couple of party girls out to enjoy life. And he's thinking he paid you to be on his side."

Laughing, they hugged then exited the small haven to face the big bad wolf.

CHAPTER 30

Loss of Appetite

Back in her room, dinner was not sitting well for Gracie, it had been hours with no word from Jeff. At loose ends, she disconnected the call to Jeff trying to fight back her anxiety. Why didn't he answer? Nothing made sense at this point so she dialed her brother.

JJ swallowed hard as he answered Gracie's call. "Hi, sis. Are you in a quiet place, sitting down?"

"Yes. You said call after the dinner. We're in our room because Bailey demanded a shower to purge the touch of Pliant." She tersely added, "I tried calling Jeff, but he's not responding. I'm irked that I can't reach him. You were second on my list. What don't you want to tell me?"

JJ sighed. "Gracie, Brayson found Jeff beaten by unidentified assailants. His battered body didn't appear bad enough to leave him at a local hospital, so Brayson risked his cover to bring Jeff to the on-board infirmary. He's got a few stitches and busted ribs, which are sore as hell, I suspect."

Gracie's world rocked. She sat down hard and inhaled. "JJ, you're telling me this now? You knew before I went to dinner and said nothing?"

"Yep, because I knew you'd march up to the man who ordered him worked over and blow your cover. Likely Bailey's too. The nurse told Brayson that, because of the concussion, they wanted to keep him overnight. He suggested Jeff would get released in the morning."

Fear and anxiety overlaid her anger. Tears flowed down her cheeks. "I can't go see him, right? This is all my fault. Dammit! Poor Jeff. He joined me to help out, now it's cost him."

"Gracie, get ahold of yourself. This isn't the time to crumble. If we give up now, Pliant gets away with his illegal dumping and beating up Jeff. Usually, you're all about justice. But understand, we are down one team member because he got caught sleuthing on Pliant. We can't afford any more mistakes."

"I know you're right. Argh. I need to see him. He means more to me than this job."

JJ scratched his head in annoyance and replied, "Yeah, we thought you'd say that. Use the twisted ankle routine to get into the infirmary as your excuse. You can tell Pliant you wanted a clean bill of health on the ankle to reassure him there would be no lawsuit. I do advise, though, no overt visiting when you get inside."

Gracie's voice held her normal lightheartedness. "Thank you both for helping him." After a few more sniffles, she cleared her throat and straightened her shoulders as if adding a mantle of armor. "We're going to get that crook. I swear it!"

JJ commented, "Looks like Keith uploaded some excellent evidence from today's scuba tour to the secure website. We're on the home stretch. Please be careful. Just so you know, we aren't the only ones fuddling with the on-board video surveillance recordings."

"What do you mean?"

"I mean, we aren't the only ones prowling the video feeds looking for the comings and goings of persons of interest, my adorable sister. Look at the video we parked up on our website from this morning. Pliant's men showed him a video before he sent them into town to lean on Jeff."

Gracie pulled it and quickly accessed the footage. Groaning she said, "A hall video of Keith coming out of our cabin. We need a damage control story."

"Correct. I can create a feed with him knocking on the door and being admitted unless you three want to play summer lovers together. If it comes up, laugh it off and tell Pliant he clearly didn't watch the whole feed, just the incriminating portion. Bailey needs to be alerted to discuss it as an unwanted advancement that she dismissed with a hearty slap."

"Bailey and I need to discuss this. What a mess. I can help her with the story and talk about her drinking too much. He lost his room key or something."

"Okay, but no more mistakes. Jeff's beating means Pliant's goons are checking up on everyone and everything. I get you're both resourceful, talented, and in love, but no more risks."

"Yes, JJ. You're right."

Bailey came out of the shower area and drew up short by Gracie's torrent of tears. Bailey fretted, "Your female sixth sense was right, wasn't it?"

Gracie could only nod as the waterworks flowed.

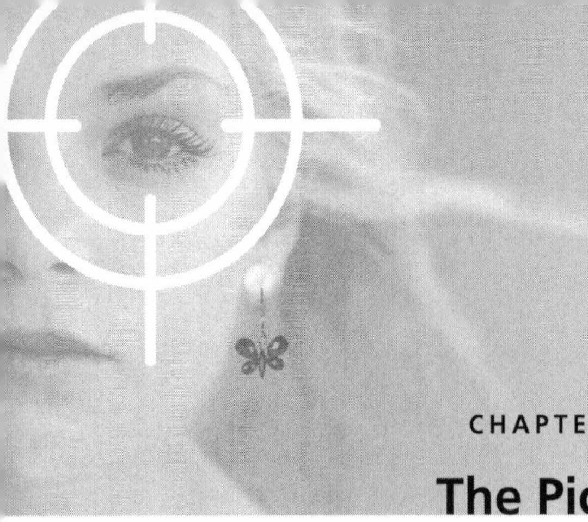

CHAPTER 31

The Pickup

Gracie struggled with fear for Jeff's condition before she realized she needed to get it together. She freshened her makeup and changed from her dinner clothes to something more casual. She outlined with Bailey how they should approach the clinic. Minutes later they set out toward their destination.

With Bailey as her lookout and support, Gracie hobbled into the infirmary. "Good evening. I've wrenched my ankle wearing the wrong shoes." Hanging her head in shame and flashing a rueful expression, she added, "I'm hoping you have an ace bandage to keep the swelling to a minimum. Do you have a brace or something I might use to support it enough to walk around the ship?"

The nurse smiled and then lowered her eyes with a hint of sympathy. "Why don't you have a seat and remove those boots. I want to check it and see if we need x-rays or to bring in the doc."

Gracie noted the disdain in the nurse's voice for the boots and muttered, "I guess no one likes my choice of shoes."

Murmuring and glancing around, Bailey helped Gracie remove her footwear.

Gracie grinned toward the nurse. "Am I your only patient? If that's the case, I am glad for you that with the size of this ship, you aren't inundated with other foolish tourists sabotaged by their stylish footwear."

"We have limited space. We try to get guests back to their rooms after we're done. We do have one sad fellow we're keeping an eye on here until morning." Gracie noted the direction the nurse's eyes noticeably flickered.

The nurse probed her ankle. "You don't even need to see the doctor. I think it's sore, not broken. Let me wrap it for you. I recommend a couple of pain relievers before you turn in."

Once Gracie got wrapped, Bailey bent to assist with adding the boots. A sudden noise echoed down the hallway. "Sounds like you have more customers arriving. Bailey can help me finish this up, then we'll get out of your hair. Can I use the bathroom before I start the hike back to my room?"

The nurse nodded and pointed the way to the lavatory around the hallway to the right of the room.

Gracie stood and added with an angelic sincere expression. "You've been so kind. Thanks."

The nurse nodded with a grin, then turned toward a frantic mother leading two wailing children who sounded like a band of wild Indians. Bailey remained seated to respond if the nurse commented on the extra time her friend was gone.

Gracie vanished toward the target then slipped into the interior room. She stopped short of the covered figure who rolled his head to see who approached. Gracie's heart caught in her throat; clearly the cat got her tongue. Jeff's body reflected the intense pain, but she was happy his face wasn't injured. The bandage highlighted his head injury and his wrapped torso both swollen and bruising around the edges not covered.

Jeff smirked. "Hey there. Some folks have said one must have an accident before a pretty girl will notice them." After a second, he added, "Is this pickup line working? Will I get that dinner date I've been pestering you for? I promise you an evening of dancing as well, and a quiet drink at…"

Gracie sobbed, reaching for his hand. She raised it to her lips and gently brushed it. "Jeff, please don't make fun! I'm so sorry you're hurt. You poor thing. I recall using that same line when we first met. But the difference is, I didn't get knocked down and worked over trying to help out your friend."

"Gracie, I need you to go back to your room. I'm fine. Please let me deal with this without disrupting the case. We're close to ending this. Don't blow your cover like mine is. If they catch you here it screws up lots of work, likely to the point of no repair. I remember what happened to other folks who tried to get this jerk. I'll be back in my cabin in the morning. Keith is coming to fetch me after breakfast." Squeezing her hand, he added, "Remind me to put Brayson on my Christmas list for getting me back to the boat."

Through ragged breaths and sniffles, Gracie delivered a little kiss to his forehead before moving to leave. The nurse looked up as she closed his door.

Gracie smiled and sat to finish putting on her boots. Signaling to Bailey they should leave, she told the nurse, "When I left the bathroom, your patient was mumbling for water. Since you were busy, I helped him to a sip from the glass by his bed. He took a small drink and then closed his eyes. I hope that was okay."

The nurse smiled gratefully and returned to tending the children. The instructions she shared with the mom sounded well-rehearsed.

Gracie tried to keep a lid on her emotions, but a few tears slipped away.

Baily slumped as she watched the video. Slowly she handed back Gracie's phone, lamenting numbly, "They worked Jeff over, and the hall cameras caught Keith coming out of our room. That's just great…amateurs-are-us. Any other mistakes I need to know about?"

"My guys believe they've scrubbed the ship's videos and the feeds to Pliant's data warehouse, to show Keith showing up just minutes before, drunk looking for some sugar and forcing his way in. You slapped him and sent him on his way."

Bailey nodded. "I can use that episode with Keith as my excuse not to have drinks alone with Pliant. I'll use the whole 'I don't really know you well enough' routine. I agree, wholeheartedly, Gracie, we need to stick together like glue. I've got a suspicion we're not finished dealing with this scumbag yet."

Gracie nodded and reassured her with a quick embrace. Gracie tried to remain busy but the imagery of Jeff on the infirmary cot plagued her and amplified her guilt.

"Girl, we are a team and we can do this," Bailey confidently concluded.

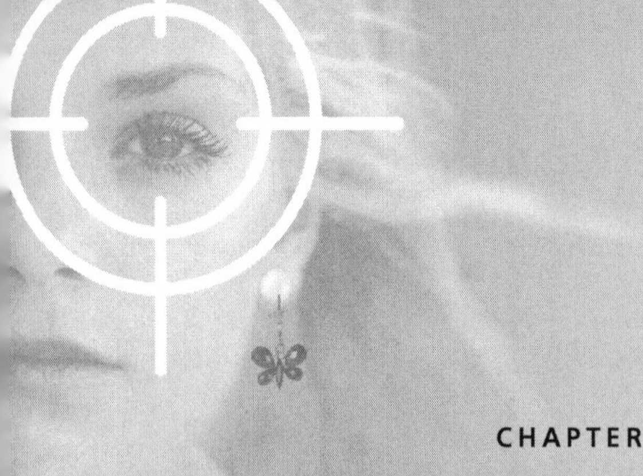

CHAPTER 32

Tightening the Noose

JJ connected the video conference and greeted, "Good morning, all. Thanks to your collective efforts, there is enough evidence to start proceedings against Pliant Industries for fraud and violation of the trash disposal contracts for two states. We are also catching the ear of the Department of Justice for violating the Environmental Protection Agency's trash disposal best practices. Keith, those last photos from your snorkeling outing finalized the proof for viable international environmental case. I'm glad you added the latitude and longitude coordinates to permit authorities to locate the chopped useless grade of plastic forced into giant bricks and secured under water with old fishing nets. Setting up plastics manufacturing for housing material as a front for single purpose weapons on any of these islands is atrocious. Maybe the authorities can get to the sources with your details. Dumping non-recyclables into the ocean allows Bailey's environmental advocacy team to launch an inquiry with teeth."

"JJ, there's more going on here than just illegal dumping," Jeff protested, holding his ribs, still uncomfortable with some movements. "I've tracked several legitimate building permits with associated loans. Bailey and Gracie tracked down a fully functioning used plastics processing plant. Keith and I uploaded pictures of the sample output of their processes, which are onboard the ship. At each port, more are removed from the pallets by Pliant's men and we suspect used to entice the various leaders at each stop. A new twist on door-to-door selling. These appear to be single-purpose weapons and we hope your experts can confirm that suspicion. I believe there's more going on than just illegal dumping."

Gracie added, "We've noted the younger dinner guests, supposed students, shepherded by Pliant's creepy brother, who boarded the ship at various ports. They vanished after we tried to talk with them, and JJ hasn't found them on the onboard video feeds. Bailey spotted the universal sign for help from one of the young girls. And the glaze in their eyes suggests possible drugs, or worse."

"Boy, talk about creepy!" Bailey shuddered. "Pliant came on to me at dinner last night." She rapidly moved her fingers and her distorted features reflected on the video feed. "Icky."

At her statement, Keith made a growl then an angry shadow passed across his face.

"Keith, don't be worried," Bailey continued. "Gracie helped defuse the situation and change the conversation. If we are finished gathering evidence, let's fold up our tent and go home."

Keith shrugged his shoulders and shook his head. "We have a few more days to add evidence. As long as we have kept our covers, I recommend we stay the course. I'd like to know more about the plastic weapons, see if we can locate the ammunition, and names of the buyers for these products. They will likely be of interest to the authorities. I'd like to see if we can reveal the entire product cycle of manufacturers, sellers, and buyers, if possible."

Jeff, unable to easily nod agreement, delivered a thumbs-up to indicate his comment to support the goal.

Bailey smiled. "Gracie, you and JJ have resources who are good at photo reconnaissance and data analysis. After this is all over, can we connect and share the contacts? I'd like to know how they work like a finely oiled machine."

"Bailey, this is your show," said Gracie. "I've got a chance to go through Pliant's accounting ledger, which may answer additional questions you can use in the case. I can't do this alone. I need Bailey with me. If we can confirm Pliant's business model that Jeff's deduced from his research, he's down. If the ledger entries back that up presumption, then he's out. The charges could keep him tied up in legal trials that hopefully end in a long jail sentence. At the very least, I believe Bailey's team will have a stronger case."

JJ looked across each facial expression on the call. "Sounds to me like you'll want to continue the project. All except Bailey."

"Hey, wait. I didn't say I wouldn't stay the course. If we can stack up more evidence against this slimeball—count me in."

JJ suppressed a gratified smile. "Just keep low profiles."

JJ called his team for an update. "Brayson, thanks for getting Jeff to the infirmary. I know Gracie is grateful as well. And nice work filming the loading of the shipping vessel containing the packaged plastic goods last night." He chuckled. "Tell Clarence he did a great job. The ship is registered in the Bahamas to a fictitious shell company out of the Bahamas. The topping on this sundae is that Pliant Industries controls the ports-of-call for it."

"Any idea where it's headed, or the buyer?"

JJ grinned. "Pliant's finished goods get shipped to Bandar Abbas in the Strait of Hormuz. Apparently, the radical insurgents there are buying single-purpose guns and rocket launchers with bitcoin. Bitcoin mining is quite the cottage industry in that region. Those governments have the ability to sidestep the sanctions the western powers leveled at them."

Walking the money trail through, Brayson mused, "According to Jeff, at a couple of the island stops, Pliant's people withdrew lots of currency from the ATMs. It's not a big stretch to believe they're using bitcoin funds in exchange for the U.S. dollar. Seems like the ideal way to buy, influence, and underwrite weapons trafficking. Pliant has created a successful, complex, business model. Nice detective work, JJ."

"I'm going to upload all these findings to the storage link and text Gracie," JJ promised. "The money laundering Pliant's doing, on top of everything else, should get him incarcerated for a couple of decades. Brayson, please keep an eye on my favorite sister and her team. We can't afford any mistakes this close to success. I'm confident he's positioned for the take-down. Sadly, that's when folks grow too confident and the rug gets yanked."

"Sir, yes, sir. Brayson and company are on the job. I agree, but this one's in the bag." Brayson cleared his throat. "JJ, Gracie is your only sister, right?"

JJ rolled his eyes and chuckled as he disconnected the call.

CHAPTER 33

Changed Plans

Pliant advertised his jovial mood by whistling a happy tune as he finished buttoning his island motif shirt in anticipation of his visitors.

Both Maxwell and Fred approached him cautiously. Maxwell held out his smart phone and said, “Boss, we’ve got something for you to take a look at.”

Pliant glanced at the grainy video and shrugged. “Don’t waste my time, Max,” he said, then added a sneer.

Maxwell straightened. “We’ve got this guy coming out of YOUR Bailey’s cabin yesterday morning, early. It so happens he is also the cabin buddy of the man you had us work over. Come to find out, their cabin assignment is the one next to that of your dinner guests.”

Pliant frowned at his men. He felt anger coursing through his veins, then turned up his chin and jerked his head in a dismissive attitude meant to remind them who was the boss.

Fred took a breath, looked at the floor, and muttered, “This morning I pulled a video segment of your two girls going into the infirmary. The one named Gracie was limping like she did for the yard manager. The room she ducked into is where the guy we worked over after he somehow got back on board. We’re still working on that one.” Fred took a breath and stood a bit taller, as if readying himself to sink or swim with the next comment.

"Something about the guy's expression when we worked him over nagged at me. I reviewed every bit of footage from this cruise. Then I got an inspiration. I found and scanned that Internet footage of your guest when she spoke at that conference in Amsterdam." Max pulled up the video snippet on his phone and pointed to the image with his beefy index finger. "There, next to her, leading an attendee away who got too pushy with Gracie. I think that's the same jerk-weed. I recalled the incident specifically, because when guests get unruly around you, it's how me and Max divert people."

Pliant turned up his lips realizing at least one of these dinner guests was hiding her agenda. The men moved two steps back. He clenched his hands into fists, then bellowed, "Crap. I'm the victim of yet another con to get inside my business. Fine." He clenched his teeth and added, "I'll fix that broad, and Bailey as well if she's two timing me with bullshit too. I'll invite them to my room and see if I can get the truth and identify where their loyalties lie."

"Yes, boss." Max indicated, not making eye contact. "What do you want us to do in advance of their arrival?"

Fuming, he paced. "Search at least one of them, maybe both, for devices." Pliant slapped the meeting table hard enough to make the papers bounce. "She wants proof of my operational numbers. I'll show her proof she'll never forget." He rubbed his hands together, mentally listing the steps he was planning. "Gentlemen, make all the needed arrangements so I might treat our guests in the special ways they so deserve." Pliant dismissed them with a wave and narrowed his eyes in resolution.

Gracie and Bailey exchanged hopeful glances at each other as they made their way to Pliant's suite. Gracie felt assured and lengthened her step with confidence. "Once we get our hands on the accounting information, we're in the home stretch, girlfriend."

Bailey nodded as Gracie knocked on the door. It opened immediately, almost as if he'd been waiting by the door for their arrival.

Gracie thought Pliant's expression resembled a shark impatiently waiting for chum to hit the water. Her stomach grew uneasy.

Waving them inside, he stated, "Gracie, the consummate finance professional, so glad you could make time for me." He extended his hand and gripped hers a bit too tight. "Bailey, you're an inquisitive surprise, and constant companion to the esteemed speaker. Welcome." He tried to shake her hand as well, but Gracie bumped her buddy aside.

"Oops. Sorry, Bailey." Gracie giggled.

Pliant extended a hand into his cabin. "Thank you both for giving me some time."

The earlier sureness eroded as they acknowledged each other with an exchange of wary glances at the odd, overtly friendly greeting.

Gracie looked around. "Mr. Pliant, this suite is lovely and spacious compared to ours. Do you get to select the décor?" She ran her hand across the figurine on the side table. "Unique."

"No, they simple have well-appointed suites for a price. Everything has a price, I have found," Pliant sneered.

Gracie saw the meeting table with a view of the ocean piled with stacks of papers and a laptop. "I presume we're meeting there. The view is a definite distraction. I think I'll keep my back to it until we finish." Gracie turned to circle the table. Suddenly two of Pliant's guards materialized from the shadows. They seized the girls' bags.

"Hey, what's up?" Gracie shouted. Ignoring her, the nearest man pushed her into a chair.

Bailey added, "I thought we were on the same side."

"Shut up and we'll see," Pliant said.

The bags on the table in front of each girl got scanned. Moments later, the camera/trackers were triumphantly pulled out for display. "Told you, boss," Max declared and shook his head. "Sorry."

Gracie trying to buy time, noticed Bailey blanch, and became furious. She realized even the ploy Bailey established was lost. She jumped to her feet.

Reaching her full height with an enraged expression, she appeared like a storm cloud about to unleash lightning. "What the hell? You asked me over to review your ledgers to confirm business viability and possibly provide recommendations for additional loans. Your goons grab my stuff like a search and seizure operation. Really? And you want my support?"

A stone-faced Pliant looked at Gracie as one looks at a fire ant before crushing it to avoid its bite. "My associates have orders to scan everything from the rooms I enter to the people I deal with. I'm naturally suspicious of electronic eavesdropping devices, thus they're very adept at identifying those sorts of technologies. I didn't want to believe it when they first told me of your deception. I suppose seeing is believing." Pliant nodded to his associates who used a scanning wand around each girl and ripped their hairclips. The offending clips and devices from their bags were unceremoniously smashed into tiny pieces. Gracie's tension grew when she realized the exits were blocked. No one outside knew what was occurring in the suite. Gracie steeled her expression in defiance and noticed Bailey follow suit.

Pliant sneered. "You're not really here to judge whether money should be lent, are you, Gracie?" He spat her name as he said it.

Before she responded, each of Pliant's men held the girls securely from behind. In a fluid motion, a rag soaked in ether got placed over their mouths and noses to minimize the struggle and neutralize a noisy response.

Before the ether removed her resistance Gracie planted a foot-stomp to the instep of her assailant. She went limp in hopes that her weight was too much for Fred to continue supporting on the damaged foot. The momentum careened them into the wall. As one, they slid down. In a fog, she heard him yelp in pain. Worried he'd retaliate and strike, she focused on staying aware. Almost thankfully she heard Pliant's orders.

"They're inventory. No damaging the merchandise." He dispassionately added, "Make certain they're out. And I don't want them bruised or abused. Secure them in the cargo hold with a sedation-drip attached. We'll off-load them at the next port. I know our friends will pay top dollar for two beautiful whores. Their fate is sealed. No one will find them."

And then Gracie was out.

CHAPTER 34

Out of Touch

JJ was busy reviewing and categorizing the files on Pliant to help build the complete package when his monitoring equipment sounded an alert. It appeared like an out-of-distance notification, which is easily adjusted. He extended the allowable range to adapt to the movement of Gracie or Bailey. Seconds later, his chest seemed like it was getting crushed when he realized his error.

At that exact moment on the ship, Brayson attempted to adjust his notifications and roared, "Dammit!" He rechecked his equipment twice before he slammed a fist on the table. "The signals are dead." He grabbed his phone, sent a text to one number, and placed a call to another. As soon as the call connected, he snarled, "JJ, we need rescue protocol started now. The signal didn't fade from the power drain—it vanished."

JJ calmly stated, "I saw it fail, Brayson. I tried to trace it back. I'm scanning the video feeds deck by deck to see if I can find them. Alert Keith and Jeff they're in danger."

"I'll caution them to let us do our work. I've enabled the secondary protocol for assistance."

"Put eyes on them and let me know. I'm afraid Gracie and Bailey's cover got blown. They could be anywhere on or off the ship if that's true."

Keith signaled the friendly bartender his order. Then he aided Jeff into the plush seating of their favorite bar watching every action to help if needed. Jeff concentrated as he gingerly got settled. Keith admitted, the man caught his breath but didn't complain. Keith sat and tapped the fingers of one hand on the table.

The dim lighting and soft, smooth jazz in the background music hadn't failed them as a quiet place to talk. Guests rarely congregated in this remote location until after all the other bars closed.

"You got slammed, man. So sorry. What did Gracie say?"

Jeff winced as he shifted. "She noticed right away I looked a little worse for wear. She got mad when I made light of the situation. She thinks I need some warranty work." He chuckled. "Let's change the subject. Did you order the painkillers?"

Keith looked toward the bartender and smirked. "Two Fireballs neat for you and a beer for me, coming right up."

A few minutes later, a petite, perky blonde bartender appeared with drinks. She leaned over to set them down. She whispered, "Hi. I'm Marian. I was asked to deliver a message. Do not return to your cabin. Brayson is securing a safer spot for you two. Gracie and Bailey are missing. We're trying to get a fix on their location. Wait here. Act nonchalant for any video cams sending feeds to Pliant's team. You are both likely targeted so please don't try being heroes. Brayson or I will deliver word as we receive it."

Keith's first emotion was disbelief. He watched worry flash across Jeff's face, certain his face reflected the same. He noted that Marian's body blocked their expressions from the camera behind. He mentally went through a list of what he could do, coming up short.

She continued, "They know about Jeff. Hence the painful lesson. Keith, they've got you on camera coming out of Bailey's cabin at oh dark thirty a few days ago with a very early time stamp. In the eyes of Pliant, your intentions are suspect. Make no mistake, you've both got targets on your backs. We'll find them and set up extraction. Please follow my directions for everyone's safety."

Keith grabbed his drink, trying to appear relaxed and toasted Jeff. "I don't like this. Who the hell are you, and what is a Brayson?"

Jeff placed a steady hand on Keith's arm. "Brayson, and now I guess, Marian, are our guardian angels. Brayson's the ship's photographer. He brought me back to the ship, how I don't know. Keith, they're our support team. Gracie brought them in to help behind the scenes. She hoped we wouldn't have a reason to meet them."

With some difficulty, Jeff pulled out some cash and handed it to Marian. "Please, keep 'em coming. This is just for you, ma'am." He quietly added, "Water them down so we can be useful if needed."

"That's riot, sir. I think my next career is bartending." She stood taller and loudly added, "Thank you guys. Just wiggle or wave when you want a refill."

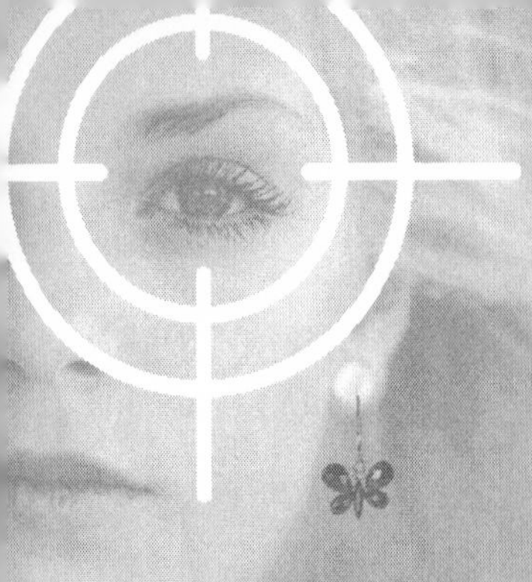

CHAPTER 35

Condemned or Retrieved

Two drinks later, Marian surreptitiously delivered a folded note while collecting the empty glasses. Jeff read it then shared it with Keith. Jeff rose, gripping the table exhibiting wobbly legs and all.

"Sorry, 'ol buddy," he slurred. "One too many drinks for me."

Keith jumped to assist. "No worries, man. I'll help you back to the cabin so you can rest."

They progressed to the elevators, swaying out of the way of fellow passengers with assorted comments of *sorry* and *excuse me*. Keith pressed buttons for three different floors. Exiting at the second stop, the two men walked the short distance to the designated suite. If the instructions held true, the re-mastered video feeds masked their journey.

Brayson opened the door, waving the men inside. He closed the door and pointed to the table and chairs. Brayson shook hands with Keith. Jeff said, "Thanks again, Brayson."

"You're welcome. Hi Keith, sorry to meet you like this. Thanks for following directions. The video feeds looked clean. We have a call in a few minutes to get an update. Hopefully we'll receive answers."

Brayson made the connection and the screen on the television came to life. "JJ, we're here."

"Gentlemen," JJ offered with a grim expression. "Guys, I've got video footage of Gracie and Bailey heading towards Pliant's suite. Plus, I had the signals of their journey from their wearables. Plaint's techs scrubbed the entrance and exit telemetry of the visual feeds. I suspect they wish to use the *not me, man* if questioned."

Jeff and Keith groaned.

"You're saying you've got nothing?" Jeff groused.

"JJ," Brayson interjected, "talk faster so these guys don't get their panties in a wad."

JJ patiently added, "The techs were smart enough to scrub the closest video feed, but not all the other cameras of that captured segment. Various cameras picked them up on their journey to the belly of the ship freight area, or dungeon, if you prefer. Even in wheelchairs and wearing big floppy hats, I'd recognize Gracie's hand jewelry anywhere. Yes, they scrubbed the video at the storage area door, but might as well have posted a flashing neon sign saying look here, they're in the cargo hold."

Jeff staggered to his feet. "Then let's go get them."

Keith nodded agreement as he stood, supporting Jeff at the elbow.

Brayson clucked his tongue. "Without a plan for extraction? Jeff, you're only at fifty-percent after being a punching bag. There are at least two of Pliant's thugs watching them, not counting the crewmembers who are on Pliant's payroll. We charge into the cargo hold area to secure the girls, we put you, and them, at greater risk."

"Brayson's right," JJ added. "Pliant's people at the next port got alerted to accept unwanted debris which I think is specifically the ladies. Pliant won't dump them overboard while at sea and risk getting anything picked up by the ship's electronic safety systems. I suspect they'll drug them and add them to the sample pallets. That way they can unload everything in broad daylight.

Both girls are lovely and potentially valuable. Pliant wouldn't do anything where he could get implicated. His onshore unit can handle the distasteful portion of the exercise after Pliant sails away."

"This, in a word, sucks," Jeff stated. "What can I do?"

Keith's expression intensified. "What can we do?"

Jeff inclined his head in agreement. "There must be something."

"Guys, we've been reviewing options." He straightened and added, "If we rush this criminal and his team, they'll panic. They could dump the girls overboard or fight us with their single-purpose weapons. We're confident there's a cache of ammunitions for demonstration purposes that none of us located. We need better odds and less risk."

"I breathed a sigh of relief to find them alive. We know their whereabouts." JJ looked eye-to-eye through the screed and insisted, "We need to work together and not become emotional."

"Guys, are we good?" Brayson asked.

Jeff and Keith nodded with a set to their jaws that reassured Brayson.

"Alright, shortly the cameras will use a looping video feed of the empty hallway, for Pliant's watchers to enjoy while we head down to our staging area close to the cargo hold. We'll rendezvous with my partner, who is finishing up our additional gear. We need to move quickly and quietly through the blackout areas of our route. Don't make eye contact if we bump into anyone along the way."

"Can I assist Jeff to the staging area?" Keith asked.

"Better let me navigate alone," Jeff stated, "in case we happen to cross paths with other passengers. It would make them wonder and remember me being helped along."

Brayson nodded. "Agreed. Remember we need sneaky not squeaky." He looked both men in the eye, and added, "To that end, I'm sorry, but no elevators. We have stairs and specific hallways to negotiate. We need to stay close but not together."

"JJ," Brayson said, "we're ready to start the video loop. Lights out in five, four, three, two, one." The suite plunged into darkness, matching the equally darkened hallway. Brayson led the way.

CHAPTER 36

Show Time

They made their way toward the destination in silence with no encounters. Exactly eight minutes later, Brayson unlocked the cabin door planned as their jump-off point. Jeff, the last to enter, closed the door and leaned back, struggling to catch his breath with his taped ribs.

Brayson patted his back. "Great job. I imagine that hurt like hell, but you kept quieter than a mouse."

After locking the door, Brayson ushered them toward a figure hunched over a table working on something.

Marian peered at the two men, then returned to her project. Her arm twisted indicating some sort of adjustment. She lifted the item and faced them. Their faces reflected surprise at the crossbow in her hands.

Jeff stared incredulously at the item, rough in fashion but looking extremely durable. "Where on earth did you learn to make such a functional device?"

Marian chuckled, "Air Force survival training school."

Keith reached out. She grinned and handed it over. He twisted and turned it to study her improvisations. "I've been through survival training, too. They never demonstrated how to build a crossbow. How'd you get that guidance let alone practice?"

She beamed with a bright smile forming on her bow-shaped lips. "I liked signing up for the extra credit lessons."

Keith shook his head unwilling to accept the flippant answer. "I, for one, would like the details."

Marian sighed, and began, "My uncle brought a crossbow back from Vietnam after his tour of duty. He'd done a lot of work with the Montagnard guerrilla fighters. They showed him how to make a crossbow out of ironwood and twine. These crossbows were frequently deployed as unmanned booby-traps. My uncle showed me how to make them when I was ten. It was my introduction to weapons, and I got hooked for life."

Brayson intercepted the trip down military memory lane. "Our plan's all about stealth. My crossbow-wielding, Air Force sniper buddy needs to get close enough to dart our targets. The last time I used this much tranquilizer, the subject stayed out eighteen hours. That's the same amount used to sedate an enraged buffalo on the African Savannah."

"From my training," Keith reflected, "you're right, but it won't take effect immediately. Someone needs to dance with them until the drug kicks in. Is that where we help?"

"Yes, and you're with me. In Jeff's battered state, he's behind us as the second line of defense. I hope you're okay, Jeff, with covering my favorite partner, Marian."

Jeff confidently nodded. "I can do that. Hand me a weapon."

Brayson rocked back and admitted, "We brought our usual semi-automatic HK-MR762A1 weapons, but the necessary 7.62 mm ammunition got confiscated during boarding. The captain has a problem with passengers carrying self-defense weapons. Those HK's have been turned into some very nice window props because there is no ammunition." Brayson intently stared at Jeff. "WE are the weapons."

A slightly dejected expression crossed his face, then Jeff nodded.

They gathered around the lettered graphical mockup of the target area on the flip chart. Brayson emphasized each step with his hands. "We'll come in through this remote entrance marked D and follow the path. Keith, we need to get them to freeze for a moment with their backs toward Marian." He pointed to Marian, and continued, "She'll be here. We need them close. There's a single feather glued to the top of the filled needle, to make it fly straight and penetrate. The preference is for her to dart them in the buttocks. She's sentimental about shooting jerks in the backside."

Marian laughed. "Yeah, but this time it won't be from seven hundred yards with a fifty caliber."

Both men eyed her with a mixture of unease and admiration. Marian beamed as she gently patted the crossbow.

"We keep their attention on fighting with us, not reaching for the dart," Brayson continued.

They exchanged looks of acknowledgement, understanding, and confidence before they high-fived.

Brayson declared, "Let's do this."

Jeff's adrenaline must have kicked in as he moved better and appeared in less pain.

Appearing like shadows dressed in black, they swallowed and took a breath at the cargo hold door. Keith sensed the beads of sweat forming on his forehead as he stood ready to pick the lock. The hallway was silent with a slight tinge of disinfectant in the air from earlier housekeeping.

Marian noticed Jeff's watch and whispered in his ear, "Can you turn your watch face to the inside of your arm under your sleeve? It's a possible spotlight giveaway in this low light space or inside."

Jeff quickly complied. "Thanks," he whispered.

Keith's mouth went dry. He hesitated a moment as he picked the lock then nodded as they stealthily pushed through the door. Single file, the four entered with no more sound than a cat's paw on carpet, moving around the large items and using them as cover. His mind focused on his military training to steady himself, prepared for anything. He briefly realized fighting on foreign ground was different being in position to help rescue Bailey.

Marian signaled she was in position. Brayson and Keith moved out in opposite directions to encircle the pallet. True to form, Pliant's men stood guard, but were obviously not expecting company. One of them had started to nod off while leaning against another pallet.

Keith positioned himself behind the men and simultaneously hit them hard on their backs. The force of the blows drove them towards Marian. Brayson hit hard from the side, and for a moment it looked like they'd won. Maxwell rolled and bounced to his feet away from Marian. The first dart landed home. Marian stepped into the hooked loop at the front of the crossbow and pulled the makeshift string with all her strength into the locked position. She lifted the weapon to load another tranquilizer.

Fred, dazed, didn't recover his balance. Keith leaped onto the man, driving him backward with punches designed to motivate him to retreat. Fred cursed under his breath and favored one foot.

Brayson spotted Maxwell reaching for the dart on his back. Max, facing away from Brayson, never saw the spin kick that landed on the end of the projectile to finish delivering its payload.

Keith turned to see that Fred had gained his footing, finally aware of the attack. The man pulled out his weapon ready to shoot Keith but suddenly grabbed at his neck. Marian had darted him in the throat, and he went down with a thud.

The team approached the shrink-wrapped container. Brayson produced a razor boxcutter and enlarged the plastic opening.

Inside, Keith spotted Gracie and Bailey strapped to a pallet. He scrambled to one side to check vitals. He was tempted to rip out the drips, but resisted. "Jeff, turn your watch face so I can count heartbeats in a minute." He concentrated and tallied for Bailey, repeating for Gracie. "Their breathing is shallow, but they have strong pulses. I'm going to take out the drips, then we can figure out how to move them safely."

Jeff held his watch still.

"Here are some large Band-Aids," added Marian, handing the wrappers to Jeff.

"Tear off the wrappers, Jeff, and hand them to me one at a time. Then we can release their bindings. They will remain out for a while, so we need to brace them."

Keith scooped up Bailey and stepped to the side, holding her close, waiting for instructions. Jeff tried to lift Gracie but realized he didn't have the strength. Brayson stepped in to take her from him.

Brayson handed over his phone so Marian could send a text.

Have the goods. Need video cloaking to exit.

Seconds later a text reply arrived.

Six two and even, over and out.
Video blackouts to cover your way are in motion.
Leave the location sensor on until in the safe room.

Keith was still on his adrenaline high, stopping where Marian indicated before she vanished. He turned to see Jeff follow Brayson, who handed him Gracie. "Wait," Brayson whispered, then he disappeared.

Less than a minute later, Brayson and Marian returned with the wheelchairs they'd stored close by.

Marian said, "Jeff, place Gracie into this chair so I can get her secured for the trip out of this place."

He complied and helped secure the seatbelt.

Brayson grinned. "Keith, put Bailey into the other chair, then help me restore order in here. It's a shame to waste those drip taps, don't you think? I mean, here are these poor chaps that need to rest, and by all accounts, they are first in line."

Keith chuckled and replied, "Oh, yeah. Waste not, want not, has always been my motto. Plus, it would be good manners to seal the pallet once these goons are situated. I'll try to come back later and see if we can find anything incriminating if you want."

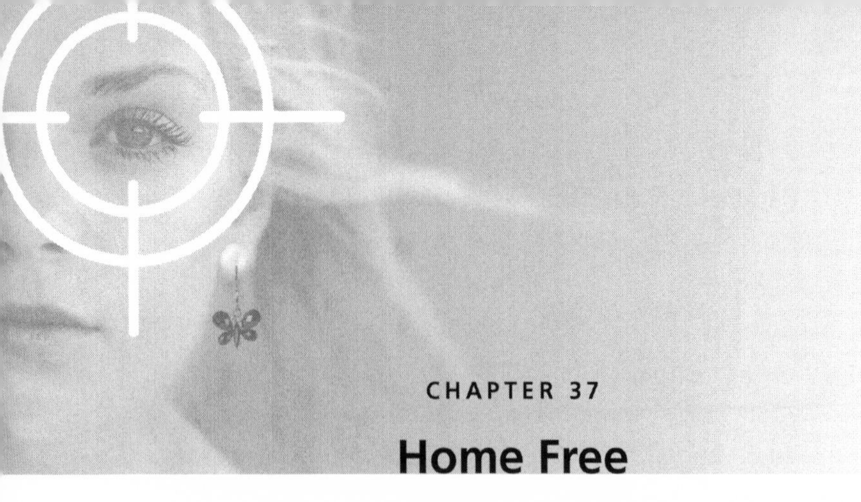

CHAPTER 37

Home Free

Jeff knew JJ would erase the hallway video feeds as soon as he and Keith navigated the wheelchairs to the safe cabin. Marian and Brayson took off to get supplies reminding them to stay inside the cabin. Jeff felt exhausted and weak after making the long, emotional trek. His heart ached each time Gracie's head flopped from side to side in her unconscious state. He worried about permanent damage, both physically and mentally.

"Keith let's move them one at a time and get these wheelchairs folded and out of the way. It's a little cramped in here."

Jeff, with the help of Keith, lifted Gracie and carefully placed her into bed. He covered her with a sheet and then assisted Keith with Bailey. Keith took their vitals and made notations in the notebook on the bedside table.

"How are they doing?"

"Their breathing is shallow. You can tell by their abnormally pale skin that their blood pressure is a bit low. Both temperatures are low, plus their skin is cool."

"Would it help to massage their legs or arms to increase circulation?"

Keith tilted his head. "That's not a bad idea and it may help the drugs move through their system a little faster."

"Okay," he indicated and started a light massage of Gracie's limbs. Keith copied the idea, and they established a thirty minute or so routine.

Jeff straightened Gracie's waves with his fingertips and traced her perfect features, then adjusted her blankets. Frustrated, he wiped his face and touched his sides, gauging the tenderness of his damaged ribs. He sighed. "We've been at this a couple of hours. Brayson or Marian could have run into trouble and we wouldn't know it. Maybe we should call the infirmary and ask for a medic to come to the cabin."

Keith moved closer and rechecked their vitals. He updated the details on the notepad. "I'm worried too, man. But they haven't done a dramatically negative turn. As long as they hold stable numbers, I think we watch them until the others return."

Jeff noticed the worry lines in Keith's forehead appeared more pronounced as he caressed Bailey's peaches and cream cheeks that today appeared more like sour milk.

"As long as you don't think we should call."

"They're okay," he replied. "No fever, so no infection. Slightly low blood pressure, though it has gone up a bit with the massaging. I recommend we stay the course. The less crewmembers we engage, the less chance of our whereabouts getting exposed."

The door slid open along with the whoosh of air and scent of the sea. Marian brought in food which was on the balcony table.

"Sorry it took me longer than planned. Glad you stayed put. We wanted to move the food on the outside rather than via room service. Remember," she admonished, "our exit strategy is to keep them out of sight until we dock. When these lovelies wake, they're going to need to get refreshed. Why don't you unpack the bags and pick out some new outfits I placed in the closet? I'll help them change, or you can." She waggled her eyebrows trying to encourage them to lighten up. "It obvious you can undress them, but how about the reverse?" Marian chuckled.

Brayson entered carrying another platter of food. "Pliant's people have access to the corridor camera feeds. It wouldn't do to see you wandering around the ship. Marian and I don't have targets on our backs so we can continue to do the recon, avoiding this hallway and door, of course. We purchased a couple of rooms on this side of the ship, which allow us access to this suite from the balcony. The moment Pliant doesn't get an expected check-in, a full-scale search will begin."

Brayson's device vibrated. He looked at the message. "It's from JJ."

Pliant contacted his folks onshore.
He requested increased security.
He discovered his men.

"Darn, I thought we'd have more time," Keith muttered. "We almost got away with it."

"They still don't know your whereabouts," stated Marian.

Jeff stood and winced, then took a breath. "I need to get into our suite to pack the evidence I found but wasn't able to upload. We'll need it to build a tight case."

"Nope." Brayson shook his head. "You hid it from prying eyes. None of us can risk trying to get there. It's on the other side of the ship where we don't have any safe rooms. Please wait until after we speak to the shore authorities. I've a few additional resources to meet us in port, too. After Pliant's in custody, you can get your swim trunks and sunglasses." He patted Jeff's shoulder.

"You said you darted them with as much juice as needed for elephants," Jeff argued. "Plus, they were on the drips and useless to Pliant for at least a day. I don't want to risk losing the proof I hadn't uploaded, plus Keith's film cases are vulnerable. Even if the room got ransacked, they might not have found everything we hid." Jeff looked at Gracie, sensing the tears filling his eyes. "I can't bear to watch them not moving. The vitals are good. Marian's here and ready to clean them up. You get JJ to cloak the cameras in these twilight hours. We go, pack, and return with everything. Keith, you up for this?"

Keith nodded with a resolute expression. "I need to extract Bailey's stuff from the safe. This bastard can't get away with any of it, especially after hurting our girls."

Brayson frowned. He did not care for this option in the least. Then his shoulders slumped. Jeff watched his fingers fly over the phone screen, sending a text. Seconds later, a response returned.

Brayson stared hard at both men. "I think it's a mistake. But you'll be clear in five. You have a twenty-minute window where JJ can mess with the cameras. That's it." He faced Jeff. "I hope your ribs can tolerate the climb up one level to the hallway. Return the same way. Keith, you stay behind him going up and in front coming back." He handed them a room card. "This key will get you in and out of the cabin above. You have your key, right?"

Jeff nodded.

"You're all set," Brayson indicated. "But it won't keep you out of trouble if they are waiting for you."

Jeff paused to listen at the door of the girl's suite. "We'll grab a bag, some personal things, and the documents from the safe and under the bed," he whispered. "Then we'll backtrack to our cabin."

Jeff swiped the key and they entered the dark room, quietly closing the door.

Inside the cavity of the suite, a lamp illuminated and a familiar voice boomed, "I knew you'd hit this room. I'll get a bonus from the boss for getting you two this easy. You're fools. We already cleared all your junk."

Keith shook his head in disbelief and spat, "Jonas the pimp. I thought you left at the last port. What are you offering now?"

Jonas smirked and pointed his weapon. "I have a plastic one if needed, but I like the reliability of my Walther. She holds six 380-caliber bullets. I don't miss, and it gets messy fast. I have four expendable heartbeats. I recommend you cooperate. You might get a chance after a little fun with my girls. They're going to show you their talents while I film." In Spanish, he stated, "*Es hora de que las chicas les demuestren lo que pueden hacer.*"

Sophia nodded with no expression, and turned on another light, exposing her and Elena's nakedness. Elena moved toward Jeff while Sophia approached Keith, each with tears in their eyes. They tore away the men's clothes with flashes from a camera capturing poses. Jeff felt like a prop in a choreographed play with no emotion from any of the actors. The compromising shots were meant to degrade the targets.

Elena whispered in broken English, "If we do this, families no punished."

No sooner had the short film started than Jonas laughed at the images and turned loose the goons. Since Max and Fred were out for the count, two other gangsters pummeled the victims, with fists hitting like pistons from a racecar engine.

Jeff maintained awareness more like an out-of-body experience. He saw Jonas' evil grin of victory while accepting the beating. Keith resisted both until one of the men grabbed him from behind and allowed the other to place a perfect kick to his solar plexus. Jeff winced on his behalf as Keith crumbled to the floor—lights out.

Through a slit of his eyes, Jeff watched Jonas slash each girls' face with a razor for effect, fortunately with not a lot of blood. He motioned for the girls to continue their date rape film for future blackmail insurance.

Jonas maniacally laughed as the scene unfolded. He stated in Spanish, "Add bites and scratches on their hands to prove you fought. Hit them with your fists and kick them for your freedom… More helpless looks toward the camera, chicas. Elena, take his hand and place it on your breast but pretend to resist. Look terrified and beg with your eyes in this direction. Juries can't resist inaudible pleas. When they find the drugs in your system, the verdict will be swift. Your families will be safe—for now."

"You two get out of here and make everything ready for transport," demanded Jonas. "Once we dock, the disposal unit will deal with these amateurs."

Jeff succumbed to the darkness and sleep his body demanded.

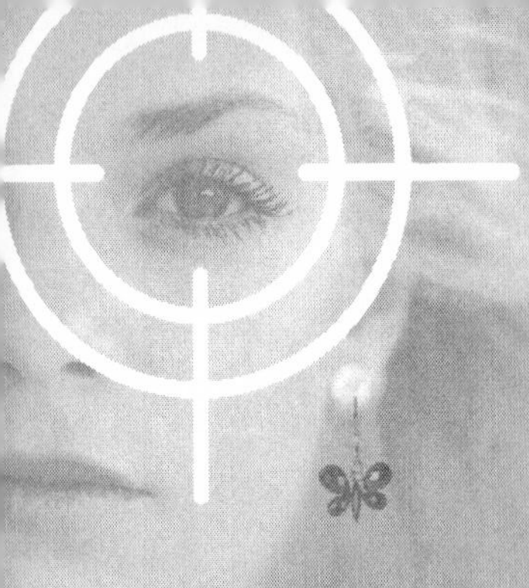

CHAPTER 38

Everybody Goes Home

Brayson shuttled between the two rooms. Marian finished the sponge bath and redressed the still-unconscious girls in clothes she had in her suite upstairs. Brayson felt his forehead tighten as time ticked by.

Marian frowned. "They should be back by now."

"No, they shouldn't have left," Brayson barked.

He launched a call and enabled the speaker as it was answered by JJ. "Rescues-R-Us. Got a couple of missing boneheads? JJ, here, how can I direct your call?"

"I've got eyes on both rooms from the feeds. No sign of anyone since they entered the suite going on thirty minutes ago," replied JJ. "Hey, wait. Pliant's at the door to Gracie's suite. He got let in by a woman wearing next to nothing. But wait, did I see that correctly? She has cuts on her cheeks."

"What, more players? Where'd they come from? The boys must have walked into a trap. I'd bet they're captives. What do you want us to do?"

JJ groaned, then snarled, "Gracie and Bailey should be okay for a while. In the off chance they wake, leave a note in lipstick on the bathroom mirror, to stay put. Here's what I want you and Marian to do: Remember that improvisation routine number we worked out? Find the ingredients. Mix and load the stuff into a spray bottle. Then I need you to..."

Marian rapped loudly on the door of Gracie and Bailey's suite. "Housekeeping." When no one answered, she used the master housekeeping key and let herself in, pushing her cart. She made a low whistle at the shambled state of the room. Seconds later, thumping, scuffling, and cries of pain resonated from the walls of the adjacent suite.

She chuckled suspecting the reason for the noises. "Nothing like vinegar and bleach squirted in the eyes to slow an ass down." She slipped through the balcony and forced the door open. "Housekeeping."

She heard loud thumps as she stepped into Jeff and Keith's suite through the balcony door. Her eyes immediately stung as her nostrils reeled from pungent odors of bleach, vinegar, blood, sweat, and excrement. Even a seasoned veteran like Marian had to suppress her gag reflexes.

Brayson stood over the sight-challenged Pliant and Jonas, both laid out on the floor. Two young girls sported terrified looks as they grabbed sheets for covers. Keith was moving but incoherent. Jeff was out cold.

Brayson gave each a pick-me-up-cocktail-shot that had them cognizant in minutes.

Marian cable-tied the slimeballs. She turned to the young girls. "Are you okay?"

They nodded with tears running down their faces, mumbling obscenities in Spanish while looking at Jonas and Pliant. Marian handed them warm washcloths for their faces.

Marian calmly added in Spanish, "Take it easy, girls. When you catch your breath, I'd like to know what happened to your faces, and if you can give me any details on the events for the last hour."

The girls nodded and asked to use the bathroom to clean up.

Jeff roused and blinked a few times, then scooted to a sitting position. "Be careful of those two. They look innocent but fought like wildcats while we were held at gunpoint. Jonas delivered orders in Spanish. I think the girls were threatened or even drugged."

Keith nodded agreement shaking his head as if to clear it. "I don't see the Pliant henchman," he groaned. "I bet he sent them to coordinate with their shore contacts. There are two loose bastards that pounded and kicked the hell out of us. I want a piece of them…once I can stand."

Brayson called JJ and turned on the speaker. "JJ, we got 'em. Two Spanish-speaking girls, possibly drugged, are here as well. They look like the ones we saw onboard in the dining room with Pliant's brother, though definitely injured."

"Yep," Marian added, "both the girls were in the dining area a couple of nights ago and appeared slightly glassy-eyed but walked on their own."

"We got Pliant and Jonas tied up for the authorities," Brayson said. "Um, their vision is messed up until they get a saline rinse. Keith said he thinks two of Pliant's flunkies might be running for contacts when the ship docks in the morning. Jeff and Keith need some recovery time but are ready for transport."

"The port authority's aware," JJ confirmed. "I alerted the ship's security team to help facilitate. I'm trying to identify Pliant's brother. The onboard pictures didn't capture his face. Get our guys and those two unfortunate girls back to our safe room. Oh, make sure you bring all the contents, especially electronics. If there's a weapon, throw it over the side so no one gets hurt. When you text me the all clear, I'll alert the feds to grab any of Pliant's men when you dock. Nice work."

Brayson disconnected and grinned at Marian.

"I'll help the girls get changed when they finish cleaning up," she clarified. "Brayson, can you run next door and grab any clothes left behind, please?"

When he returned, she called through the door in Spanish, "Girls hurry up, we need to go. You'll find some clothes outside the door, please get dressed." She smiled at Brayson. "Thanks, honey." She kissed him on the cheek. "Move Jeff and Keith and I'll bring Elena and Sophia. I've got some salve to help their faces."

The weary group cautiously retraced their steps to the safe cabin. Once there, Marian noticed Gracie and Bailey stirring. Marian and Brayson maintained a watch on the group of six until the ship docked.

CHAPTER 39

All Ashore

Maxwell raced down the hallway in the bowels of the ship, nervous that the clock was ticking since the boat docked. He paused and looked back at Fred. Maxwell sneered with disgust at Fred who limped along at a snail's pace. They needed to work together, but he resented returning to the scene of his failure. He was grateful to the second shift guards who found them and brought them to Pliant for recovery and instructions, only no one was there when he regained his senses.

Maxwell groused, "Can't you move any faster? We have maybe an hour before the captain can clear the authorities and extend the gangways. Everything's going to hell in a hand-basket if we don't get rid of those weapon samples and the ammo. Even without instructions from Pliant, I've been with him long enough to know the steps to sanitize the operation. You have too. I'm not risking slammer time for evidence we can extract."

"That broad didn't stomp down on your instep, Max. Lighten up or I'll show you how it feels. I should-a sampled her goods before we put in the drip taps. The shore disposal unit wouldn't have known that I had broken the seal and sliced a piece off the loaf. They still could-a gotten good money for her, even used."

Maxwell studied Fred thoroughly annoyed. With a snort, he demanded, "Let's swing by and get our crewmember stooge with the keys so we can empty out the shit before the port authority guys board. Unless, of course, you want to reminisce more about your missed romantic opportunity."

Fred gritted his teeth as the pain intensified. Leaning against the wall, he produced a small vial of white powder and power-snorted more cocaine. Now boosted, he picked up the pace to get to their crew stooge, who turned as white as year-old paste as they neared. He looked around to see if anyone was about, then faced the men.

Maxwell growled, "We need access to the cargo area to move…some product out for our next customer. Let's go."

The man lowered his head and murmured, "What're you doing here? The port authority boarded even before we docked. Your boss is being interrogated along with his lieutenant. An alert was sent to the entire staff to cooperate with the authorities…"

In one swift movement, Fred pulled his military grade carbon steel blade and placed it point first, on the crewman's stomach. He deftly sliced off a button with a slight twist. "Don't you dare move."

"Fred's having a bad day," Max smugly offered. "Do as we ask or yours could end on a lousy note. Keep your hand away from the silent alarm if you like your fingers."

The man moved his shaking hands into the air.

Maxwell hissed, "Hands down. Stop trying to signal the video pointed at your back. Now laugh like the joke was funny or he'll gut you, boy. We need to get in the space, now."

The crewman's expression appeared resigned. He grabbed the keys tersely griped, "Come on."

Following the standard route, they arrived at the locked door undetected. He opened it and gestured for them to enter. Fred grabbed his arm and shoved him inside. "You're leading us out when we finish." Fred added a nick from the knife to the side of face that appeared like a shaving miss. The man flinched but said nothing.

Maxwell shook his head and offered, "I warned you; he's having a bad day. Now you know, he's willing to share."

As they got to the pallet Maxwell recounted the instructions: "You help us open up the pallet and bag the items we indicate. Then we exit by the crew entrance. After—"

Three U.S. Marshals stepped out of the shadows with their weapons drawn. The lead ordered, "Nice work, Deck Cadet, we'll take it from here. Uh…you with the knife, my 9-millimeter will drop you before you blink. Put it down unless you want a body bag."

Fred swore but complied. Dave took the opportunity to stomp on his injured foot. Fred collapsed to the floor in agony.

"That's for slicing me, you bastard," Dave stated.

Brayson launched a FaceTime to JJ. "It's a wrap. The feds arrived aboard early as you suggested. The bad guys are in custody. They snagged the missing two in the cargo hold trying to destroy evidence. Everyone is awake, though bruised and shaky."

"Too bad about Pliant's brother slipping away," JJ lamented. "I did identify the man, because he's the same one who evaded me in Magnolia Bluff when I was on vacation. His name is Mateo. He's Pliant's half-brother, and he specializes in human slave trading. Another loose end to follow up on."

"JJ, Marian must have gotten the connection from reading old files. She mentioned she thought she forgot something. She reads and remembers every report, from every CATS case. Who would have thought these two guys were connected."

Changing the subject, JJ said, "How's my sister?"

Brayson chuckled. "She's practically on fire trying to orchestrate the final closure on this mess. One minute she barks orders, the next she gently caresses Jeff. Then she works her magic on the two girls. She got them to tell her everything from trafficking plans, people involved, and points for the distribution. Marian's taking notes while Gracie runs the emotional rollercoaster from A-Z."

"This is my surprised look," JJ commented with scrunched features. "She's always successfully multitasking, especially after a great night's sleep. I'm glad everyone is alive. Any last details I need to address?"

"I think we're good, sir. The core team is recovering so there isn't anything else we can do here. Marian and I are heading out as soon as the protective custody rep takes Elena and Sophia."

"Well done to you and Marian," JJ added. "I'm looking forward to your debriefing over a cold one."

Brayson chuckled and disconnected.

CHAPTER 40

Time to Go

Brayson found it difficult to keep up with their charges as they bounced around on the gangplank. “Honey, can you try to keep close to the girls while I snag the luggage, please?”

“These two are a handful, so yep.” In Spanish, she added, “Chicas, we need to grab our luggage. Please stay here.”

Brayson suspected the crowd of happy people felt like freedom to the teens. He appreciated their enthusiasm as they pointed to the luggage masters who distributed bags to the torrent of passengers like a choreographed Broadway hit. Taxis and tour busses filled up in rapid succession then pulled away, adding to the vibrating din.

He successfully grabbed their luggage and shepherded the group to the side of the pandemonium to hear himself think.

The young girls alternated from Spanish between each other and broken English to converse with Marian. They frequently giggled as they spoke between the languages, often making mistakes trying to get information. Marian delighted in the activity and the girls’ excitement.

Brayson felt like a caged animal. “Honey, we’re getting close. Are things clear for the girls?”

She grinned and nodded. “I think so.” Then she tapped the side of her head with realization. “Girls, I almost forgot!” Marian pulled two pairs of snappy designer flip-flops from her tote. I got a pair for each you from the ship store as a memento.”

Brayson enjoyed the look of satisfaction and the sweet murmurs of *gracias* from the stunned young ladies.

"Since you're going to be in this country," Marian added, "you need to dress like you were born here. I'm sure the loaner clothes will soon be replaced with styles and sizes more age-appropriate. But these designer flip-flops, flower tops and all, go with anything. My gift to you. I hope you enjoy them for a long time."

They grabbed the sandals then swarmed Marian with hugs, tears, and thank you murmurs that Brayson understood. He savored the scene, committing it to memory.

A voice called, "Mr. Morris. Brayson Morris?"

Brayson looked up and squinted his eyes, sifting through memories for a match to the face of the man. "Yes? I'm here." He lifted his hand, then pushed Marian a bit behind him. In turn, he heard her move the girls behind her body. He didn't recognize the man who shouted or the other walking alongside. A slight sensation of apprehension filtered through his mind, but they were meeting officials. They both dressed the part of official types with light suits and groomed hair.

The two men approached at an even pace with friendly expressions. One flashed a badge that caught the early morning sun and reflected into Brayson's eyes. Rolling his eyes, the man said, "Finally we found you."

Marian casually surveyed the men, and advised them in Spanish, "Girls, put on your new shoes and you'll be set for your next adventure."

Both stopped next to Brayson in casual, friendly stances. "Whew, I've never been asked, but if someone wants me to tell them what organized chaos looks like, I got a mental picture after this. I'm Tony Goodwin, CPS, and this is Mitch Crawford. We can take these girls from here to the processing center downtown. You must have some pull, Brayson, to get them to the top of the processing list. We have a temporary family for them both signed up from Boca. They're on their way to the center to sign the papers. These two will be in a loving home in no time."

Looking at Marian and Brayson as he offered a hand to each in appreciation. Then he sincerely stated, "Thank you for getting them this far." He then asked in Spanish, "Are you girls ready?"

Smiling, they nodded with pleased expressions. Each gave strong embraces to Marian and Brayson.

Brayson watched the agents weave through the throng, each guiding a girl to the waiting requisite sedan. Tony got in the driver's side and merged out into the traffic that swallowed them within moments.

Marian was gazing toward the departed vehicle when his phone rang. Brayson answered, "Hello."

"Brayson, where are you guys? This is Rachel with the child protective services team here to accept Elena and Sophia. Give me an idea of your location so we can connect."

He felt like he'd been shot in the pit of his stomach and gripped Marian closer. "What are you talking about? Why are you calling me—did you forget something?"

Rachel objected, "We don't know what you or the girls look like. I got a cell number and was told to call and arrange a meeting spot."

Brayson slowly closed his eyes, feeling ill. "Two men were just here. One said his name was Tony Goodwin and the other was Mitch Crawford. They said they were with the CPS. I can give you descriptions and—"

Rachel roared loud enough that Marian overheard. "CPS doesn't send men to collect young girls! We always send women so there is no chance of— Can you describe the car? Tell me you got a license plate number at least."

Feeling out of control, Brayson shouted, “We got nothing! They walked up, called us by name, flashed a badge, spoke Spanish to the girls, then they all loaded up in a black four-door sedan with heavily tinted windows. In this human zoo and endless identical vehicles, you have as much chance of spotting them as you do a runaway ameba. Dammit!”

Marian patted his arm and calmly launched an app on her mobile phone. Nodding when the app delivered the request, she turned the screen so Brayson could see the display.

Brayson studied it momentarily then snapped his eyes to Marian, making a mental note to lavish attention on her at the earliest opportunity.

She batted her eyes, feigning innocence. “I placed trackers on the flip-flops as a precaution. Give the CPS people the location and the dual codes so they can triangulate and intercept.”

Brayson looked at her feeling relief and adoration for his brilliant wife. Taking a deep inhale, he conveyed, “I’ve something better than a license plate number. My partner had the foresight to put tracking chips on the girls. Tune to the frequency I’m about to give you and enter these codes. Ready?”

Rachel demanded, “Your partner’s a genius. Give me the codes, please.”

Brayson dialed JJ and flipped to video when he answered. “JJ, I screwed up. I got played. Two phonies conned me into letting them take Sophia and Elena. Marian had the foresight to plant tracking devices on them so at least we have a chance of locating them. Our phones aren’t powerful enough to track the signal, but Rachel with CPS has the codes.”

"I got the text," JJ replied. "I'm on it. I know you'd rather stay and engineer a rescue, but I want you and Marian to head home. I'll feed the reconnaissance information to CPS. At this point it's their fight, not ours."

Brayson, nearly overwhelmed with guilt, sputtered, "No wait, it's my fault they got grabbed. I need to…"

"How about following orders," interrupted JJ. "Stop thinking everything's your fault. Pliant's guys had all the taps in place from the port authority ship-to-shore conversations including the CPS discussions. They planned it perfectly, based on insider information. The four of you were ambushed. Marian had a fabulous back-up plan, which is why you team so well. Get over blaming yourself. It's an old habit you need to break."

Brayson seethed, "I'm not supposed to feel lousy because Elena and Sophia got grabbed on my watch?"

"I know you internalize a lot on these assignments. I need you to remain objective. You and Marian snagged a great win. We've all done everything we can, now we need time. Accept well-earned praise and head home. Everything's in motion. I'll text Gracie with an update. Talk soon."

Marian smiled at him and tucked her arm through his. "Can we go home now, honey?"

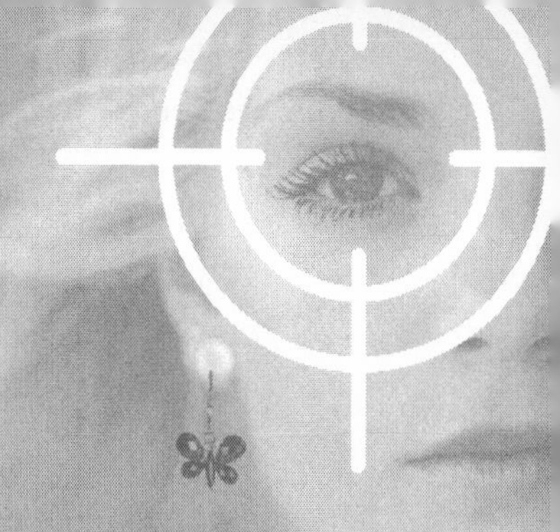

CHAPTER 41

Harsh Pain Great Gain

Ready to disembark, the passengers assembled on the main deck by group number with their belongings. The noise levels rose and fell as new friends exchanged information and wished one another well. Gracie stalled at the coffee shop, grabbing a cup of tea. Seeing Bailey, she waved. Bailey grinned and worked her way across the area toward her bestie. They exchanged a quick hug and air kiss. Gracie spotted Keith doing bag duty and finger waved, receiving a smile and salute in return.

"Gracie, glad I you spotted me in this madhouse. With our early flight, I was afraid I'd miss you. We could have only pulled this off together, along with your behind-the-scenes team. Keith and I feel bad that Jeff got hurt. They exchanged information to stay in touch. Give him an extra hug from me. He's a keeper. We'll team up again soon."

Gracie felt a wave of sadness that their adventure was over, but knew it was time to move on.

"This bedlam is wild," she said with a grin. "We're a little worse for wear, but we got him, girlfriend. Your ecology group seemed delighted with the evidence we gathered. Pliant will be locked up for a long time to pay for his outrageous activities as an ecological gangster. Perhaps your team can do the cleanup oversight and improve the plastics recycling processes. I do hope some of the manufacturing plants will continue to provide jobs for locals." Gracie blinked as tears threatened to fill her eyes.

"Me too." Bailey agreed with a nod.

An announcement reverberated through the deck with several numbers called.

"Ah, that's me and Keith. I gotta go, Gracie. Talk soon. Let me know, if you can, where those two kids end up. I hate to think or imagine how awful their fates could have become as someone else's property. They looked so vulnerable."

Bailey's comment made Gracie feel ill inside, but she nodded noncommittally based on JJ's text message moments ago. Gracie thought, *there is no need to tell her that part of the puzzle fell apart. It would dampen her high spirits.*

"Bailey, come on, sweetheart." Keith's voice carried over the crowd.

The friends hugged. "Call me," they said in unison and laughed as they parted to their next stops.

Gracie, a little sad, reflected how much she'd miss her friend. She walked toward the elevator to go to the onboard clinic. She and Jeff were scheduled to exit via ambulance to the hospital for a final check-up by a physician before heading out. She beamed and answered the incoming call. "Hi, Lance. Nice to hear from you. What's up?"

Lance's deep voice reverberated through the phone. "You know it's funny, Gracie. I know I owe you the favor, but I'm calling to ask you to help someone else if you can. I'm used to having transport issues with my big cats but when I see the same thing for humans, alarm bells go off in my head. I think you just might have the resources to assist."

Gracie wrinkled her nose as concern gripped her chest. "Go on."

"I have a local friend who gets me transport when I have to move animals. Anyway, he was working to get me some trucks, and crossed paths with this surly outfit leasing most of the vehicles I need. My buddy was trying to reason with them when this nasty tempered Hispanic character named Mateo, signaled his bodyguards to rough-up my friend. This Mateo character demanded to know what we needed the trucks for. When my friend insisted my cats were more important than regular cargo, the fight started. This Mateo guy had no sense of humor." Lance inhaled loudly as if collecting his thoughts. "I know what you're thinking, but there is a point to this story. Something hit me as wrong, so we watched the trucks move out and discreetly followed them. They caravanned to this old warehouse district north of Miami and started loading up what looks to be teenagers. Now why, we asked ourselves, would you treat human beings like animals instead of loading them into nice tour buses?"

Gracie, grim, shook her head and tersely asked, "Can you send me the address, plus any photos or license plate numbers? You may have stumbled onto the distribution case I'm working."

Lance sighed and chuckled. "Already in-flight ma'am. I sent all my info to Jeff's and your phones. I went back to the truck rental place to ask questions. No one wanted to help at first. Then, after I told them who I was and showed my credentials, people fell over themselves spilling their guts."

"That's terrific, Lance. What did you do to persuade them?" Gracie chortled as she kept walking. She pictured the young Lance that Jeff introduced her to when they'd arrived. It seemed like ages, not merely one long week.

"I wanted full disclosure on this Mateo character so I decided to pretend to be a private detective. I had played one years ago named Thomas Mauser and keep a card in my wallet. I handed over my business card and they read it out loud in disbelief, but laughed: *Tommy Gun.*

Gracie furrowed her brow and adopted a serious tone. “Lance, you realize you’re describing a human trafficking situation, right? Any thoughts on where they came from or where they’re headed?”

“Gracie, I sent you everything I got. Except…” He added a playful tone to his words, “I discovered the caravan was heading to Texas, because I was told I can get the trucks once they return. Gracie, it would please me if you and Jeff could help those poor, scared kids. They reminded me of the animals I rescue.”

“Darn it,” Gracie murmured in frustration. “Lance, thank you for calling. We’ll do our best to help and let you know.” She ended the call and thought, *we saved two but dozens more are being carted away. Sounds like Mateo is still running his business.*

Gracie texted all the details to JJ with a promise to call after speaking with Jeff.

She entered the clinic and eyed the nurse, who said, “Ten minutes, Mr. Wood.”

Gracie grinned. “How’re ya doing, Mr. Wood? They’re letting you go to the hospital in street clothes?”

“Yep, the doc thinks they’ll just do a once-over and release me. We’re headed to emergency at Baptist Health South Florida. They promised extra tests and a lollypop if I cooperate. Since our flight is scheduled for tomorrow, Brayson took our luggage and got us a hotel room.”

“Wow, that’s terrific.” She moved next to him hugging and then possessively kissed him on the lips. Stepping back, she spotted the slight grimace on his face.

He hooked his arm around her waist. “Gracie, I’m okay. Just a lot sore. I’m glad we got Pliant. Can’t believe what that jerk was doing to the environment. I know Bailey and her group will make the right changes.” He squeezed her side and inhaled her sweet scent. “I’m proud of you, honey.”

"I think we did good, Jeff. I couldn't have any of the success without you. Sorry you hurt so much. Hopefully you'll heal soon."

"Gracie, it pains me to admit that perhaps I don't belong in your world, sweetheart."

"Don't belong in my world?" she protested. "Good grief! They've botched your medications and now you're delirious! We agreed to return to New York together. And…your word is your bond as you've told me so many times, Mr. Wood."

"Gracie, you were born into this role. You've trained for it. It's second nature for you. I thought I could be in, but all I am is a lawyer expecting everyone to show courtroom manners. I've only fought arguments in front of a judge; I don't want to be fighting for my life. You got knocked out, then manhandled into a pallet with a narcotic drip. Here you are ready to chase the ones who got away. I'm struggling to get into a wheelchair because I was playing out of my league. If I can't defend myself, how can I ever defend you? The beating was my wake-up call."

The nurse pushed in a wheelchair and assisted Jeff to get settled.

Gracie grabbed the handles and murmured close to his ear, "That is not how this story ends, mister. I will be with you while you're checked out. Then we'll have an informed discussion at the hotel later. No, is not an option. Together we can work this out."

Gracie watched Jeff struggle to hold back his tears. He whispered, "I'm ashamed and angry at myself for being useless up against those goons. I can't hardly believe you would still want me in your life."

She swiped her tears of frustration from her cheeks. "We've both trained for our professions. That doesn't mean we can't learn or train for another. Understand you have a training deficiency, so we are going to cure that, or find a sweet spot where your expertise can be optimized, like research. I can't believe you'd think me so shallow as to dismiss you because of different skillsets. You remember that phrase people say to each other now and again *for better or for worse*? I'm proud of you. I want us to work this out. I want you healed. I want to teach you what you don't know, and learn from you. I'm not prepared to watch you wheeled out of my life."

Tears now streaming down his cheeks, Jeff quietly petitioned, "Gracie, if you're sure, then I'll try my best and teach you anything I know."

Wiping the excess leakage from her eyes and beaming, Gracie demanded, "It would please the court to accept your petition, Mr. Wood. The plaintiff is now remanded to medical care for the near term and is to accept all affection lavished upon him by one Gracie Rodreguiz."

Gracie noticed the mood lightening as Jeff slightly chuckled.

Gracie stepped from the exam room when JJ called.

JJ's voice resonated in her heart. "Hey. How's Jeff doing? You two have been through a lot on this assignment. I wasn't sure what his mind set would be after it was all said and done."

Gracie squeaked, "JJ, he's worried he's not good enough. The beating he took resulted in more than sore ribs. When I protested and told him we could make it work, he grew silent."

JJ sighed. "Yeah, Brayson and I worried he would wig out. You know how lawyers are, always arguing their points of view to a logical conclusion. I'm glad his petition was denied. We kinda like him. Plus, we already know you've fallen for the man. I guess this means I've got another person on my Christmas card list.

"Gracie, he's damaged and now scared. The physical stuff gets the aid first, but it sounds like he has psychological damage as well. You'll need to let him build back faith in himself. You'll need to get him help in both areas. If you're sure you want this, then don't wait too long. If you let him close those wounds himself, you'll lose first mover advantage."

"You're right, JJ," She announced. "Yes, I want to do this. While his body is physically recovering, I'll get him into counseling to make sure no demons lurk in background mode. I'm not giving up without a fight."

"Ah, there is my powerful and determined sister. I think that's a wise approach. Please use some finesse, okay? It would be insulting if he thought you pitied him. Aunt Petra once told me about the emotional demons she battled. She couldn't deal with anyone after her accident because she feared the pity. You guys stay the course, and all will be fine."

"JJ, you always know how to make me feel better." Then she recalled something. "JJ, that man we helped before we boarded the ship with the animal issue, Lance? He reached out with information about Mateo. I texted it to you, after you didn't answer my call."

"Everything we can do to find him is being worked. It's a long shot, but good information."

"Maybe we can find the guy and get him prosecuted right along with Pliant. What a family. Argh." Then she confessed, "I'm sorry this call has been all about me. How's Jo?"

"Awesome. For the record she was afraid we were at opposite ends of the spectrum, but decided we are better together. She loves her career and recognition as the top fashion model in the world. I promised her she could have that life as long as she wants it. I'll be here. Funny though, after every photo shoot she sends me a printed catalog that is signed special for me. We've got the best of both worlds right now. Best of all we communicate."

"There, see? I knew she was a fighter," Gracie commented. "You guys are a hot ticket item."

JJ continued, "I sit staring at those photos knowing we are building a life together." He confessed, "Just so you know, I'd never demand that she give up on her life's passion. Curious enough, she feels the same way about my work. I mean, go figure."

Gracie sniffled. "You're not going to sing that song by Lonnie Lupnerder *If You Love Someone, Set Them Free,* are you?"

JJ clucked his tongue. "It was originally stated in a poem by Kahlil Gibran — *If you love somebody, let them go, for if they return, they were always yours. If they don't, they never were.* And yeah, I'm going to say that, so you won't just give up. Every couple of days or weeks I get a text message along with a cute photo from her and I reciprocate. Perhaps a little healing and space for you and Jeff would work. If you don't think so, you might recall how our family friends, Zara and Buzz, fixed their lives. Their relationship went to hell in a hand-basket for a while, but ultimately, we watched them get married and ride off into the sunset."

"I hope it continues to work for you two. I'll take what you said under advisement. Thank you, my wonderful twin. And thank you for not singing Lonnie's handcuff song."

JJ smirked. "I gotta let you go. Off to meet Jo and see what our next chapter becomes."

"I believe in happy endings, JJ."

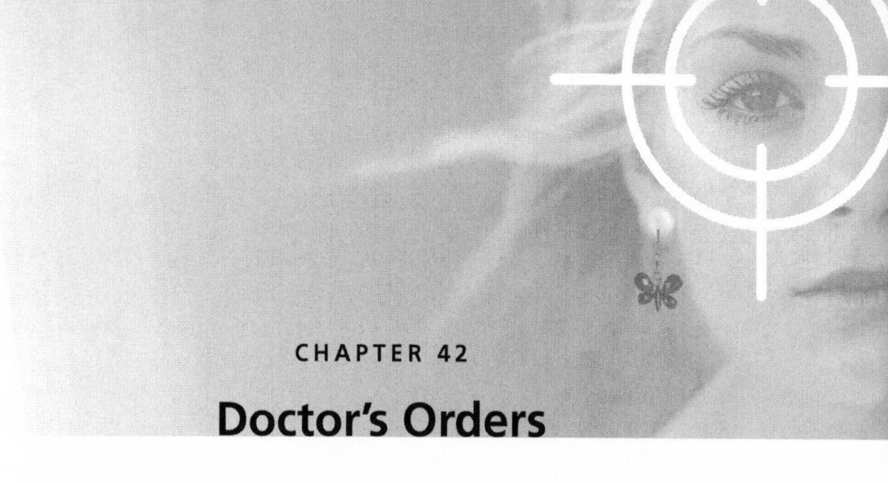

CHAPTER 42

Doctor's Orders

Gracie rode in the ambulance with Jeff to the Miami Hospital. They held hands, though he kept his eyes closed as if to focus on warding off the pain. The EMT monitored all the vitals and gave her a thumbs-up as he made notations on the chart. The lack of expression or involvement by Jeff disconcerted her. She believed the two beatings he received compromised his spirit. Still, she wanted medical opinions. The extensive research on PTSD helped her understand more about the possible demons he battled, but their frame of reference substantially differed. Understanding what he wanted and needed to overcome any doubts became her focus.

Gracie asked the trauma nurse inside the exam room, "Ma'am, can he have more for pain relief? Each movement seems to hurt."

"Gracie, it's tolerable at present," Jeff stated. "I want to hear and understand everything. I can't do that doped up. I promise I'll ask for something when it hurts too much."

Gracie felt like she'd overstepped. "I'm sorry, Jeff, I don't want you in pain."

"Trust me, honey, I am a big boy who can speak his mind."

She squeezed his hand and smiled to his closed eyes. Gracie realized she was pushing and kept quiet. He needed control of his care. "Of course, Jeff. I'll try to stay quiet."

Jeff clasped her hand, acknowledging her concern. "It's all good, honey."

The nurse returned within the hour and inserted the test results into Jeff's file. A short time later, Dr. Duane Mosier came into the room. "Mr. Wood, I'm from our trauma ward, and was asked to come chat with you. I'd like to have a short discussion with you in private, if you are up for it."

Jeff nodded. "Gracie, how about you grab a cup of tea, honey. I'll text you when we are finished."

Gracie felt dreadful leaving, but she acquiesced. Rushing to the cafeteria to grab a cup of tea, her phone buzzed with a text from JJ.

Gracie, give him space, he needs to control his destiny too.

She read it and replied:

I know, but I don't want him to think I'm deserting him.

Her phone chimed again.

He might in the short term, but it won't last.

Gracie sniffled and dabbed her checks to blot the tears. She knew she was out of her element.

JJ, I think I'm pushing too hard.

She wanted to fix everything.

Nope. He needs to find his own way. That's different.

Gracie realized she had a hard time not being in charge.

Okay, I'm going to think through my next steps, I'll let you know the outcome.

With that comment, Gracie set the block text command. She'd never done that to her twin before, but she needed to think.

Thirty minutes later, she received a message from Jeff to please rejoin him. Gracie took a deep breath and decided he should lead the discussion. She would show her concern for his wellbeing. The monitors kept an unexpected cadence to their conversation. She felt as long as the machines matched her heartbeat she might survive.

"Hi, sweetheart. How are you after speaking to Doctor Mosier? Was it a good discussion?" she asked a bit too perky.

Jeff opened his eyes and searched her soul before he spoke. She realized he looked forlorn. "Gracie," he began, "you're a powerful force and an incredibly independent woman. I've never known anyone like you, certainly not with your background and list of accomplishments. Here I lie, in pain, worried about looking weak in your eyes and unable to protect you like I want."

She smiled encouragement, but remained silent, keeping her gaze on him.

"I was raised to be strong and the provider, which I can do from an earning perspective without a problem. But, hell, you don't need my physical protection because your training taught you to kick most everyone's ass and take numbers. Heck, even after being drugged you look fresh as a spring day while I feel like yesterday's trash that hasn't been picked up."

Gracie caressed his cheek and kept an even expression. She didn't want to sway him in any direction, but rather let him flow in his direction.

"Jeff, we're different as salt and pepper, but I think combined we're good. We balance one another."

Jeff looked away as if gathering his thoughts and added a rueful smile. "You may be right about us mixing well. However, until I work through my issues, I'm not useful to myself or to you."

Gracie's eyes threatened to give away her heartache. She took a deep breath. "I have to respect your perspective, even if

I disagree. For me, life is not about being the same, but rather about following your heart. You captured my heart a long time ago and it is yours to enjoy or destroy. I'm not ready to give up, but I will give you space to heal and reflect."

She pressed a paper into his hand and sadly smiled. "The paper contains several practitioners you may wish to consult. You need to orchestrate your recovery in a way that fits your desires. The last thing I want is to force you to choose because I do or do not want something. I do feel responsible to offer options for you to take or ignore.

"These doctors are at your disposal and I will remain outside of all discussions without your specific requests. You are a special man whom I love, and who was subjected to wrongful beatings, but thankfully survived. Yes, our team will track these jerks and hopefully bring them to justice. I wish we'd all been spared the horrors of this trip. But please remember, nothing you did or said will convince me that that you are not the bravest man I know. Courage is not winning or fighting or even getting to the finish line first, but rather about honor. I have never met a more honorable human being. I wanted you to know that before I give you the space you want. You're the conductor of your own destiny and I will respect that. You can always reach me, but know too, that I love you with my heart and soul."

Gracie leaned over and gently brushed his lips with hers, then squeezed his hand one more time before smiling and walking out the door.

When the door shut, Jeff shut his eyes wishing there had been a different outcome. Then the nurse bustled in with discharge papers, transport via private plane to New York City, and a referral from Doctor Mosier to see a colleague in the next couple of days. He dozed until the driver to the airport arrived.

Gracie arrived at her apartment in New York. She took out all her anger on her things. None of those mattered when her heart was bleeding rivers of blood. She'd protected herself for so long from being hurt, and here she was in agony. After thirty minutes of exhausting rage, she took a breath and collected herself.

"I need to go to work in the morning and get my mind off my relationship failures. In the coming days, I'll focus on my strengths and pick apart the rest. Resigned, she grabbed the broom and dustpan to clean up her mess. Grinning with the last scoop of debris, she admitted she would not go down that path again any time soon, but it had felt good in the moment. Then her phone notified her of a text message.

> Are you finished?

She frowned.

> Yes, JJ, I forgot you had eyes in here.

Her phone chimed again.

> That and your block on the phone doesn't work for me, Gracie. Nope, and never will. Give Jeff some space, I'm proud of how you handled the situation and kept yourself together. Consider this your virtual hug.

She kissed the screen, resigned to waiting. Then she showered and climbed into bed, determined to keep distracted for as long as possible.

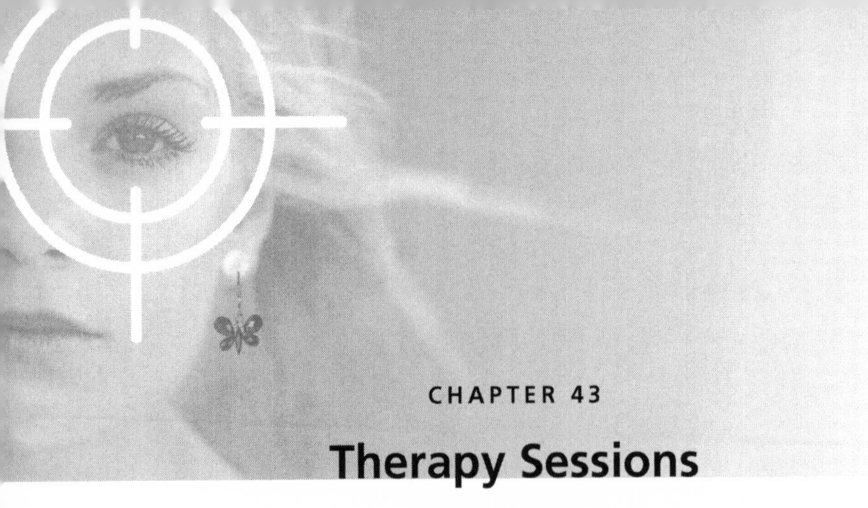

CHAPTER 43

Therapy Sessions

For the next several days, Gracie arrived bright and early to her office catching up on those items delayed due to her travel. The white tile floor covered with silk Turkish rugs offset the dove-grey furnishings, which hinted at business and refined elegance. When a client came to work, she used the table and grey leather chairs near the windows permitted a stunning view of the skyline. Keeping busy was easy. Her jammed calendar contained meetings and work activities all day. The long hours put significant distance from her feelings after Jeff's email sent the day he got released from the hospital. She'd kept it to reread often. She heard the soft whirring as the clock's mechanism started the tribute to her favorite song by Tchaikovsky. She hummed the tune her grandfather thought helped her go to sleep. Stretching, she decided to pull up his email, read it one more time, and delete it.

> *Hi Gracie,*
> *Thank you for your help, encouragement, and love. I have a few weeks of PT to gain full mobility. The doc promises I'll fully recover and the tenderness will lessen over time. I ran into a veteran in the hospital who has had a really tough time. As a Navy Seal, he did some hard stuff. Funny, like*

you mentioned regarding your background, he said his training helped his abilities, but pain is pain. Mark and I've had a couple of insightful conversations, and formed an unexpected bond. He has no other family so I think I'll help him as a friend. He suggested I speak to his shrink, which just so happened to be one of the recommendations on your list. We connected. I've had a session and will continue, I think.

I know you have a crazy work schedule, so catch up and help the world. You are one special lady I won't forget. I need to do this on my own, Gracie, so please move on with your life and be happy.

Jeff

The waterworks trailed down her cheeks and onto her blouse. Scrolling one more time, her mouse cursor hovered over the image of the trashcan. She shook her head in acceptance and permanently deleted it. Grabbing a tissue, she sopped up her tears and blew her nose. She took a sip of water and rubbed her forehead as if to stall off a headache. Then she dialed JJ.

"Hey, do you have a few minutes?"

"I do. What's up?

"I know Jeff's hospital bill was paid, but can you please make certain that any ongoing treatments are taken care of and not tied back to me? You said he needed space and he told me something similar, but I don't want him financially impacted because of me."

"Easily done, sis, and already in the works. How are you?"

"I'm done being angry. I have lots of work, though I wish he would have taken the time to listen to my thoughts about having him work the research angle for R-Group. His logical mind and ability to put puzzles together, especially with older documents for legal cases, is something we need."

"Good. Work is good. You're right though, he's a smart, articulate man. He'd be a great addition. Perhaps after he gets back on his feet and sorts things out..."

"Maybe."

"I'll let you know if anything significant changes for him. I love you, Gracie. You may recall that Jo and I had a similar impasse at one point. Time may be your friend."

She yawned into the phone and giggled. "Not right now, it's not. I'm headed home and don't have to be back here until nine. Thanks, JJ. Goodnight."

"Goodnight, Gracie. Rest well."

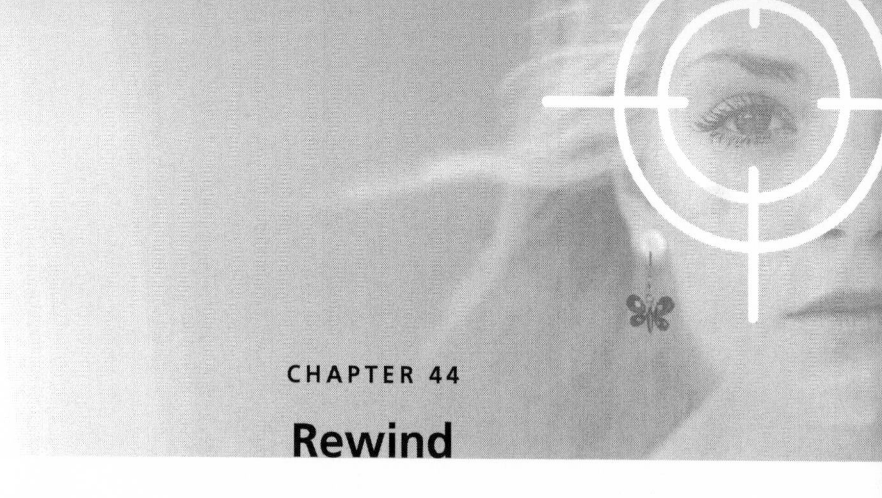

CHAPTER 44

Rewind

Several weeks later, staring out the window of his high-rise apartment in Manhattan, Jeff propped his sore leg on the brown leather couch. He absentmindedly rubbed it as the therapist advised. The late afternoon sun cast shadows that continually changed, offering unusual visuals on the adjacent towers. As quiet and peaceful as it was watching the early evening lights come on here and there, a heavy blanket of melancholy draped over him. He mumbled, "I should have done it differently. I should've taken it more seriously when JJ called and offered me the research job. The offer letter delivered yesterday was generous, but I didn't accept it. I don't think I could work with Gracie and not want more." He released a resigned sigh.

Jeff was startled back to reality at hearing the obnoxious apartment door buzzer. He reached for his walking stick, stood, and plodded toward the door to find out the identity of the unexpected visitor. As he limped, he grumbled, "You'd think after all this time, I'd be getting around better than this, but nooo."

Jeff caught himself before opening the door and tried to look out the peephole as a precaution. All he saw was grey. Growing suspicious, he loudly asked, "Who's calling?"

A gravelly man's voice replied, "I got a delivery from *Dump it on the Doorstep* for Mr. Jeff Wood. It's all paid. I need a signature to get my tip."

Confused but willing to accept the delivery, he opened the door and mumbled, "Not sure this is a good idea. I wonder what Gracie would recommend."

He was rewarded and astonished by the sight of Gracie, who promptly chided in her normal voice, "She'd-a said don't answer it, dummy."

He felt shocked, pleased, and stunned at her comment and shook his head.

After a few seconds, she smirked, "Okay, I'm glad you answered it. I've got all the fixings for your veal parmesan forte that we'll cook. I wanted the wine to be special. I took the liberty of securing a nice zinfandel that should pair deliciously. That is, of course, if I may come in."

Gracie grinned. Jeff felt nearly undone and awash with emotions. His eyes threatened to overflow, but he took a ragged breath. "I keep special wine. Just because it comes in a brown cardboard box labeled Vin-ordinaire doesn't mean it's second-rate. I happen to like it with my raisin bran or my special recipe of Velveeta-based mac-n-cheese."

They burst into laughter.

Jeff slid to the side. "Gracie, please come in. I'll carry the box to the kitchen."

Observing the cane he clutched for balance, she raised an eyebrow and grinned. "I'll take the package. You close the door." She glided in and added, "If it's not too much trouble, can you please open the wine? I want to sample while we cook."

"I would deem it an honor, my dear." Jeff went to work. In moments they were at the counter in front of the cooking area with their wine.

They each took sips before Jeff wrinkled his features and protested, "How did you get into this building without me being alerted? I pay for a high-security facility. Are you some cat burglar? And how did you do that trick with the male voice, Miss Magician?"

Gracie took another sip and sighed. "This is where I went wrong before. Telling you too much, too fast, but not preparing you for collateral damage. Forgive me for being selfish, but I still wanted you in my life. I should've not put you at risk. Truthfully, I wanted you with me. I'd like us to try again, please. I'd like you to accept JJ's offer. It's not working for me, but for his group."

"I'm sorry I ran from Miami," he confessed. "I was scared. I've never been frightened for someone else. It was my mistake that led them to you." He caressed her arm. "My world is empty. I've felt miserable ever since. Yes, I would like for us to try again."

Gracie clicked their glasses and took a generous sip of wine. "Hey, our meal isn't going to cook itself. Aren't you starved?"

She went into the kitchen, methodically taking items from the grocery bag while Jeff leaned against the fridge behind her. She stopped in mid-unloading to face him. Gracie set her determined expression. "For my organization, I orchestrate digital covert operations around the planet to help people. So, yes, I can be a cat burglar when needed. It's easy to disable a building security system to get in, then turn it back on. I used a special program on my phone to record my voice and morphed it into a husky male voice based on the response I wanted you to make."

Jeff noted Gracie's eyes almost blazed, reflecting her confidence. "I must be decisive and calculating because the criminals I'm up against are cold and ruthless. You've only known the other side of me, so I understand why you were unsettled when you saw me in that combat state. I've got to be able to tell you things for your trust and withhold some stuff to keep you safe." Her eyes softened, as did her voice. "Can we make this work, Jeff? I want to try."

Jeff studied her a moment then rallied. "Did you bring your toothbrush and toothpaste? I know you don't like my brand."

Gracie chortled. "You're all about romance, honey." Holding up the items in question, she added, "I was hoping you'd ask me to stay."

Discussion Questions for

Enigma Tracer

Book Club Leaders ...contact Charles and/or Rox to participate in a special meeting to discuss the book; the concepts; and the evolution of the series. We always encourage readers to post individual reviews on Amazon.com. And thank you.

In-person gatherings are possible if you are in the North Texas region. Otherwise, Zoom is always an option.

Group Discussion Questions

Did the ending pull you in? Did you want more?

- Were you satisfied or disappointed with how it ended?
- How do you picture the characters' lives after the end of the story?
- What was your top takeaway from Enigma Tracer?

What do you think of Gracie's role leading the international information broker—R-Group?

- Do you know anyone like her?
- Do you think that there are women like her today?
- Do you think it's important for a woman to be able to physically defend herself?

What do you think of JJ leadership of the CATS team?

- Do you know anyone like him?
- Do you think that there are men with honor and commitment today?
- Do you think a caste system remains between men and women in technology?

Who was your favorite supporting character?

- Why did you like them?
- Did you find them believable?
- Did they have relatable character flaws or were they too squeaky clean?

Do you think Pliant was a realistic antagonist?

- Did he get his just desserts or would you have liked something different?
- Have you crossed paths with a person like this?
- What would you do in a similar situation if you were the leader?

What risks did Gracie take that should have been avoided?

- Should she avoided being with Bailey?
- Does it take a village to right this type of injustice?
- Was she a hero or a victim and why?

What themes surfaced in the story?

- Have you ever been in a situation where you needed someone to save you?
- Have you ever been in a situation where you did not want someone to save you?
- Have you ever had to step in and help someone out of a dire situation?

Read a snippet from the second book in our new series

Breakfield
and **Burkey**

Enigma Forced

CHAPTER 1

Promises Failed

Inside the diesel truck, the dashboard and its associated attachments vibrated and rattled from the ride on the uneven road surface. Like an old man wheezing from years of smoking, the air conditioner worked to deliver warm air in fits and starts.

"Stop messing with the radio dial, Miguel," sputtered Toby, not taking his dark brown eyes off the dusty road. "There hasn't been a signal we could grab for at least an hour. Listening to static is annoying."

Miguel slicked back his oily black hair with his fingers then rested one hand on top of his grimy knee visible through the worn jeans. "We've been on the road for nearly eight hours for a trip you said would be six hours tops," he whined.

"Hell," Toby groused, glancing at his buddy for a second. "We lost time at the weigh-station when you decided you wanted to drive, and killed the engine. These trucks don't always start right up, plus the officials eyed us for the additional smoke we blew. That took an hour. I was surprised they didn't open the doors after looking at the papers, but the inspector did remove boss's envelope from the clipboard before waving us through."

The truck lumbered through another small one-gas-pump Texas town with no stoplight. Speed limit signs were present in each of the rural cities with cruisers strategically positioned to act on speeders. Toby shifted into a higher gear as he fidgeted on the cracked vinyl of the bench seat.

"Why don't you admit we're lost, Toby. This piece of junk has no tunes, GPS, or air conditioning. I hope those melons and avocados, or what's ever in back aren't melting, or we won't get paid."

Toby's teeth banged together when he nailed the pothole. "I used the map boss provided when we got the rig at one this morning. It was lots cooler before the sun came up. I got us from outside of Brownsville to San Antonio on a decent highway. If you hadn't spilled your Dr. Pepper on the map, we could have followed his directions to Pflugerville." Toby slapped the seat and caught his finger in the torn vinyl. "Ow." He shook his hand. "Then there was the damn detour that put us on this two-lane road that announces slow as we approach each city limit."

Miguel's head bounced against the seat at the next pothole. "Hey, watch where you're driving. You could miss the holes if you tried. This is one rough ride. In the next town, let's stop for petrol and ask directions. Maybe we can get food and a couple of waters. It's not even noon, and I'm sweating in this sauna."

"You stink too," Toby stated with disgust, wrinkling his nose. "I hate the idea of stopping and being even later." He toweled his forehead with his filthy handkerchief then tried to reposition himself on the seat to ease his stiff back. "Maybe asking for directions would help. I'll pull the rig into this adjacent parking lot. I'll walk to the store for water and directions. You get the hot air all to yourself." He parked the rig and set the brake. "Don't touch anything while I'm gone. Don't go anywhere. And don't turn off the engine. I'll take our map. I'm sure they got a pencil."

"Remember, you promised to teach me to drive a big rig when this job's over. I think I'd like driving freight in this country. But not this piece of crap."

Annoyed, Toby opened the door into the inferno of the August morning with the sun blazing overhead. The sweat evaporated from his skin as he hopped down and slammed the door. Smoke randomly billowing from the exhaust stack on top of the cab. He walked around the building to the front door with a view of the regular gas pumps. Toby noticed a few cars were there but no one outside refueling. He decided folks must be inside enjoying the cool air. Turning back to the business at hand, he oriented his map to make it a quick conversation.

He started to push the door to enter. Inside, a hand pulled back the door and grabbed hold of Toby, yanking him into the store. He fought to keep his balance, but his worn boot soles slid him into a display rack, like a skater on ice. Several items plopped to the floor with resounding crunches. Then there was stillness. He felt the jarring pain from a solid object banging on top of his head. His knees gave out as he crumbled to the floor atop several chip bags that exploded from the impact.

A demanding man's voice with a Mexican accent, growled, "Stay down on the ground, mother f*****."

Toby's hand reached for his injury as he tried to move into a sitting position. He caught sight of the revolver rising and felt the blow smash down on the same spot.

Toby expelled his breath. "Ooooff." Then he grunted. Lying mostly on his right side, he peered through his eyelashes but everything seemed blurry. His head pounded, so he shut his eyes hoping that would ease his pain. He heard the voice again.

"Diego, I got another one. What's taking you so long?"

A second accented voice came from farther away, echoing as if in a closed area. "I told you not to use names, stupid! You just created another problem. It's bad enough the cashier can't open the damn safe. Now these people know our names, Chico."

"Sorry."

"Never mind, get his wallet, too. We're going to take all the money we can, including anyone who stops."

Toby figured it was Chico who pulled him up by the armpits and waved his gun. He shoved Toby toward the edge of the checkout counter. Toby noticed several folks sitting near him and holding their knees. They gave him a quick look reflecting fear, before hiding their tear-streaked faces against their chests.

"Gimme that wallet from your back pocket, mister. Then sit down and shut up." Chico demanded.

Toby's vision cleared enough to see Chico's hand waiting to receive the wallet while he pointed his weapon to the floor toward the others. Without thinking, Toby grabbed the man's wrist and yanked hard, slamming the man into the corner of the counter, knocking out his breath. Toby recognized he stood half a foot taller, so he continued pulling and shifting the tension to keep the man off balance. Chico fought like a ravaged coyote and swung his revolver over, delivering two rounds in deafening rapid succession. Toby released his hold on his killer, falling dead with blood rapidly pooling on the floor.

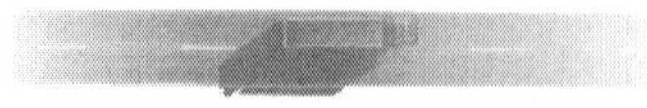

Multiple screams and cries sounded from the hostages.

Chico bellowed, "Anyone else want to be a hero?"

Behind him, the glass doors exploded, and three police burst in. "Freeze! Hands empty and in the air!" one officer commanded, shifted cautiously to the right. Another officer sidled left while a third maintained her position at the opening.

Stunned, Chico ducked behind the hot grill counters.

A man chuckled from nearby on the floor. "Good. The silent alarm worked. Cops arrived in less than fifteen minutes."

Chico identified the man and grinned. In a blind rage, he shot the man, then turned toward the storefront in time to receive two rounds in the chest from the policewoman. The impact drove him into the hot food area. Several things jarred loose and joined the dead killer on the ground.

Moving cautiously, the other officers methodically walked the aisles. Diego popped up and fired several wild shots. He was shot twice in succession. Once in the chest by the officer, Jose. Again, in the head from the officer, Steven.

Jose hollered, "Who else is here?"

One of the hostages yelled, "We're behind the counter. There were only two of them. Thank you for saving us."

Radiating heat waves rose from the black asphalt in the parking lot. The three officers huddled in the shady strip outside the storefront where local citizens were boarding up the broken windows, while others swept up the chards of glass debris.

"I hate store shootings. The follow-on questioning goes forever," complained Jose.

"At least the coroner loaded up the last of the bodies and we finished questioning the hostages," Brenda proclaimed.

Steve nodded. "We'll get back to the office, fill out the final paperwork, and see what turns up on the dead guys. The wallet of the man who entered toward the end, according to one witness, contained no identification. A rough map located in his shirt pocket was penciled on brown paper. Not even a cell phone on him. Strange."

Brenda's shoulder radio barked, "Brenda, have you accounted for everyone? We identified the robber's car, but based on the body count there should be one or two more vehicles. Can you confirm?"

Jose wrinkled his forehead and fretted, searching the parking lot. "Steve, circle to the back and see if there is anything we missed. The hostages gave their statements, then left. I only see one vehicle."

Steve returned, shaking his head. The rig parked in the abandoned parking lot belched black smoke, and its idling tone changed, capturing his attention. "Hey," Steve pointed, "that 18-wheeler in the parking lot on the side could be his. It's still running. Let's go take a look."

Jose opened the driver side of the cab. The stale hot air took away his breath. Seeing no one, he climbed up and turned off the engine. Leaving the door ajar, he jumped to the ground and walked around to the rear of the trailer. He saw the heavy padlock securing the opening and slapped the metal. "Damn. I hope there's nothing perishable in there. We're going on two plus hours since the shooting."

He advised dispatch over his comm link, then froze. He frantically waved to Brenda and Steve. The two officers rush to his side, meeting at the open cab.

"What up, Jose?" Brenda asked.

"I heard something after I banged my hand on the rear, then again after talking to dispatch. Tell me what you hear, or call me crazy." Jose slapped his hand against the trailer. Within a second, a plea for help echoed from inside. The officers stared at Jose who suddenly felt ill.

"Steve, go grab the cutters from our car," Jose ordered.

Steve ran off.

"You're perfectly sane," added Brenda. Beating on the side of the trailer, she yelled, "We're coming to help."

When Steve returned, he and Jose used the tool, and had the lock broken in seconds. Jose lifted the rod and swung open the door on the right, while Steve grabbed the door on the left. Brenda rushed to the opening and stared at the scene inside. An indescribable stench bellowed from the opening along with moans and cries. The cargo was heaped in groups with a few clustered near the side walls.

Jose backed away and took a breath of fresher air. "Dispatch, we need more EMTs here now, with saline drips. Send the coroner too. We found a freight trailer full of humans, some still alive.

"Steve, go find blankets, and all the water you can carry. Tell those workers to help lay blankets in the shade even if it's under this trailer." Shaking Brenda to get her to focus, Jose said, "Go see if you can find the manifest for this rig in the front."

Jose hopped in noting random movements of arms and legs. Those he found alive, he moved to the trailer opening so others could place them on the ground. An anguished cry got trapped in his throat, and tears filled his eyes at the sight of a small toddler lying on the trailer floor with a puddle of blood under her head. Her lifeless, glassy brown eyes stared back at him. It took several beats for him to move on, searching for survivors.

Brenda joined him. Together they moved several of those breathing so helpers could lower them into the shade to await the EMTs.

"Hey, buddy, are you okay?" asked Steve when the next young victim was positioned for retrieval.

"No," Jose admitted. "I'll never be okay again. That little girl looked like my daughter. I kissed her this morning before school."

He felt Brenda pat this arm. "We're all these people have right now," she whispered. "I'm so glad you heard their cries for help."

He nodded and retreated to the depths of hell to find more bodies. "Dispatch," he sobbed into his comm, "we need more help, and we need it now." He felt his anger and frustration explode as he roared, "Call every surrounding town. We need EVERYBODY! They can't die like this. KEEP the damn media away."

CHAPTER 2

Righteous Outrage

Gracie blinked away brimming tears, unable to believe the news flash. She twisted strands of blonde hair around her finger, and the second read jolted her sensibilities.

Fifty miles north of San Antonio, Texas, authorities found an abandoned 18-wheeler. Inside was not the fresh produce suggested by the manifest, but humans packed like sardines. Survivors got transported to undisclosed destinations. Authorities estimated only a third of the undocumented immigrants survived. All reports suggest they remain in critical condition. Dehydration claimed the lives of the aged and infant travelers, locked in the box trailer baked by triple-digit temperatures as the summer heat wave continues.

Reeling from the harsh reality, Gracie leaned her head back and pressed her fingers to her eyes. "Human trafficking. I don't understand how anyone but a monster could do this," she mumbled. Her thoughts returned to the cruise, where she got briefly captured and her friends hospitalized. They all recovered physically, but the memory would remain forever etched on her brain. Her fingers pounded out a message to JW on the keyboard to get some action from her European team. Moaning her frustration in not getting a quick fix, she reached for her cell and called her twin.

"JJ, I hate being head of a fourth-generation information business, like the R-Group, and feeling powerless when atrocities like in the news this morning. Do you feel powerless at times, too?" Gracie took a breath with ideas churning. "Can your CATS resources find out more about the top headlines this morning on the human trafficking event near San Antonio, Texas? As Uncle Carlos would say, my Yaqui Indian senses are tingling like crazy. It appears Mateo's business model has surfaced again, on wheels."

"Yes, Gracie, my team's on it. ICABOD flagged the news feed. You're right. It looks like his handiwork or an evil copycat. We tracked the rental of the rig back to the same money source that rented transport out of Miami last month. The inside tip Lance Pope shared with you is paying dividends. We'll work that angle. But Homeland Security is pushing to keep it under wraps. With only this one report, I'm not sure why the media isn't outraged by this horrific crime against humanity. Nobody deserves to die like these immigrants did--except for that trafficker Mateo."

"I sure hope Sophia and Elena are not among those unfortunate victims," she lamented, remembering when she met the pair at dinner on the cruise. "Is your right hand, Brayson, aware? He was on the cruise when the girls were traveling with Mateo."

"He checked that angle immediately," said JJ. Nothing in the info we looked at for the living or dead suggested the girls. I think their captors had other ideas for those two. Remember, the truck came from Brownsville, not Miami, where Sophia and Elena disappeared."

Gracie closed her eyes with relief and sadness that they were still missing. "JJ, we need to focus on locating Mateo and ending his wretched business model. Recruiting teens for sale or prostitution is bad enough," she spat. "But wholesale importing of people for fun or profit is-is…I can't think of something bad enough to call it."

"I agree, it's hateful," JJ agreed. "Can you get your team to start tracing the financial angle? As some reports suggest, these victims pay in advance, sign up for paying in any way possible or smuggle drugs. There're payments to multiple sources to turn blind eyes from somewhere. The dangling promises that life in the United States is milk and honey persist. In some third-world countries, people mortgage everything and beg, borrow, or steal to achieve the American dream. The exploitation of refugees is a disgusting business model. Where is the money going, and how do we intercept the endpoints? Mateo and others in the business must have a weak link. Are the credit cards that could provide leads used in the truck rentals?"

"I've asked our cousins, Satya and Auri, to track the information, JJ, including rental payments over the last year. JW is supervising. Sometimes they get stuck, and he needs to write additional computer code to get them on course again. He wants to locate the origin as this is likely not a new business, just growing. Granger is augmenting ICABOD's processing power in real-time. I suspect Mateo uses cryptocurrency to launder his income, but that's a lengthy search algorithm. We found crypto purchases completed with stolen credit cards bought off the Darknet." Gracie shifted uneasily in her chair and quietly asked, "How's the new contractor doing?"

JJ laughed. "Jeff's doing well. It's nice that he's low maintenance, especially while dating you."

"Hey, I'm easygoing, too," she chuckled. "We're working through our issues. Jeff hasn't complained about his work, so thank you for adding him to your team."

"Jeff's smart enough to know you and I talk often."

"I know," she chuckled. "I need to get back to work."

"Me too. Good night, Gracie."

"Night, JJ. Thanks."

Jo clutched her tote, entered their cozy rooms decorated in warm, vibrant colors, and locked the front door. “Hey, JJ,” she called, “sorry I’m a little late, honey. Traffic was a bear.”

Resigned to a standard workout with JJ before dinner, she headed toward their gym, hoping to surprise him. Not hearing a response, she went to their bedroom, buoyed by the welcoming atmosphere of their home. The workday melted as she inhaled the fresh scent of flowers while she put things into the laundry and changed into her exercise clothes.

Jo admired JJ’s muscles undulating while he threw spinning side kicks, elbows carefully aimed backward to halt his imaginary adversary. He added deadly frontal jabs in an effort to destroy the punching bag. It spun like a marionette master was controlling it for an unseen audience. JJ abruptly stopped, sweeping his longish dark wave away from his eyes. He knelt on one knee and hit a button to initiate a new session.

JJ snapped his head and body up to focus on three spring-loaded projectiles rocketing towards him at ninety miles per hour. Jo gasped, her heart racing while the blunt missiles zeroed in on him. She beamed, watching him sidestep each with lightning-swift movements, grabbing them in midair and tossing them to the floor.

Jo walked behind him as he retrieved the objects, knowing he was aware of her presence. “I worry when you place yourself in harm’s way, but I love watching you.” Reaching her arms around him, she leaned into his back. “I’ll never move that fast. Those darts travel like a major league pitcher’s fastball.”

He spun her around, hugging her back. “Nope, but you are fast enough for everyone to admire your form. Besides, I don’t use the programs often. I need to keep my reflexes sharp, just in case.”

Jo kissed him and gently caressed his cheek. “Sorry to be late again. Do we have time for me to work out before supper?”

“Of course.” He waggled his eyebrows and kissed her nose. “I love working out with you anywhere, anytime.” He turned on the music she enjoyed while they sparred. “We’ll do stretches. Then let’s do an easy session for your muscles and balance. You have another shoot tomorrow.”

She nodded agreement and caught her mane of mahogany hair into a scrunchy, centering her mind on her body, smiling at their reflection in the mirror.

JJ laughed. “Honey, even in a gym, you look hot. No wonder you’re so successful as a supermodel. Any out-of-towners coming up?”

“No, only studio shoots for a couple of weeks, then maybe a session in Mexico. Let’s do this, I’m hungry.”

He pulled her limbs, extending gently insistent tugs to find stress points. “Jo, I need to talk to you about our Magnolia Bluff adventure. Something happened today. I want your perspective. I’m hoping we can discuss it during dinner.”

“Sure.” She groaned in appreciation as her shoulder popped into the joint. Inhaling, she said, “I knew I held that position too long for that last outfit.”

Thirty minutes later, she felt invigorated. “Sweetheart, you’re the best,” she said, adding a kiss to punctuate her statement. “Let’s go eat.”

Arm in arm, they went upstairs. Pulling items from the refrigerator, she set up a tray of fruit, cheese, and cut meats while JJ poured wine. He carried the wine and food outside to the patio. The balmy air caressed her skin. She tugged off the hair tie and shook her mane. She switched on the perimeter lights. The table looked inviting. The fragrant white flowers appeared almost fake. Bending, she smelled a couple and deftly snapped off a few with her manicured nails. She added the flowers to the small vase in the center.

"There. Perfect."

"Yes, you are, Jo." He pulled out her chair and kissed her shoulder when she was seated.

While toasting one another, Jo asked, "So, what happened today, honey?"

JJ seemed to collect his thoughts but frowned. "We think the human trafficking monster, Mateo, has resurfaced. It appears that he has broadened his business model to include wholesaling."

"Wholesaling?" Jo cocked her head and leaned forward, grabbing a piece of cheese and an apple.

"A large group, nearly a hundred immigrants. From your experiences, I wanted to hear your ideas on the possible end game for whole families."

Chewing the morsels, she thought back to her captivity, and her harrowing escape after her parents died. She had told JJ all the details of her background when they found the poor souls in Magnolia Bluff. She shook her head to chase away the negative memories. "If my insights could help, then let me try. To put it simply, JJ, the trafficking leaders promise you to hope for the future and agony looking back. That was how my parents and other families originally got captured."

"From what we've discovered, most people in this latest fiasco sold everything. They borrowed, jumping at the chance to escape the horrors of their lives only to get trapped in a box truck in the summer heat of Texas. We've found promises to pay and send money back home once established in the states."

She lifted her glass for a sip with her hand trembling. "That must be the incident I heard on the radio. So tragic." A heavy somberness penetrated her heart. "People try, and monsters take advantage. Why do you think Mateo is involved?"

"Some of the descriptions track back to those we experienced. Plus, we have recovered some surveillance shots from the Brownsville border that appear to show him exchanging packages of what I suspect is money. Still searching for details." JJ scarfed a few of the delectable tidbits.

Jo wiped her mouth with her napkin. "I recall comments suggesting Mateo returned over the border to his ranch. Mexican officials were unwilling to divulge details. Did you ever learn more about that location?"

"No, but I love the reminder. I need to follow up on that avenue."

"If the next shoot is in Mexico, perhaps I can find some additional intel."

JJ swallowed the last of his wine with the remainder of the beef. "Honey, if you go to Mexico, you'll have company."

"Your Uncle Carlos, I know," she chuckled. "Let's take a nice warm shower and fall into our softer-than-a-cloud bed. I've got a mid-morning start tomorrow."

"I'll do the rubdown, but I promise to wake you up early."

Grabbing the tray and flowers, she said, "Deal."

CHAPTER 3

Promised Delivery

A crude, aging trailer, parked in front of a decrepit warehouse, looked abandoned. Several emaciated dogs wandered here and alert to every movement while scavenging food. Inside the trailer, Rodrigo kept his temper in check by using his large beefy fingers to knead the stiff tendons in his neck. He turned his soulless cold black eyes toward the seated man. "Miguel, I don't understand. How did you make it to this drop location without the driver, truck, or, more importantly, my cargo?" Rodrigo straightened his shoulder holster to remind the man of the gun under his arm.

Nervous sweat beaded on Miguel's face. "We stopped to get directions," he sputtered. "Toby left me in the cab. He went across to the store for directions and water. It was so hot. A few minutes later, I heard gunshots. Then police cars raced into to the parking lot. Three officers got out. One was carrying a metal pipe. He ran straight for the glass doors, which exploded on impact. They entered with guns drawn. Seconds later, I heard more gunfire so I jumped out of the cab and ran. I was scared. I didn't know what to do. I didn't think it was a good idea to hang around and explain to the police. I hitched a ride telling the driver the area I needed. He dropped me off a couple of blocks from here. I was glad I remembered the address. Please help me."

Rodrigo cast angry glances at his two silent associates. He clenched and unclenched his fingers, getting madder by the minute. "Why didn't you drive the truck? You had the keys. The engine was running."

Miguel sobbed. "I don't know how to drive a rig like that. You gotta believe me." He looked at the man, then offered, "Why don't we just go and get it? We aren't that far, maybe half an hour. I can show you. Your cargo should be okay. It wasn't at the store parking lot. Maybe Toby is okay and waiting for me."

Rodrigo sat at the computer and clicked the keyboard, searching for news. His eyes grew wide as he saw the breaking news story about the 18-wheeler, its cargo and the shooting fatalities. He shook his head in disbelief at the sudden turn of events.

A long moment of silence got interrupted by Rodrigo clucking his tongue in annoyance. "Too late. You should have tried to leave with the cargo. Now I need to call the shipper and explain this mess. I think I know the next step, but let's hear it anyway." In a practiced fluid motion, Rodrigo placed a call and put it on speaker.

The man's gruff voice barked in a thick Spanish accent. "Why is my timetable running behind, again? You should-a called two hours ago. What's the hold-up?"

Rodrigo's fingers drummed on the desk. "It's a total write-off. The rig and all the cargo are in the hands of the authorities not far from here. The report suggests Toby took one too many bullets in the head."

"What? How the hell did that happen? Why is it a total loss? And who knows the details?"

"I have the driver's riding buddy, who ran from the scene. He knows too much, or nothing, so not a complete write-off."

"Damnit. Wipe the scene clean. Burn it if you must. We can't use that location as a processing point again. Start looking for another location at least a hundred miles away. I'll destroy the financials and alert the buyers," the man insisted.

"And the runner," Rodrigo asked. "The whiney one?"

"He's useless. Kill him and add him to the fire. Screw-ups and losers aren't needed in my operation, ever."

Nodding, Rodrigo disconnected the call. "Men, you heard the man. Clean everything with the standard bleach wash as we are on our way out. But first take our friend here out in pieces so the dogs can eat. Then add the body to the inferno. We leave in an hour."

Rodrigo pulled out his .45 caliber Colt.

"You weren't going to pay us, were you?" Miguel shouted.

"No, but you will." He pulled the trigger twice, sending two rounds through Miguel's teeth to make identification impossible if any remains were recovered. "I'm sure the dogs are gathering."

Breakfield – Charles works as a data/telecom solution architect and supports digital security, blockchain solutions, and unified communications. He enjoys writing, studying World War II history, travel, and cultural exchanges. Charles' love of wine, cooking, and Harley riding often provides writing topics.

Much of his personality comes from his father who served in the military for 30 years and three wars. Charles grew up on multiple bases and different countries. The multi-cultural exposure helps him with the various character perspectives they bring to the series. His personal ambition is to continue to teach Burkey humor.

Burkey – Rox is a Customer Experience Specialist who works with businesses around the world. As a gifted speaker and accomplished listener, she bridges the chasm between business problems and technical solutions to optimize business productivity. She has written technology papers, white papers, but launches into high gear when plotting our next technothriller or short story.

As a child, she led the other kids with her highly charged imagination generating new adventures with make believe characters. She is proud of being a Girl Scout until high school, and contributed to the community as a member of a Head Start program. Rox enjoys her family, learning, listening to people, travel, outdoor activities, sewing, cooking, and thinking about how to diversify the series.

Breakfield and Burkey – began their partnership writing non-fictional papers and books. They formed a business partnership to share stories as fictional story writers. They recognize storytelling is an evolving method to share excitement, thrills, and insights to today's technology risks.

They are passionate about leveraging the real technology into fictional writing. The variety of characters have attributes from the many people who crossed their professional paths add that depth. Admittedly, Breakfield often asks interesting people he meets if they thought about being an evil cyberthug or femme fatale in their series.

Both authors have traveled to many places around the world. These travels are pulled into stories that requires real knowledge of specific locals. They enjoy well-rounded thrillers that include levels of humor, romance, intrigue, suspense, and mystery.

They love to talk about their stories at private and public book readings or events. Burkey conducts podcast style interviews with a couple of author groups, and enjoys extracting the tidbits from authors, especially new ones. Her first interview was, wait for it, Breakfield. You can learn where they will be from the calendar on their website.

EnigmaSeries.com has information on the Enigma Series, 12 books, 10 short stories, audio books, book trailers, and the newest series Enigma Heirs releasing in 2023. They have proudly earned multiple awards for their fictional creations.

We are also part of the Underground Authors group writing cozy mysteries/murders in the Magnolia Bluff Crime Chronicles. We are committed to providing an installment for Season 2 and Season 3 to accompany *The Flower Enigma*, released in Season 1.

Please provide a fair and honest review on Amazon and any other places you post reviews. We appreciate the feedback.

Other stories by Breakfield and Burkey in
The Enigma Series are at **www.EnigmaBookSeries.com**

We would greatly appreciate if you would take a few minutes and provide a review of this work on Amazon, Goodreads and any of your other favorite places.

Season 1 Magnolia Bluff Crime Chronicles

Made in the USA
Middletown, DE
21 March 2023

26728252R10158